THE GATE

THE IMMORTAL COIL SAGA

BOOK ONE

BRANDI
SCHONBERG

First Print Edition 2022

Published in the United States by Lights Out Ink, LLC.

ISBN: 978-1-914152-06-1

Cover design by K.M. West Creative

Lights Out Ink is an independent publisher of serialized, digital, and printed fiction.

Visit www.lightsoutink.com to discover our full library of content.

This book is dedicated to my husband, Rio. There would be no Amarynn without you. And to my children. May her story give you strength.

PROLOGUE

THE BANMORROW CLIFFS

*T*he stone was just that — a stone.

Permeated with crystalline veins of blue, it was a simple, white rock, but she held it in her pale hand like a dragon's egg — a precious thing. The air around the woman's slight form pulsed, thick with energy, magical vibrations palpable in the moonlit night. Wind whipped her hair, tearing past the craggy outcropping above the shore. A clutch of ancient trees clung to the ledge just beyond her, refusing to give up their purchase on the cliff.

A mage stepped out of the shadows of the grove and picked his way along the rocks towards her. One hand gripped a staff of carved driftwood and inlaid pearl. The other clutched his robes to keep them from tangling underfoot. Unsteady in the gale, he took his time in his ascent before finally standing to face her. He cast his gaze toward the cloudless sky, then out to the roiling waters of the sea below them.

"You are certain?"

She nodded. "It must be now."

"But the raids have ended in the north. We have time."

She shook her head. "We are depleted of fighting men, and when another Kingdom rises against us, we will fall."

She lifted her hand, exposing the stone to the full moon's light. The mage stepped forward and raised his free hand to cup hers. They withdrew into themselves, both of their mouths moving and forming different words, but together in their silence. A glow radiated from the stone while a fine mist coalesced around their outstretched hands. The crystals within groaned and swelled, shedding the plain rock encasing them.

The woman's hand trembled in his. The mage only recognized she was faltering when she stumbled forward. He braced himself against his staff, preparing for the inevitable strain he would bear if she failed. She grasped onto the staff as well, her chest heaving.

"Dyaneth, stop!"

She opened her eyes. Tendrils of icy power danced through them, and she lifted her chin defiantly. The wind picked up in response to her. She drew in a slow breath and squared her shoulders.

"Now, Regealth!"

"It is too much. We must stop."

She was panting with the strain, and he sensed the coming onslaught of power would be too much for her to bear.

"Now!" she hissed through clenched teeth.

The mage dared one last look at the woman before him. The very stars in the night had descended to adorn her hair, while the chilled light of the moon bathed her in an otherworldly glow. At that moment, she was the sky.

He had no other choice but to drown himself in the magic of the deep as a massive wave crashed against the cliff with a roar. Lightning tore through the sky, flashing in a surge of unbridled energy. The collective force knocked both mages to the ground, and the stone flew from their grasp.

And just as quickly as it had happened, it ended.

Dyaneth lay in the soft seagrass, unmoving. The stone rested beside her, pulsating and undulating.

Regealth crawled to where she lay.

"Dyaneth!" His voice was a ragged whisper.

Her eyes opened for only a moment, and she smiled. "It is done."

Regealth picked up the stone in his trembling hands, marveling at its transformation. What had once been just a rock, fallen from the cliffs above Banmorrow, was now a crystal that contained more power than any one wielder could imagine. He could not drag his gaze from the depths of its many-hued blue facets and the worlds they held within. On this very night, they had made the impossible a reality.

Dyaneth's slowing, shallow breaths dragged his attention from the stone. She lifted one hand to caress the crystal.

"It is what we wanted, yes?" she breathed.

Regealth lifted his chin. "It is the true gateway. It is our hope."

Her eyes drifted closed, her hand dropping to the ground.

"Dyaneth!" Regealth dropped the stone and clutched her shoulders. "Dyaneth!"

He lay his ear to her chest, listening for sounds of life—her heartbeat, like an echo, faint and slowing. Panic writhed deep within, and he pulled her to him, her head resting heavily against his shoulder. His hands trembled as he cradled her, her golden hair tangled in his fingers. "What do I do, Dyaneth? What do I do now?"

She managed one last ragged breath.

"Bring them."

CHAPTER 1

*C*rack!

The wooden staff collided with the warrior's back with sickening force. It knocked the wind out of her as she fell, sprawled out on the ground. Her fingers curled in the dirt while resisting the urge to reach for her blade.

"Goddess, take me. I won't fight you this time," she whispered.

Her face was streaked with blood, her skin crossed with fine, silvery scars barely visible in the evening light. A dark-brown tattoo swirled an intricate pattern on her left temple, one fine line curling just under her eye.

The back alley where she lay smelled of piss and pig shit, muddy from the recent autumn storms. A crowd had gathered to see what was going on, wagers already being made before the first blow even landed. Three ragged men circled her, weapons in hand. The big, burly one twirled his staff as he laughed to himself.

"Little girl," he sneered. "You don't look so deadly to me."

She pressed her forehead into the ground and let loose a half-hearted chuckle, spitting the mud from her mouth. "I never do."

No one in their right mind would have engaged with her if they knew who she was. By all accounts, she was no more than a young, cocky upstart with a stolen Legion short sword. She picked fights with any ignorant wretch she could find, and to ensure anonymity, she had let loose her signature war braids and left her infamous broadsword and two daggers behind at the inn.

The gathering onlookers cheered for the trio of cutthroats. She turned her head just in time to see a handful of street urchins elbowing their way to the front of the crowd. So much for a quick end. This was a full-blown spectacle now.

The little man with the sword was emboldened by the public support and leaned in close to whisper, "You're nothing but a girl!"

She couldn't see the third man, but she could feel him behind her. He was quiet, and she counted on him to hit his mark with his pair of mismatched daggers. She exhaled slowly, fighting the instinct to defend herself. He stood over her, then brought his daggers down with a grunt. She gasped as the blades penetrated her sides, carrying the thick poison paste she'd spread over her skin just before picking the fight.

The mage had been specific about the concoction seeping into her bloodstream — she could not inflict the poison upon herself, or the magic would not hold. Of course, she could have paid someone to do it, but she had to maintain some dignity even with a death wish. While she hated for it to end like this, it wouldn't matter soon. She smiled, silently thanking Nyra, the Goddess of Night, for hearing her plea as the spreading fire of nightshade infiltrated her blood.

Her limbs weakened as the poison slithered through her body, creeping up to lick at her heart. She forced herself to relax, to give herself over to impending death. Numb heaviness took hold of her limbs, but a pinprick of immortal magic pulsed in her belly. Doubt flickered in her mind as the spell took hold and began to fight back the deadly assault.

"No, no, no," she groaned, the pain screaming through icy magic as muscle and flesh repaired themselves. She sucked in slow breaths, her rage rising. It had taken three long months of searching to acquire the nightshade, and she had done everything exactly as the dark mage had instructed. It should have worked. She should be dying.

Strength flooded her body as anger and frustration exploded through her limbs. Her hazel eyes glazed over with the familiar rage of battle, and she flipped over onto her back. Two of her assailants fell in the space of a breath, her throwing knives squarely embedded in their chests. Only the big lout with the staff remained standing. She jumped to her feet, drawing her short sword.

The crowd around them froze, dumbfounded, as they realized who she was. No one could withstand those injuries and then stand and continue to fight. Her scars and tattoos were visible now, and her long auburn hair was as wild as her eyes.

"Do I look deadly now?" she growled as her sword tore through the last man's distended belly in one swift movement. His mouth opened with a gurgle before he crumpled to the ground.

Amarynn sat at the table and stared into her wooden cup. Next to her, leaning against the wall, was her broadsword, Frost. Belted at her waist were a Legion short sword and an ornately-worked dagger. The smoky inn was loud, bustling with northfolk trying to escape the cold. A fire blazed in the hearth while bouts of raucous laughter cut through the chatter of serving girls and kitchen noise. She absently glanced up and out the window. The autumn winds howled through the cracks in the walls.

The faces of the men she'd cut down just moments before flickered through her thoughts. Absently, she scowled at the three thin, fresh scars glistening on the inside of her forearm. Damp blood clung to the cuff of her sleeve. Essik, the first of her kind, had shown her how he commemorated each kill with a cut of his own, and his empathy resonated with her, though she was loath to show it. Her early scars were in hidden places, under clothing, or next to more prominent battle scars, where they would go unnoticed. After twenty years, there was no space left on her flesh to hide them, but they would fade and become barely visible, just like the thousand others scattered over her body.

A peal of laughter brought her attention back to the room and her dilemma.

Why had the nightshade not worked? That vile trickster of a mage had sworn on her life it would. She had heard stories about the mage's abilities. But those stories came from the living, not the dead. Realizing the absurdity of her faith, she snorted to herself and drained her cup. Her life wasn't even about living. Her kind were creatures built for destruction. She, and the eighteen others like her, were only good for war and death. Though she didn't want it anymore, her forced, immortal existence was like a suit of lead armor she could never remove.

Without warning, the inn door crashed open, caught up in the bluster of a brewing storm. Two men — the apparent leader, dressed in a long, oiled coat — pushed through and briskly shut the door behind them. Shadows hid their faces. The pair slowly made their way to the fire, surveying each table they passed. Halfway to the hearth, a serving girl approached them, but she was turned away by a gesture from the leader.

Amarynn slumped into her chair imperceptibly, drawing back into her heavy cloak's hood. She eased her left arm beneath her right. The thunderbolt and circle brand was old and faded, but it was a mark bore by all of her kind. One of the men paused when he neared her, and she casually drew circles on the rough-hewn table with her thumb. Only a moment passed before he continued toward the back of the common room.

The two men reached the fire, and the taller of them turned. "We are looking for someone."

The room stilled for a moment; she tensed. Hushed conversations and raucous laughter quieted as the patrons turned to look at the man who was speaking. Although the alley brawl had happened several hours ago, it had been poor planning on her part to choose a location

4

near a crowd. The trio of men she had cut down were nothing but low-life thieves, and they were dead now, albeit with half the town standing witness. Though she did her best to remain anonymous, all the tales of her prowess on the battlefield meant a low profile could be exceedingly difficult to maintain.

"Five silver pieces for the Traveler called Amarynn."

She stiffened while the room remained silent. Her eyes stayed firmly cast on the table, her fingers now toying with the handle of her cup. Moments passed like hours. She carefully lifted her eyes to survey the room. Most of the patrons shook their heads, but she could have predicted it would be the pig-nosed serving girl that gave her away with a glance in her direction. The tall man leaned over and whispered to the other, who inclined his head in agreement. The two men strode toward her table, the tall one following the other. As they neared, the firelight illuminated their faces. She sat back, her hood falling away from her tangled mass of dark, red-brown hair.

Both men sat down opposite her. The eldest offered a greeting.

"Fine evening, isn't it, Rynn?"

"Hello, Bent," Amarynn smirked. She looked at his companion. He pushed up his sleeves, and there, just below the bend of his elbow, on the soft underside of his forearm, was a fresh circle and bolt brand — only about a few months old by its look.

"I don't believe I know you," she said. Her left hand drifted under the table to rest on the hilt of a second dagger she had strapped to her thigh.

Bent glanced at the other man and said, "This is Aron."

She studied the newcomer while a minute passed, then finally, she turned her attention back to the older man and broke the uncomfortable silence. "Who sent you?"

"Your King." Bent leaned in on his elbows and waited for her reaction.

"You mean *your* King," she responded, furrowing her brow.

5

"Rynn, when are you going to stop this madness? You are a subject of the Kingdom, and you have been for twenty years. Karth is your home." Bent shook his head and leaned in closer, lowering his voice to a warning growl. "And Lasten is your King."

She placed her elbows on the table and came nose to nose with the burly man. Her voice was a low hiss. "I am free. I wasn't born here, so I am no one's subject. I did twenty years with the Legion, and I owe *no one*."

She settled back in her chair, her eyes glinting with heated anger. Bent reclined with a deep sigh, studying the woman across from him.

She was a Traveler, a human pulled across dimensions through powerful magic by a mage called Regealth the Gatekeeper. She was a conscript in the Legion of Karth with no other loyalties, no past, and no other future but the one created for her by the King of Karth. "Lass," he began, "you will always be Legion. And right now, you are a deserter."

Amarynn groaned. "Couldn't you have just let me be?" She looked down and picked at the tankard handle in front of her.

"These are dark times," Bent said.

Her eyes flicked up briefly.

"I need a solid Blademaster at my side, and there's none more solid than you. Your Kingdom and your King need you."

"I couldn't care less what your King needs," she mumbled.

"*I* need you," he implored. "Rynn, lass, what else do you have?" His voice was gentle, almost fatherly. For a moment, she wavered. These past months, the time spent on her own had been lonely and painful. For the last twenty years, Bent was the closest thing to a father she had ever known. Now he sat in front of her, aware of where she had been, what she had seen, asking her to put her life back in service of a King to whom she held no loyalty.

She looked away and pretended to consider his request. A pained expression clouded her eyes, and she rubbed her temples. "I want my life back. *My* life."

"The Legion is your life, Rynn. Life as a Traveler in Karth means you want for nothing, girl!"

The corner of her mouth curled up as she glanced at Aron. "No? You're a Traveler, Aron. Do you have your own life?"

"Oh, yes," he said. His quiet tone held the tiniest hint of a lilt. "We are elite. What else could be as grand?" His bright blue eyes held her gaze, challenging her. She started to look away, but something odd in the way he looked at her held her for just a moment longer than she would have liked.

She quickly looked back to Bent. "We don't have lives, Bent. We're not given that option, remember? So, instead, I think I will find a cottage or a cabin in the woods and stay *especially* drunk." She drained her cup.

Bent wrinkled his nose in distaste and stood. "Just like Essik, then?" He shook his head. "How fortunate it is you cannot die, girl. A drunkard's death is especially miserable. I've never known you to walk away from a fight, lass. Why now?" He placed his hands on the table, his face hovering near hers. "Remember — you're not the only Traveler in the world. Stop acting as if you are! And, as a deserter, I can't help you if you are found out."

The serving girl who had betrayed Amarynn's identity hurried to the table. "My five silver — where is it?" she demanded of Bent, and the aging Legion commander dropped a handful of coins on the table as Aron pushed his chair back and stood and stepped away. The girl scrambled to pick them up, but Amarynn's hand shot out and grabbed her by the wrist. Amarynn glared at her, then released her wrist and swept the coins off the table onto the floor, pocketing one for herself. Wisely refraining from comment, the serving girl scrambled to collect the remaining four coins beneath Amarynn's dark glare, then swiftly disappeared into the crowd.

"We'll be at the outpost barracks tonight, but we are leaving for Calliway at first light," Bent told Amarynn. "You can keep hiding or live the life you've been given, even if you don't want it. You were bestowed the gift of immortality, lass. It is like thievery not to use it. Besides, what a sad waste it would be to spend an eternity in the mines!" Bent crossed his arms and leveled a hard stare. Behind him, Aron edged through the crowd.

"Are you threatening me?" Amarynn asked softly, challenge flashing in her hazel eyes.

Her old master turned and followed Aron out of the inn without another word. Behind them, the portly innkeeper scurried to close the door against the relentless wind.

Amarynn sighed and dropped her head into her hands. She'd fled from Legion service over three months ago, but she could not find her place anywhere she went. She was an immortal Legion Traveler who had seen three wars and countless bloody battles, but her worst fears weren't of blood and pain. She feared, never knowing what could have been. While other Travelers reveled in their power to destroy, she took no joy in death-dealing. It was true, she was the best of them all, but she was certain there had to be more for her than blood and steel.

What if Bent was right, though? What if the only place for her was at the other end of a blade? Killing was the only thing she was good at, the only thing that distracted her from her pain. If he were offering her a way to return without penalty, she would be a fool not to take it.

She lifted her empty cup and called for another. A different serving girl handed her a wooden tankard as she stood. Amarynn swallowed the sweet liquid in one gulp and hefted her broadsword over her shoulder. She strode to the door, opened it, and slipped out into the night.

CHAPTER 2

Amarynn watched the garrison entrance from the shelter of a copse of trees. Light rain pattered softly on the leaves. The heavy wooden gates clattered open, and a cluster of men, led by Bent, rode out. Next to her, her golden mount whinnied, sensing the energy of the other horses. Amarynn placed her hand on the horse's broad, muscled neck. Like before every battle, she shifted back and forth on her feet, weighing her options as she inhaled the cold forest scent deep into her lungs.

To accept Bent's invitation and return to Calliway was to return to the very thing she hated, the person who had made her who she was. But Bent was right. To stay here in this back-mountain outpost and remain in hiding was no better. She would never be happy — certainly would never know peace. How would she explain her youth while those around her withered and died without giving away who she was? Given enough time, her very being would always betray her, and then, what would it all have been for?

Amarynn tightened her leather gloves and rechecked the girth of her horse's saddle to put off the inevitable. The time had come to decide. She rested her forehead against her mount's neck, breathing in his familiar scent of leather and horsehide. Returning to Karth would mean she must face the King. She must bury the rage she felt for Lasten and return to the Legion, killing and defending in his name, again and again.

Her horse quivered and pawed at the earth. Amarynn stepped back. "You're ready, aren't you, Dax?" she asked, ruffling the gelding's mane. "You want to see your friends again, don't you?" He snorted and pranced in place, and Amarynn chuckled. "My boy, you've always been the smart one." She reached up for the pommel and swung herself into the saddle. The massive battle horse stilled with practiced intensity as she found her center and balance, awaiting her command. Dax was the best she'd ever trained in her twenty years with the Legion, and they had been together for the last ten. She thought he might be ready to step away from the frenzy of battle, but feeling his eagerness now, maybe not just yet. She smiled to herself and gave two short whistles. Dax took a step and then moved forward through the trees, stealthy as any predator, winding around saplings with practiced ease. Amarynn leaned low to his neck as he stepped out of the tree line and turned him toward the road. A cloud of dust still hovered in the distance where the group of riders had been. She pulled him to a stop, but Dax fought the bit, eager to catch up to the others. Amarynn rubbed his neck once more, dug her feet into the stirrups, leaned closer, and breathed, "Go."

The seasoned warhorse hugged the edge of the road as he gained speed, his hoofbeats masked by the soft, damp ground. The wind whistled, cold and wet, past Amarynn's ears, the singularity of the sound drawing her focus away from the decision she had just made. Her breathing synced with Dax's pace, and she relaxed.

They rounded a bend and saw Bent's party ahead. The two men in the rear glanced over their shoulders as Amarynn and her massive mount barreled toward them. They parted, allowing her to reach Bent and Aron in the front. Amarynn squeezed with her knees, and Dax slowed to a trot when she pulled up alongside them. Bent turned his head in her direction, a smirk on his lips. Amarynn eyed him for a moment.

"That confident, were you?"

"Rynn, lass," he said, "I know you well enough." A smile tugged at the corners of his mouth as he eyed the horizon.

"And?"

He pursed his lips and nodded towards Aron.

"And you hate it when I'm right."

Without another word, Bent kicked his horse into a gallop. Aron and the other men followed.

Amarynn pulled Dax to a halt and fought the urge to turn and ride back the way she came. She absently scratched her forearm. Scars always itched for a day or two, even the little ones. Dax shook his head with impatience, and she turned her attention back to the riders ahead. The wind picked up; dark clouds were gathering above the tree line.

"Time to move," she growled.

She squeezed Dax's sides, and the horse launched himself forward. Like it or not, she was heading home.

The sky had darkened, the sun just dipping below the horizon when the riders stopped for the night. The heavy storm clouds that had gathered earlier had drifted to the north, granting the riders a reprieve from the ever-present northern rains. Amarynn unsaddled Dax while the men set up camp, giving him a good rub down and a piece of honey brittle from her pocket. "You are too easy to please, you know that?" she laughed, giving his big ear a gentle tug. He snorted, and she stepped away, leaning down to retrieve her bow from her saddle. Dax watched her as she made for the trees, then dropped his head and wandered untethered, grazing on the grass and clover in the clearing.

She felt restless.

A hunt would do her good — help her regroup.

Before she ducked into the hedges, she watched Bent barking orders at the men. They hadn't spoken since she joined the men on the road, but there was something comforting about being in his presence again. She sighed and slung her bow over her shoulder, padding skillfully into the quiet shadows.

Stars were appearing in the sky, and the first moon was peering out from behind the retreating clouds when Amarynn returned and deposited her small quarry of rabbits and hedge hens by the fire. She grabbed her pack from where her gear rested and rifled through it, retrieving an oiled leather wineskin. She raised it to her lips and pulled the cork out with her teeth. She took long gulps until she felt warmth spread from her belly to her limbs.

"That's a piss-poor haul, lass. Clearing the cobwebs, were you?"

Amarynn glared.

Bent chuckled and clapped her on the back. "Come, sit!"

She reluctantly followed and sat down beside him, taking another drink. As she swallowed, she noticed Aron seated across the flames, staring at her with his unnerving blue eyes. She wiped her mouth with the back of her hand.

"Who is he, really?" she asked Bent, nodding her head in Aron's direction.

Bent snatched a piece of jerky from his bag, then turned toward her. "Crossed a few months ago, the day after you left. Regealth had a difficult time with it, I was told. It took the old man at least a month to recover. Aron was completely wild, that one. But the King says the crossings have to be done—"

"None of it has to be done," Amarynn muttered between bites.

Bent scowled at her but continued, "King Lasten had him sent to me. Strange, it seemed. He kept babbling on and on in a language no one could understand. He had his wits about him, too, unlike you. He could even handle a blade! I'll tell you, in all my years with you Travelers, I never saw anything the likes of that one there. I figure the King thought if I could handle you, it must be my specialty — managing the difficult conscripts." He flashed her a grin.

"Language?" she mused. "I didn't even know I was human when I woke up." She wrinkled her nose at the memory. "Even walking was new. How could he manage a sword?" She studied Aron more intently, the firelight casting shadows across his face.

Bent raised an eyebrow. "He couldn't do a damn thing with it, but he most definitely knew what it was for!" Bent pulled up his sleeve to reveal a two-inch scar, still red and puckered from its recency. He flashed a sly grin. "Don't be jealous. The one you gave me was bigger!"

She half-heartedly returned his smile. Bent, and Bent alone, was the only reason she had survived being chosen to travel from her world to theirs — wherever this world was. He had been patient with her but never soft. Bent had helped her learn the language, the customs, and most importantly, he had been her Blademaster. More than once, she had been on the edge of escape, and every time he had been able to convince her that she had a purpose and value. While she loathed the Kingdom and the King they served, she bonded with the Legion and, most significantly, Bent.

The fire hissed and crackled, sending showers of sparks into the clear night sky. Both moons had risen, and their combined light bathed the bedrolls and grass in pearly blue. Amarynn, Bent, and the others gathered around the fire finished off a fat rabbit and two hedge hens before Bent broke the idle chatter. He gave Amarynn a long look and lowered his voice. "You need to know that the Legion believes you left on my orders."

"You lied for me?" Her eyes widened.

"I gave you the space you needed to see your way back where you belong," he said.

"That might have been the stupidest thing I have ever heard you do. Lasten has always hated me, and if he found out you lied, he'd have your head on a pike."

Bent laughed out loud. "Oh, I'm sure he would have!" He glanced around the fire and scratched his nose. Most of the men had begun to retire to their bedrolls, but he lowered his voice even more. "The truth?" He cast about to make sure no one was within earshot. "Regealth sent me to find you."

Amarynn snapped her head around to face Bent full-on at the mention of the mage's name. She held her breath for a moment. The whole story Bent had woven at the inn about needing her at his side, fighting for King and Kingdom — it had been a fabrication. She took a moment to consider what she had just heard.

"He knows how to do it?" Her voice was barely a whisper.

"He knows something. What, exactly, I don't know. But whatever he found was enough for him to send me out here," he glanced around again, uneasily, "after you. He was insistent."

Amarynn knew he would never have come for her otherwise. Bent knew she was too skilled to be caught — he'd trained her well. She considered the new information tumbling inside her head. Regealth, the mage who had brought her here, had learned something that could return her to her home, her *real* home. And no one could know, because if King Lasten even suspected the old mage had found a way to undo the very magic he had been ordered to create, there would be a heavy price. Even hinting at her desire to shed her Traveler status was a risk in and of itself.

She never quite understood why, but the old mage had always seemed to have a soft spot for her; he had vowed to help, despite the cost. So, she had put her fate into the mage's hands, never really believing there might be a way.

Bent looked his protege over to be sure she understood his message. Rising, he patted her shoulder and trudged toward his bedroll. "I'm going to sleep while I can," he said. "You should, too."

"Sleep?" she breathed. Her mind was spinning out of control. She felt her pulse racing as the anxiety of inaction washed over her. How could she sleep now?

Bent stepped out of the firelight's reach while Amarynn tried to calm herself, to remember that her actions would be watched. Now, more than ever, Bent's life and position were in her hands. No one could know of her desertion — if they did, it would be his end. She knew she had to follow his lead, to be patient.

The flames were slowly dying, embers crackling and glowing. Across the fire, Amarynn studied Aron. He was still staring, but this time into the flames. His dark hair fell haphazardly across his right eye, brushing the pale ivory skin of his cheek. It didn't appear he had eaten a thing, and he didn't look tired at all. Oddly, he wore no fur or warmth against the nighttime chill of the northern hills. Whereas most men still up and about were bundled in their cloaks and hoods, he seemed perfectly comfortable in the cold. Amarynn pulled her cloak tighter and watched him intently when he suddenly lifted his chin and locked gazes with her.

She took in his peculiar eyes, unable to pull her gaze from the unfamiliar energy emanating from them. They were the strangest color she had ever seen — an icy blue marbled with silver. Finally, she broke off her stare and stood, turning toward her bedroll. She picked up her wineskin, which had fallen behind her, keeping her back to Aron as she drained its contents, trying to recover her composure. Aron's gaze remained unbroken as she lay down on her bedroll.

The twin moons were full and high in the sky now, diminishing the light of the stars, their pearly glow replaced by a blue-green sheen over the entire campsite. Amarynn settled in and pretended to sleep but kept one eye open just enough to monitor the newest Traveler. Eventually, he stood and then disappeared into the shadows that surrounded their camp. Amarynn rolled onto her back, her thoughts spinning with Bent's news. Maybe there was some hope to be found in his words. Perhaps she was riding back to Calliway to her demise, but it could be on her terms this time.

The two moons, Ahai and Ban, had lowered to the treetops before she willed herself to breathe normally again. She watched the stars fading in and out of the inky blackness until she resolved to sleep.

CHAPTER 3

Amarynn awoke with a start. Sweaty hair stuck to her face and shoulders. Another dream. She sat up and rested her face in her hands for a moment before reaching to untangle her hair and re-braid it. She had only slept a few hours, but she'd had enough. Years of Legion training had made sure she could function on even the smallest doses of sleep.

Stretching, she rose and started to pack up her bedroll. She whistled a long trill, and her mount came trotting over from the edge of the clearing. Dax tossed his head and whickered in greeting. Amarynn rubbed his velvety white nose, then pulled a piece of honey brittle from her pocket. She held it out, and he gently lipped it from her palm. She gave him a quick rub on the neck before saddling him, securing her pack and broadsword.

Surprisingly, the rest of the camp was nearly packed up. A young new recruit — as indicated by the short sword belted to his side — trotted over and handed Amarynn a tightly-rolled brown canvas.

"Your bedroll?" he offered, unsure.

Amarynn pointed to her saddled and loaded mount. "Is that a bedroll already tied on my horse?" The young man stared mutely. "Are you blind?" she hissed.

"I-I-I'm sorry, my Lady!" he stammered.

"Lady? I am Blademaster to you, harpy *puke*!"

The soldier's wide-eyed stare made her wince. She did not intend to be cruel. She stalked past the soldier, who nearly fell over himself while trying to back away.

Bent, standing close by, howled with laughter. "Ha! Now there's the lass I know!" He slapped her heartily on the back as she passed, then retrieved his horse, where two more soldiers were finishing securing supplies to his saddle. Within minutes, the entire camp was mounted and on its way.

The riders traveled for a day up and through the Dark Mountain pass, then began their descent into the forested foothills that stretched from the bottom of the mountain range to the rolling farmlands surrounding Calliway. They pressed hard, and in two days' time, found themselves following a small stream — a tributary of the great Arnell River. After a brief stop to water their horses and eat a meal of jerky and biscuits, only a handful of minutes, Bent signaled for the group to mount up. The main road that led into the capital city was only a mile from the stream.

The Travelers guided their horses through the trees and finally onto the road. They broke into a comfortable gallop toward the west, toward Karth and its capital city of Calliway. Mountains rose on the horizon, softened by the low clouds of winter. The air held a bite, and the smell of pine trees seemed to lace the mist like a subtle perfume.

Amarynn felt a mixture of excitement and dread. Returning to the city meant familiarity and relative comfort. Still, it also meant dealing with her departure and committing to a necessary lie if she wanted to protect Bent and herself. She would, no doubt, be questioned by the King. The story her mentor had given her was that she was on a mission to uncover dissent in the north, and she must produce evidence of her efforts. King Lasten was a shrewd man and no thinly-veiled story would do. She and Bent would need to solidify their ruse before entering the city gates.

As if reading her mind, Bent sidled his mount beside hers and motioned for the group to slow to a trot. The two of them pulled ahead in order to speak privately.

"We're almost to the city gates, lass."

"Aye. I know what we've discussed," Amarynn replied. "I'm to say that with these peaceful times, I was growing bored and itching for something new, something like what Ehrinell and her assassins do. You thought to broaden my training by giving me an extended mission in the north, where we've been hearing the whispers of possible rebellion. But I was impatient and left without your knowledge."

"And what will you report?"

"That the trouble was nothing more than rabble mouthing off and that I dispatched the bastards in full view of the townsfolk so they would see what happens when talk of revolt makes its way to the King." She added that last bit with a hint of disgust. Most people were like sheep, and her patience with them was as thin as a cobweb.

"What took you so long? You were gone nearly three months," Bent prodded.

Amarynn glowered at him. They had been over this multiple times.

"I didn't think it through. People know me, and that makes quiet observation impossible. No one would ever speak ill of the King in my presence, so I had no choice but to pretend I was deserting as Essik did before me. I'm an old enough Traveler that the Madness is possible. The three idiots I killed shared secrets about me. I sent word to you to come with men, and while I waited for your arrival, I couldn't help myself. I removed them... publicly. Then we left, simple as that." Amarynn made a dramatic face. "We left a small contingency there to ensure there are no more upstarts. End of story."

The old Blademaster nodded. "That will do." He stole a glance back to Aron, who trailed them by a small distance.

The journey continued through the hills and pastures for the better part of the afternoon. As the sun began its descent into the west, they crested a rise, and there before them lay the sprawling and magnificent view of Calliway, the capital city of Karth.

The walls glowed like gold in the late afternoon sun. The city itself was perched along the Arnell River, a vast, gently flowing ribbon of green and blue that wound down the Dark Mountains on its way to the sea, a hundred miles to the south. Spires and towers of stone rose above the walls, and along the approaching road, green fields and farmsteads dotted the countryside. Calliway was positioned in the most strategically defensible location possible in this region of the continent.

From his seat in Calliway, King Lasten controlled the river and access to the only mountain pass. The climate was ideal, the farmlands rich, and on the surface, the people were content. Only a hundred miles from the sea, he held a formidable fort in the port city of Banmorrow. This extended his reach to control the trade that came from across the sea. He was an intelligent ruler, but a ruthless one as well. His thirst for power and control was insatiable, and the Travelers were evidence of his ambition.

And his fear.

Twice, Karth had been invaded, and twice, Karth was nearly lost. Forty-five years ago, when Lasten was just a boy, raiders from the sea had swarmed their coastlines and nearly decimated Karth's armies. Had it not been for Karth's possession of a water mage and their alliance with the island nation of Vhaleese, they would have lost everything — they nearly did when the war took more men than could be replaced in a generation.

The most recent invasion, at the very beginning of Lasten's reign, came from the mountains to the north, the region known as the Stone Reaches. Very little was known about the Reaches except that it was vast and lay beyond the towering Stone Giants mountain range. Its raiders were wild and fierce, some on horseback while others rode grey bears larger than the most massive bull. It was then Lasten realized he needed something bigger and stronger if he were to keep his Kingdom from ruin.

An idea formed as Lasten observed the youngest boys brought by their parents for sale to the Legion. Most cried, but the angry boys interested him most. They walked away from their fathers without a second glance, eager to find a place for themselves in a world that didn't want them. They proved to be the most loyal and hardest working of all the young conscripts.

His thought was simple.

Reach into worlds unknown and bring back bodies, forms to shape and mold into elite warriors, beings with no loyalties or ties to anyone but him. He tasked Regealth with finding a way, but the cost was high. The King's own sister, Dyaneth, a sky mage of considerable strength, was lost in the creation of the Gate. Without her, Regealth was unsure if their construct would even work, but Lasten's bloodline were sky magic sources and Regealth could draw the necessary power from any of them, though Lasten insisted he be the sole source.

In the beginning, no one realized Travelers were impossible to kill. All that was evident was the loss of all memory and faculty — "A clean slate!" the King proclaimed eagerly. The first Traveler, a behemoth named Essik, took months to tame and never fully bonded to the Legion. He deserted six years after his creation.

Though Amarynn was not the first Traveler, she was the first female, and it cost Regealth's strength dearly, more than the others. He had attempted Traveler creation by different means, and the King was furious with the aging mage for wasting his energies. It had taken longer than a full year for Regealth to recharge, garner enough magical power to reach through the Gate again, and bring another back with him. Like the legendary offspring of mythical dragons, Lasten referred to the fledgling recruits as his dragon eggs. His new warriors arrived as far apart and took just as long to acclimate to their roles as a dragon's young did to hatch; Amarynn's arrival took a more significant toll than usual on Regealth.

He even risked the King's wrath some ten years ago and brought another female, just to see if she yielded the same effect as Amarynn, but she had not. Though stealthy, with an affinity for assassinations and poisons, Ehrinell was just another Traveler, no different from those who came before her.

21

Amarynn surveyed the tops of Calliway's elegantly-constructed gate towers, watching the guards scramble as she and the men with her came into view.

Aron reined his horse between her and Bent.

"I will see you at the barracks," he said, nodding toward the city. "I'll ride ahead and announce our arrival to the King's Guard."

Bent nodded, "Aye."

Aron urged his horse forward into a trot, and then he was off, galloping toward the gates. In minutes, Amarynn could hear the distant bugle of a watchman alerting the city of their approach. She stole a glance at Bent. The aging Legion man's brow was furrowed just enough to let her know he was concerned. Her stomach twisted a bit. While she cared little for most people, Bent held a unique place in her heart. She silently vowed to do whatever it took to make sure he had nothing to worry over.

The gates of Calliway loomed just beyond a grove of trees as they rounded a bend in the road. The riders slowed to a walk as the great gates swung open to allow them entry. As Amarynn passed through, the soaring grey stone towers of the Keep and the savory smells of the market washed over her. Calliway was home, whether she admitted it or not, and she could not deny the respite she felt as they wound through the streets. The Legion barracks sat just outside the palace walls. She and Bent guided their horses past the foot soldiers' quarters to the heart of the Legion, the great hall that housed the Blademasters and the immortal and legendary Travelers of Karth.

CHAPTER 4

"How long until we are summoned?"

Amarynn tore off another piece of bread and dunked it in her gravy. She scanned the hall while Bent considered her question. Her gaze settled on a group of men at the other end of the long hall. They were a mix of Legion and Travelers, soldiers she'd served with for many years. Four of them shouted and howled with laughter as the fifth man downed a tankard of ale in one long gulp. He slammed the heavy cup onto the table and lifted his head, his brooding stare locking with Amarynn's. The corner of his lip curled in a sinister grin.

"Rynn, lass!" Bent snapped his fingers in front of her, breaking her thought.

"You didn't tell me Matteus was in Calliway," she whispered.

Bent followed her gaze.

"Rynn, leave it alone," he warned.

She slowed her breathing, fixing her ire on the grizzled man at the end of the long table. He smiled openly at her; the lack of sincerity was evident. His face was marred. Firelight rippled across an abundance of knotty scars, and his oily, black hair hung over his ears in unkempt strands.

"Amarynn!"

She reluctantly broke her stare and picked at her food, taking long breaths to steady her shaking hands. Her foot bounced against the floor in a quick, agitated rhythm.

"Would it have made any difference if I'd told you?"

Amarynn looked past Bent, focusing on the men at the other end of the room. She always felt disdain from the other Travelers, but never as venomous as they were in the past two years. She had always known she was different from the others, but she could never put her finger on why.

From the moment she had appeared on the stone floor of Regealth's aethertorium, Amarynn was raw and wild. Where the other Travelers were docile and confused at first, her anger and singular focus on destruction was a surprise. Regealth chose to call her Amarynn, an old Vhaleesian word meaning 'shining star,' to honor the unique circumstances that surrounded her crossing. At first, she had lived up to her name. She learned quickly, embracing the Legion and her role as a warrior without question. Her skill with weapons was uncanny, and her complete absence of fear in battle singled her out as the biggest threat the Legion could offer an enemy on the battlefield.

But despite being the most feared and revered of all the immortal Travelers, King Lasten had always excluded her. She received no invitations to galas and no inclusion in war councils. She lived simply and did what she did best. She killed, and she did it better than anyone. One by one, each member of the Legion elite distanced themselves from her growing anger. It had all come to a head one dark winter night.

She dropped her eyes to the table. Images of the last time she set foot in the practice yard played out in her mind, her memories clear.

A blade in each hand, she was destroying yet another unfortunate sparring dummy in the practice yard when they struck. Her arms were grabbed, pinned behind her back, while her blades clattered to the ground. She felt arms encircling her, squeezing so hard she lost her breath. They were like a vise, crushing her. She wasn't afraid for her life — death was not possible — but the pain of recovery was nearly unbearable, should she sustain what would be a death blow to any mortal man. She could smell the rank sourness of Matteus' breath as he leaned in close to her ear. "Bitch. You are nothing special. We're tired of hearing your name."

When the dagger was drawn across her neck, her body hovered near unachievable death, her blood spilling onto the cold and frozen ground. Hours passed before she was discovered.

Bent found her and took her back to his quarters. He enlisted the help of the precious few Travelers left that could still be trusted. He stayed with her as she fought her way back to the life she hated.

The old Blademaster knew what she would do.

Bent had told her stories about the other Traveler who left. Essik was in such a state of disarray, Bent said; he most likely went mad wherever he ended up. There were stories about a wild giant that haunted the Dark Mountains, howling and tormenting the folk who dwelled high up in the ranges.

Still, she was done. Why fight for a Legion that hated her? She already hated herself; she needed no help with that.

She recovered, as all Travelers do, but the moment she could walk and fend for herself, she left — slipped away in the middle of the night. She crept past Bent as he slept and left his room's warmth and safety. As she slid through the night towards the stables, every sound and shadow made her jump. Amarynn still remembered the shame she felt for fearing the darkness. Thank the gods for Dax. He was one of the only beings she truly trusted. She recalled the relief that came with his warm breath on her trembling hands as she slid the bridle over his head. He carried her away on his back with such surety and strength. She almost wept for the comfort he gave her as they made their way into the night, away from Calliway and the Legion, away from the pain, and into the unknown.

25

The fingers of Amarynn's right hand closed over the knife that lay beside her plate. Bent recognized the danger immediately, but she was on her feet so fast that he had no time to stop her.

She strode to the end of the table, the ring of her footsteps over the stone floor audible in the suddenly-silent room. Matteus kept his arms crossed, making a show of nonchalance that infuriated her. There was a collective holding of breath as she slowed her pace and stopped in front of him. The two immortals stared at one another for several seconds before he pushed his chair back and stood. He was at least a foot taller than her five and a half feet. Amarynn held her ground, refusing to look up. Her nostrils flared, and her jaw clenched as she turned to cast her derision on his cronies around the table.

"Fine night for cowards," she said quietly. The corner of her mouth tugged up in a half-smile.

None of them moved; they tried their best to look unbothered. Matteus rumbled, "Welcome back, Rynn."

She waited a full minute before turning back to him. She heard Bent's careful footsteps behind her.

"Matteus."

He wrinkled his crooked nose, sniffing in distaste.

"Who was stupid enough to let you in the gates?"

"Who would be stupid enough to try and stop me?"

Matteus stepped up to her, toe-to-toe. Her eyes were level with his chest.

"I thought we made it clear you aren't wanted here."

She inhaled deeply, a slow sneer creeping onto her face. She let the knife in her left hand fall to the floor while her right hand darted to the dagger's hilt strapped to her thigh. In less than a second, the blade was at Matteus' throat. His mud-colored eyes widened slightly, then darkened.

"You don't have the balls," he taunted.

"I've no balls at all." Her sneer turned to a smirk as her left hand swept up her belted dagger and pressed it firmly into Matteus' groin.

"I wonder if you do." She pressed harder. "Oh! There they are. We're immortal, so do you think they'd grow back if I cut them off?"

Another Traveler, Cam, jumped to his feet in Matteus' defense. "You wouldn't dare!"

Cam didn't have a chance to draw his weapon before he found Bent's leveled at his chest. "Are you willing to bet on that?" The others fidgeted uncomfortably.

An uneasy silence descended, and Cam took a slow step back. Bent lowered his sword. "I'd watch my back if I were you."

Keeping the blade at Matteus' throat, she watched Cam slink back into his chair. Matteus laughed. "Who should we be afraid of? A little thing like you?"

He purposefully pressed himself into the edge of Amarynn's blade as if he'd gladly accept her challenge. The metal pressed into his skin, a thin line of blood beading along the blade's edge. After a tense moment, he sat back down and laughed as he took another long pull from his tankard. He swallowed deeply, then cleared his throat, turning to spit at the hearth. "You are only deadly to mortals."

"As are you," She gestured to herself with a slight bow, then sheathed her daggers.

Matteus' face darkened.

She studied him a moment longer as a slow rage roiled in her belly, threatening to overtake her. Matteus wanted her to lose control, to prove their disdain for her was not without merit. Her hands clenched into fists, but she turned on her heel and walked past Bent, who sheathed his sword with his eyes still locked on Cam. She let her hand fall to the hilt of her short sword. Hushed voices and the crackling of the hearth filled the heavy silence.

"Go on, now! Run away as you do."

Her steps stilled. Matteus snickered as his men resumed a quiet chatter. Bent stood his ground at the ready, unsure of what Amarynn would do.

27

Without a word, Amarynn resumed her pace and continued, stalking past the tables and out the door.

Night was fully settled on the city when Amarynn left the hall. She was still seething from the exchange with Matteus. She needed to remember exactly why she had returned, why she had decided to insert herself back into what she had worked so hard to leave behind. There was only one person now who could convince her to stay, and she needed to see him.

She slipped into a slim passageway partially hidden in the shadows past the kitchens. A narrow staircase twisted and wound down through the walls of the castle. She took the steps quietly, making turn after turn without hesitation, on pure instinct. This passageway was purposefully tricky, hallways off shooting in all different directions, but this route had been for her use alone since she had been allowed to leave the castle some twenty years ago.

The landing at the bottom was small, the space dominated by a decrepit wooden door. She raised her hand to rap lightly but hesitated. If Bent had come for her, everything was about to change, and stepping foot into the room beyond the door would ensure it. Regealth had promised to try to find a way to undo what had been done to her, and a summons from him meant she would find out if her wish were possible or not. Either way, her heartbeat was just a bit faster than it was earlier.

Just as she resolved to knock, the door swung open just enough for a man with greying hair and a beard to step into view.

"You are earlier than I expected," he chided.

"I just arr—"

He held his hand up, and she closed her mouth. Experience taught her that arguing with Regealth was a no-win situation. She slid through the partially open door and leaned back against it to push it closed. The room had not changed in twenty years. These were the mage's chambers, not the study where he worked on matters of state. This was the room that led to the aethertorium, her birth chamber. A deep hearth glowed with dying embers opposite where she stood, illuminating two deeply padded chairs in front of it. She had spent hours sitting there listening and learning in the weeks after she had arrived.

Water spilled from a crevice in the wall to her right, near the passageway leading to the aethertorium. The crystal-clear liquid collected in a pearlescent basin, then drained onto the floor below it, seeping into the crevices in the wall. This far down in the castle put Regealth's chamber just above the aquifer that fed most of the springs in the hills to the south. As a water mage, Regealth relied on proximity to his element; he could be no closer to it than here.

"My girl." Regealth looked her up and down, then smiled warmly, a tinge of sadness in his expression.

The candles on the table glimmered and cast familiar shadows all along the walls. This was the first home she remembered. Wandering to the small table, she unbuckled her sword belt and lay it on the short bench tucked partially beneath. Her eyes roamed the room. It seemed impossible all Travelers started here as their beginning, even the brute Matteus, though none of them had stayed here as long as she had. She walked around the table before taking a seat in one of the chairs by the hearth. Staring into the embers with her elbows on her knees, she waited for the mage to join her. His robes rustled as he eased into the chair beside her.

"These bones are old," he scoffed.

She was silent, contemplating her next words. Her question was simple, but there was no way the answer would be anything but complicated.

"Why did you send for me?"

She heard his sigh and immediately knew the answer would not be what she had hoped for. She dropped her head into her hands.

The mage cleared his throat.

"I need *you* here if I am going to unlock the way back," he explained. "I tried without you, with the few Travelers like you

29

who can be trusted. Even Ehrinell helped," he chuckled, "but I got nowhere." He tapped one finger on his temple. "I believe I know why it didn't work, though."

She lifted her head and looked at him. "Why?"

"There's a very long story to be told about that girl, but not tonight." He leaned over and plucked a small decanter from a side table. He held it in the light, admiring the vessel. "Metheglin," he said, "from the Handaals. A priest I once met had it sent to me. Quite a pleasant surprise!" He poured a small measure of golden liquid into a delicate glass goblet and sniffed it.

"Why not tell me tonight?"

"Because I am tired, and now I can rest well knowing you are back. I worry, you know," he frowned and reached for her hand.

She pulled away.

"Did I come back for nothing?" she whispered. "I am to see the King tomorrow. I could face consequences."

"Lasten is not unreasonable." Regealth traced a finger around the edge of the cup.

Amarynn's brow furrowed. "You know he doesn't like me. He *despises* me. Can't you intervene on my behalf?"

Regealth set his drink down and turned to face her. "You never should have left, girl. My issues become extraordinarily difficult when you do ridiculous things like run away!" The mage's face was stern. "There are secrets about Travelers that only I possess." He leaned close and placed a hand on her shoulder. "And you are right. He does have a reason to dislike you, but it is through no fault of your own." Regealth patted her lightly and sat back. He picked up the goblet once more. "Now that I am close to discovering a reversal, he cannot know you came here at my request. That is why I sent Bent after you."

"Bent and I have already discussed this."

The mage took a sip of the metheglin. "Ah! Delightful!"

"Regealth!" Amarynn's knuckles were white on the arms of her chair as she tried to contain her frustration. "I am back. I came back for you. Can you do it or not?" Amarynn waited, but he was silent. She shook her head. "You can't give me any guarantees? Any hope? I need to know I came back for a reason."

"Trust me, girl. There is a reason. Telling you now would only complicate things. I need you to be convincing because I need you to stay." He took another small sip. "If only you hadn't left to begin with," he mumbled.

She grimaced and stood, snatching her belt and scabbard from under the table. Her exasperation and anger rose, threatening to take over if she didn't leave soon.

Regealth used his free hand to shoo her away. "Go rest, girl. Make your case with Lasten tomorrow, and do not do anything foolish. Then we can see if what I've learned is worth something."

She fastened the belt buckles around her hips and stalked to the door. She had come looking for answers to reassure her, but all she had were more questions. The one person who might have given her the hope and resolve to meet with the King (and not lose her head) had done nothing but add to her confusion. But that was Regealth. Nothing was ever easy with him. She took one last look over her shoulder at the mage, then closed the door behind her.

Amarynn knew Bent questioned whether he had done the right thing in bringing her back, as Regealth had asked. She repeatedly asked herself the same question as she climbed the twisting staircase and stalked out to the training yard. The night was crisp and clear, both moons shining brightly over the city. The barracks behind her bustled with sounds of soldiers, and part of her yearned to return to the warm glow of Bent's room. But then Matteus' smug expression crept into her mind, and she felt her rage begin to blossom.

Amarynn sliced and beat at the sparring pole for a full hour before retiring. She made her way to the stables and found Dax in the last stall, lazily chewing oats and swishing his tail. He swung his massive head around toward her as she opened the door, butting her with his nose. She gripped his ears and pulled his head into her chest, breathing in deeply when he blew softly and pushed against her. She slid to the ground, keeping one hand on his muzzle, and for the first time in three months, Amarynn, the legendary Traveler of the Legion of Karth, cried until she slid down into the hay and fell into a fitful, dreamless sleep.

CHAPTER 5

A soft nudge against her cheek woke Amarynn. She raised a hand to her face to brush Dax away, but he only pushed against her harder, his warm breath on her cheek. She groaned and threw her arm over her face. The horse stamped his foot and whinnied. Registering his warning, Amarynn's eyes snapped open.

A tall, dark shadow filled the stall door.

"You've been summoned."

Aron leaned against the doorframe. "Y'know, you look rather fetching in the straw." His expression was firm, but the corner of his mouth turned up.

She growled at his comment, then stood, snatching a fresh change of clothes from his outstretched hand. He watched her from the doorway until Amarynn said, "Do you mind?"

"Not at all."

Annoyed but undeterred, Amarynn quickly changed into the fresh linen shirt and leather breeches he had delivered, buckling her scabbard belt and knives in place.

He studied her, lingering a moment longer, then added, "Bent will meet you at the castle gate in fifteen minutes."

He left with a quick backward glance.

She started to follow, then realized she didn't have her broadsword. She exited the stable and cut across the market to retrieve it from Bent's quarters.

"Amarynn!" a voice called. A young boy elbowed his way through the throng of people in the street.

"Lucas," she smiled.

"You're back!" he exclaimed, a broad grin on his face, as he caught up to her, matching her stride.

"Aye," she laughed. Lucas was a tanner's son, and he had made himself her shadow since she'd met him three years ago. He was no more than ten years old, but he carried himself with all the purpose of a Legion recruit. At first, he'd been an irritating nuisance, but she'd developed a soft spot for the boy. She even spent some time training him in the basics of swordplay.

"Where were you?" he asked.

"On a mission."

She noticed that the boy's gaze lingered on her bare forearm, where the three new scars gleamed brightly against her skin. Lucas looked up, his expression serious.

"Who was it this time?"

She eyed him for a moment, then pressed her mouth into a hard line and looked away. "I'm off to see the King." She changed the subject. "I'll find you later and tell you all about it." She tousled his unruly brown hair. "You can show me how much you've practiced your sword stances then?"

He grinned, then disappeared into the crowd.

Amarynn ducked through the back door of the Legion barracks. Inside, she stopped to dunk her head in a water barrel to rinse away the grime of travel. She scrubbed her face with her hands and then re-braided her hair. Then, she retrieved her sword from Bent's quarters, slung it across her back, and made her way to the bustling entrance hall of the King's castle at the heart of Calliway.

The early morning flurry was well underway as she scanned the area for Bent among the carts and townspeople. She spotted him at the gatehouse, speaking with one of the King's Guard. She sucked in a quick, fortifying breath and stepped across the muddy road.

Bent gave her a reassuring smile as she walked up. "Preferred a different sort of bedfellow last night, I see." He leaned in to pick a piece of straw from her scabbard, then turned to the guardsman, "We'll be off, then."

The young man nodded, then stepped aside to let them pass.

Together, Amarynn and Bent made their way through the gates and into the ancient castle's foyer.

The castle.

For the first few weeks after her crossing, she had been convinced it was the whole of her new world because she had never been allowed to venture beyond the grey and black stone walls of Regealth's chambers. Whenever she could steal a moment from the never-ending barrage of learning and conditioning, she padded around the deepest lower levels on bare feet, letting her hands trail along the cool, damp walls. She remembered pressing her palms against the stone, trying to push the walls aside, to simply walk away.

She also remembered Regealth's kindness. He was gentle with her as if she was a rare treasure that might break. Many nights were spent in that big chair by the hearth, listening to stories and the history of Karth. She recalled when Bent arrived to take her to the Legion to begin her training. She was sure she had seen sadness in Regealth's countenance as the door closed on her way out of his chambers. Her departure from his tutelage was one of the few times she remembered feeling real fear.

Even after leaving his care, she would find the mage watching her from his tall, stained-glass window for months. His book-laden study in the castle overlooked the practice yard where he constantly observed her.

Now, she was walking back in, and if their story failed, she might never leave. As she sucked in a deep breath, the sharp, familiar tang of metal and stone permeated her senses. She exhaled. They passed two guards, one of them openly staring at her. She glared back, and he averted his eyes; they continued past. *I am Amarynn; she* reminded herself as her hand absently went to the hilt of her short sword.

She and Bent took the grand staircase up two flights to where they were greeted by one of the king's honor guards. Their footsteps rang out on the slate floors as they passed by the massive doors to the throne room. They carried on until they reached the end of the hall, where the entrance to the King's private council chambers lay open, waiting for them. She had only been summoned to this room twice — after the victory over Almanthe of Oron and when she claimed the throne of Isai, Queen of the Handaals. Her appearance had been required only for achievements until now, never under potentially traitorous circumstances.

The King was seated at the end of a large rectangular table, his son Jael to his left. The table was a carved and heavy piece, scattered with maps and papers. Two servants poured wine, scurrying between the other men seated around the King. Three of the men, deep in heated debate, shouted at one another until, one by one, they noticed Amarynn and Bent in the doorway.

"My Lord King. Legion Commander Bent and the Traveler, Amarynn." The honor guard's words accentuated the sudden tension in the room.

Jael looked up in surprise, but Lasten, examining the documents on the table, did not bother to lift his head. "Leave us."

Only Jael remained, maintaining a curious stare, while the other men and servants hastily bustled away from the table. One of the guards closed the door behind them as they left. The room was darkened, a few sconces on the walls offering much less light than the open door. Amarynn's fingers fidgeted nervously on the hilt of her dagger as Bent fell to one knee in the customary show of fealty and submission. Amarynn hesitated for a moment before dropping down to touch her knee to the stone floor, though, unlike her commander, she did not bow her head. Bent broke the silence.

"King Lasten, thank you for seeing us so quickly." He raised his head and gave a quick nod to the Prince. "Lord Jael."

"You act as though you requested this meeting, Commander." Lasten raised his head and finally acknowledged their presence. Jael dropped his eyes. The King was a handsome man, still young enough to ride and fight but not so young to believe he needed to. Traces of silver and white shot through his dark blond hair, and his face showed the unavoidable signs of age. However, he was not quite the man she remembered from nearly twenty years ago. Lasten appraised her with a mixture of disdain and calculated necessity. "Now that your protégé has so graciously returned to us, we can discuss my displeasure of being the last to know about this so-called training exercise."

He shifted his attention to Amarynn, and she forced herself to return his gaze with an equal measure of loathing and strength.

King Lasten scrutinized her with a wicked smile. He cast a glance back at Bent. "So, am I to understand the Legion is now training our battleaxes to be poison vials?" The King turned to his son, feigning amusement. "Will our garroters and silent daggers be in the training yard with broadswords next?" Lasten returned his focus to Bent. "Travelers are assigned their proficiencies for a reason, Commander." Lasten took a deep swallow of his wine. "You may rise."

As they stood, Bent adjusted his stance, "My Lord—"

Amarynn stepped forward. "I asked, My Lord." Bent snapped his mouth closed and glared in her direction.

"You say you asked to lay down your blades and try your hand at stealth?" Lasten arched one eyebrow. He pushed his chair back with a grating scrape and stood. "Makes sense, I suppose. You'd want to fill your arsenal. You *could* kill me, couldn't you?"

Amarynn's confusion seemed to amuse the King.

"Travelers are bound, My Lord." Bent cut in. "They cannot raise their hand to those that created them."

"Ah, yes," the King nodded. "There is that. But still…" He allowed his voice to trail off as he studied Amarynn; Jael watched but maintained an uncomfortable silence behind his father. "I wonder if you can tell me why you chose to undertake such a mission unsanctioned? The Legion does not dispatch Travelers without my consent." He looked to Bent. "You know that."

"Aye, my King." Bent lifted his chin, accepting his mistake.

"Travelers are the reason we hold everything south of the Dark Mountains." Lasten stepped away from his chair and began a slow pace around the table. "They are not bored children we send off to *play* at being something they are *not*." Each step accentuated his words. He reached the end of the table.

Amarynn stole a glance at Bent. His eyes were fixed forward, jaw muscles flexing. "Apologies, My Lord," he said, his voice tight. "Never had a Traveler ask to train outside their purpose. As the Commander responsible for this girl's training, I felt it to be within my purview." He cleared his throat uncomfortably. "I was wrong."

The King stopped just in front of Amarynn, and she fixed her stare on the bear and the thunderbolt sigil embroidered on his surcoat. She watched his chest rise and fall, gauging his intent by the tempo of his breaths. "Tell me, Traveler," his voice was quiet. "Has the Madness begun to set in? Is that really why you left?"

She raised her eyes to meet his stare. "No, Lord." Her words were forced. "I am not like Essik." Her brow furrowed in distaste. "I wanted to go because I wanted to learn. One battle after another has grown tiresome."

"One battle after another has gotten us where we are, girl!" King Lasten bellowed. He directed his attention to Bent, then turned and strode at a quick pace back to his chair. "Commander Bent, the Travelers are no longer under your command. My son will take on their training and dispatch. You are relieved of that duty." Jael's head snapped to his father, clearly surprised at his announcement.

Bent choked back a retort, his breath catching. At the sound of her commander's shock, Amarynn's gut seethed. The King was the worst kind of ruler. Cold and cruel. Greedy, with an insatiable hunger for more, and here she was, allowing that appetite to devour her one and only friend. She knew Lasten as a shrewdly intelligent man known for getting exactly what he desired, and this time proved to be no different. She had no choice but to give him what he wanted.

"I left."

Lasten, halfway seated, stopped, and straightened. He leaned forward, knuckles on the table. "What? Careful now," he warned.

"Lass, no—" Bent hissed.

Amarynn's hands had taken the lives of Kings and Queens with ease, without emotion, but now they trembled at her sides. She fought to control her rage, but she refused to let Bent fall. "Bent had no part in this. I deserted."

A wicked smile curled at the corners of Lasten's mouth while he straightened. "Well, now, there it is." He picked up a wooden box sitting on the table amongst the papers, unnoticed. Using his thumbs, he lifted the hinged top. Jael perched on the edge of his chair, eyes wide and jaw clenched. The King's son glanced back and forth between his father and Amarynn. Lasten, unaware of his son's distress, smiled wider as he surveyed the box's contents. He looked up at Amarynn, a satisfied smile playing on his lips. "Your weapons on the table, please."

Amarynn felt the heat rising to her face as her hand clenched the hilt of her sword. Battle rage threatened to rise but was stayed by her mentor's hushed voice in her ear.

"Lass, do as he says. We will find a way through this. But this is not the time nor the place for a fight." Bent's tone calmed her rapidly rising pulse. She clenched her jaw and took a deep breath. She pulled her short sword from its tooled leather scabbard and laid it on the table.

"And the others?" he prompted. "I wouldn't want you to make a poor decision right now." He walked a slow circle around the table, his expression throwing daggers, his smile never reaching those sharp, glittering eyes. "You must remember, *girl*," he hissed, "I am King. You are mine to do with whatever I please."

Amarynn glared at the King for a moment before his demand registered. Her eyes never left Lasten's as she pulled the twin daggers from their sheaths and then kneeled to lay them by her feet. She retrieved her throwing knives from her boots without breaking her cold stare. Twenty years of wielding her blades had made the movements second nature. She left them on the floor and stood. All that remained was the broadsword on her back. She unbuckled the scabbard fastened across her chest and pulled the great blade over her head.

"Frost is yours and no other's," she said, turning toward her aging mentor.

He nodded solemnly and sought her eyes with his own, willing her steadfastness. Bent took the blade from her hands, gripping her fingers briefly to strengthen her resolve. She turned back to face Lasten. He acknowledged the weapons on the floor and chuckled, "Defiant to the last." The King stepped forward, a thick, silver torc in his hands.

Amarynn resisted the urge to shrink back. The collar, with rounded, jeweled ends, hummed with magical energy. She could feel a magical sensation as Lasten leaned closer and placed the torc around her neck. He forced the two ends together briefly, releasing a spark that danced from one jewel to the other. The jewels hovered just apart from one another, a force both connecting them and keeping them from touching. Her strength flowed out of her, and she slumped forward onto the table.

Lasten called for his guards, and the doors opened immediately, flooding the room with daylight. On either side of her, two guards lifted her under her arms and turned her toward the door. She wanted to rip her arms free of their hold, stand between them of her own accord, and walk out with dignity, but she could barely raise her head, much less use her legs.

At a sound from the King, the men pulled her by the arms to face Lasten. He leered down at her. "I must consider very carefully what to do with you. I could have you shipped to the mines and risk your escape or—" the King paused as if in thought. "I *could* have your head."

Amarynn's breath stopped for a moment. The only way to stop the heart of a Traveler was by beheading, but it was in no way a true death. Regealth was very clear about the rules of Traveler immortality. To lose your head meant to lose your physical life. But any Traveler who found themselves in that unfortunate predicament would be lost for eternity. They would regain their memories of their past, but their souls would never be able to rest, wandering in and out of two worlds but never touching either of them.

"You will wait for my decision."

Lasten returned to his chair next to Jael. The Prince attempted to mirror his father's expression of disdain, but Amarynn noticed that the younger man's grip had tightened around his goblet, knuckles just beginning to turn white.

With a flick of his hand, King Lasten dismissed her. The two men yanked her around and made their way toward the door.

CHAPTER 6

Darkness always made Amarynn think of her crossing twenty years ago. On the stone floor in Regealth's chambers, though her eyes were wide open, she could not see anything. A ringing in her ears thrummed with unbearable intensity, and the only thing she could feel was a damp, invading chill.

In the bowels of the dungeon, there were no windows. No daylight to gauge the days and nights. This was the twisted genius of the Calliway dungeons. Prisoners were fed well, given reasonable quarters, but all in complete darkness. Prisoners would enter as young men and emerge only a year later, appearing as if they had been ravaged by a whole decade of miserable, cruel time. *The mind plays tricks*, Bent said, when Amarynn inquired about the state of men being released one crisp autumn day during her first year in Karth. Amarynn was sure there must have been more to the dungeons than just the darkness and isolation. She had to believe a King and Kingdom willing to enslave magically conscripted warriors would have more to its dungeons than that. Now, Amarynn supposed, she would find out.

Sitting on the stone outcropping of her cell, Amarynn ran her hands up and down her legs to stave off the cold. Muffled wails filtered through the walls, accompanied by the skittering feet of rodents and other vermin she could only imagine. She searched the dark, hungry for any sign of light. Finding none, she closed her eyes and tried to ignore the oppressive darkness that closed in on all sides. She could almost feel cold steel at her throat as flashes of Matteus in the practice yard permeated her senses. The betrayal of her own kind had muted her fearlessness, especially when she could not see and most definitely when she was alone.

The dungeons of Calliway castle were notorious for their isolation. She did not know how long she had been in her cell, but it felt like days. Tales of men and women driven to insanity were commonplace in the taverns and inns, but Amarynn refused to succumb to the nagging fear in her belly. She balled her hands into fists, wanting so badly to slam them into the stone but unable to because of the strength-sapping collar around her neck. Instead, Amarynn kept her eyes closed and recited the broadsword guard positions.

"Shoulder Guard, straightforward oncoming attack."

She breathed deeply, then let out a long, slow exhale.

"Heavens' Guard, swords from above."

Her hands unclenched and carefully spread out on the outcrop, fingers feeling every tiny crevice.

"Body Guard, close-range fight."

She straightened out her neck and centered her spine as best she could while seated on the uneven stone.

"Demons Guard—"

"Close range from below," a low male voice broke in.

Amarynn's head tried to snap toward her cell door, but she could only manage a bobbing nod. Echoes of the voice reverberated over the stone walls, then faded into the silence. A lantern appeared at the small, barred window, and she could see the outline of a head. The sounds of metal on metal and the scraping of a rusty lock assaulted her ears, a striking contrast to the deafening silence. Her cell was flooded with light as the door groaned open. She blinked, adjusting to the sudden brightness, and was surprised to find the King's son standing in the doorway, alone.

Shadows from the lantern played across his face, softening his features. He appeared younger than he had looked in the council chambers earlier. Less Lasten-like. He also seemed taller than she remembered in the smallness of her cell. His storm-grey eyes fixed on Amarynn until she raised a questioning brow. He quickly averted his gaze with an unexpected reticence.

"I paid attention when I watched you do your drills," the Prince said in a hushed voice. He turned and shut the door, glancing out the small window before turning back to Amarynn. He hung the lantern on a hook, then leaned back against the wall to look at her.

Struggling to slide her legs around, she pushed off the stone slab to stand, her hands gripping the stone ledge behind her to keep her weak legs from betraying her. Large sections of her auburn hair had escaped its braid and fell across her face, hiding the tattoo on her left temple.

"*Watch me*? You were second-in-command of the Legion. You know the drills. I know you trained," she scoffed.

Jael ignored her outburst and continued. "Now that my father has made me the new commander of the Travelers. I thought perhaps I would start by dealing with you and your admitted desertion."

Amarynn could not read the Prince's face. He and his father shared a strikingly similar countenance, even the same light-colored hair. But unlike the King, Jael was tall but not slender — his build matched his height. That was where he took after his mother, Queen Feramin, a huntress from the Island Kingdom of Vhaleese, far across the eastern sea. The Vhaleesians were nearly giants, built to hunt in the towering, mist-shrouded forests of the Vhaleese Islands. The Vhaleesians were usually dark-haired and pale; height was the only thing Jael had inherited from the reclusive queen. The rest of him was pure Lasten, and for that reason, she guarded herself.

"I know why you left," he said. He cast a sidelong glance in her direction to gauge her response. "Matteus has a big mouth and is a braggart. It wasn't long after that a few of us noticed you were not just convalescing, but that you were gone." When she said nothing, he

45

pushed off the wall and started to pace. "What I can't figure out is why you came back." He stopped, scrutinizing her. "You are immortal. You could go anywhere — live anywhere."

Amarynn lifted her chin defensively.

"Why?" he asked again, this time with more authority.

She thought for a long moment while Jael stoically waited for her answer, and for some reason, his patience infuriated her.

"Why do you care?" Her words were cautious. "Why does *anyone* care? I left for my own reasons, but now I am back *for my own reasons*," she challenged. She tried to step forward, emboldened, but remembered the collar and simply squared her shoulders. "If you know why I left, then there are no questions to ask. So tell me, why are *you* really here?"

"Matteus has no honor," he began.

"A shocking discovery, no doubt," Amarynn snorted.

"What he did could have been appropriately punishable by the Legion had you come forward about it."

"How did you find out?"

"Not important. I went to Bent while you were recovering, and *he* even tried to conceal the attack; Goddess knows why," he muttered. "I asked my mother for guidance."

Amarynn groaned.

He continued, "Karth has little precedent for female warriors. My mother's people, however, do. I knew not to take the matter to my father, and I had no desire to complicate things, but I would not let Matteus' crime go unacknowledged. His actions spurred your desertion."

"Well, it still doesn't much look acknowledged, does it?" Amarynn scoffed. "So, you said nothing to the King after he had me arrested?"

"I did not." Amarynn watched him take a few steps in her direction. He paused for her response, then added quietly, "I have never agreed with my father about you. I tend to side with Regealth."

She regarded him in silence for a moment. He did not entirely fit the part of a Crown Prince set to inherit a mighty and feared Kingdom. By his dark blond hair and robust features, he was clearly Lasten's progeny; he carried himself with the same strength, though he had not shown himself to be as cruel or menacing. Jael was a dutiful son, maintaining his presence as the Legion's second-in-command, and he was ever-present at his father's side, but the ruthless bite that was the King's hallmark seemed to have eluded his firstborn.

"My father is not a kind man. Believe me when I say I know firsthand." Jael looked away and continued, "But I am no good to the people of Karth if he doesn't trust me." He leveled his gaze at her. "I need to know if I can trust you."

The Prince's words were edged with palpable tension.

"Trust me?" Amarynn searched the Prince's face for some kind of sign he might be playing her, but she detected nothing.

Jael hesitated a moment more. Then, he reached into his pocket and pulled out a small, thin crystal, which he studied for a moment before he looked back to Amarynn. "Regealth says I can."

He moved directly in front of her, the warm light flickering brightly enough that she could see the steady pulse of the vein in his neck. He brought one hand to her neck and lifted the nearly-joined torc. Amarynn stiffened as he slipped the thin crystal between the jeweled ends. She felt a jolt, and her strength flooded back in a rush as the magic of the torc released its hold on her. A shiver ran down Amarynn's back as Jael's hands brushed her hair away to slowly slip the silver collar from her neck. His hand lingered near her throat for a moment.

"You spoke with him?" Amarynn tilted her head to peer questioningly at the Prince.

"He came to me," Jael said.

"What did he tell you? What do you know?" Amarynn's heartbeat quickened.

"Enough." He turned to snatch up the lantern and step outside. "Just know, I won't let you lose your head."

47

Amarynn, relishing her returning strength, quickly crossed the cell as he closed the door. She gripped the metal bars.

"How long have I been down here?"

"Four days."

"Bent. Is he—"

"He is in his quarters raging and fuming, as Bent does." He hung the lantern on a nail just outside the door, leaving the cell only dimly lit, deep shadows sliding across the floor from the bars. Jael slid the silver torc inside his shirt.

She grimaced when she heard the metal lock turn and close. Jael glanced to his left and said in a louder voice, presumably for the dungeon guards at the end of the corridor, "Our chat has enlightened me, and while I'd rather stay and soak up more of your esteemed presence, I have other duties to attend to. Please," his gesture encompassed her surroundings, "enjoy your stay in the finest Calliway has to offer before your trip to the Oron mines." Jael gave a curt bow and disappeared into the dark.

Amarynn's hand wandered to her neck where the torc had been, confusion clouding her mind. Her body trembled, but she wasn't sure if it was due to the return of her strength. The encounter with Jael had affected her more deeply than she would have thought. She didn't know Jael at all, but he'd gone to the Queen — what knowledge of her did he have that would garner such support? And Regealth! Jael's cryptic reference to the mage made no sense.

She sat back onto the stone outcropping, new questions emerging inside her mind. Pulling her legs up, wrapped her arms around them, and laid her head down on her knees. She closed her eyes and resolved to rest, regain her strength, though sleep was a long time coming.

CHAPTER 7

She did not know how much time had passed since her visit from the Prince.

After Jael left, and once she had slept for a bit, she wandered back and forth across the small cell nearly a thousand times. She recited the guards and attacks for each of her blades. She named all the Travelers in the order they had crossed. She resorted to naming each of the Legion soldiers she knew by age and rank. Finally, after what felt like days, she resigned herself to a fitful sleep.

A high-pitched wail broke the silence, startling Amarynn awake. The lantern was dark — burned out — and there was nothing but darkness again. Fighting a faint flutter of anticipation, she sat up and held her breath. She heard footsteps come closer, then stop outside her cell. There was a shuffling sound, heavy breathing, and then a sharp *clank* as something hard hit the cell floor. At a shout from guards, the footsteps ran away in the other direction.

Amarynn pounced on the space between the door and the stone bench where she lay. On her knees, she felt around on the floor until her fingers found a small bundle, roughly the size of her thumb. She snatched it up and was surprised when a metal key tied to the pile banged against her wrist.

Goddess!

Amarynn gripped the bundle, then yanked on the key to pull it free. She stood, stuffing the wad into the pocket of her jacket. She ran her fingers over the key, turning it to feel both sides.

It can't be.

She moved carefully to the door and felt along the heavy wood. There was no keyhole.

The lock was on the outside, she remembered. She reached one arm through the barred window and felt for it. Her fingers brushed against the coolness of a metal block, and she laughed to herself. The lock was just within reach. She fumbled, gripping the key between her thumb and first finger. She slid it back to the end, brushing the bottom of the lock and finding its home. Pressing it in with her palm, she twisted the key with her fingers, but it refused to move. For a moment, her heart hung in her throat. Then she took a breath and redoubled her efforts. She refused to allow a damn rusty lock to keep her trapped in this place. She grunted as she tightened her fingers and twisted again. A satisfying click reverberated off of the damp stone.

Amarynn pushed the cell door open and crept out into the passageway. It was pitch black. She tried to remember the direction she had heard the footsteps come from.

The left.

She turned. Running her hand along the wall to guide her, she put one foot in front of the other and began to feel her way out. Her progress was slow in the inky black of the hallway. Several minutes of cold breath and unsteady footsteps passed before she started to make out the dim outline of the walls ahead. Voices in the distance shouted and called to one another as she neared a crossroads in the brightening corridors, where wall sconces flickered and sputtered. Finally, she could see the way ahead clearly. She continued to creep along the darkest side of the hall toward the light. No guards appeared, which seemed odd, but she pressed on. Finally, there was movement ahead.

Instinctively, she reached for her short sword, forgetting she was weaponless. The shadows of soldiers danced along the stone ahead of her, distorted by the torchlight. It appeared there were only two moving in her direction.

As they neared, she pressed herself against the wall, doing her best to blend in with the flickering patterns. The first boots rounded the bend, and the soldier hit the ground before he knew he was falling. Amarynn had his sword unsheathed and through his side as the second soldier registered what happened. Pinning the downed soldier's back with her boot, she pulled the sword free and reached across to disarm the second. She pushed the wide-eyed guard against the wall with two swords in hand, blades crossed beneath his chin.

"Not a sound," she breathed.

The young guard lifted his chin defiantly.

"Turn your head in the direction of the exit, boy." She pulled the blades closer, tightening the vise on his neck. "And don't you dare think to mislead me."

The guard on the ground behind her groaned.

Her captive's breaths came hard and fast, and she could tell he was debating whether or not he should fight back. By the cleanliness of his uniform and his smooth face, he was obviously less than a yearling. She let loose a chuckle.

"You don't know who I am, do you?"

His blank expression was her answer.

Amarynn dropped her right hand to her side, sword gripped tight, and pinned him to the wall with her left blade across his neck. She flipped her grip on the sword and used her knuckles to push up her left sleeve. The motion drew the soldier's eyes to the inside of her forearm, where her Traveler brand gleamed. She pressed harder on his neck, and blood trickled beneath the sharpened edge. The guard grunted softly, gasped, and turned his head to the right.

"Smart move," she smirked.

Amarynn cast a glance down the exit corridor, then looked back at the soldier. Droplets of sweat had begun to form on his brow despite the chill. She could hear the other man wheezing and coughing as he started to writhe behind her; the young soldier trembled as he watched Amarynn debate what to do with them. Not ready to add two more marks to her collection of scars, she stepped back and, lightning-quick, slammed the sword's pommel into the guard's temple. He crumpled to the floor beside his comrade.

More guards were coming by the sounds of boots on stone that reverberated down the passageway. She maintained her backward grip on the right sword and switched her grip on the other. Wielding them blade-down, she sprinted for the end of the hall without any care for the pounding of her boots against the stone floor. She could see the stairwell that led to freedom, but just as she was about to dart out of the corridor to make for the steps, several guards' voices carried down from above.

Tightening her grip on her weapons, she stepped back and pressed herself against the wall, wrists crossed behind her back, with both swords pointed up behind her to conceal their metallic glint. She remained hidden in the shadows while the guards stepped out of the stairwell and took a hard right. With no more signs of soldiers near, she bounded across the corridor and took the steps two at a time.

Clearing the large doorway at the top, she was surprised to see the sky was a deepening shade of indigo — nearly dusk. Amarynn seized the opportunity of the fading light to sprint toward the barracks. A familiar, loud laugh erupted from nearby, and she started in surprise. She quickly crossed the space between the buildings and stepped inside the kitchens just as Matteus and another man rounded the corner.

Breathing hard, she made herself small, crouching inside the door behind the barrels and sacks of grain. She stowed the stolen swords between the barrels and leaned forward, resting her hands on her thighs. The lump in her pocket brushed the edge of her fingers, and she remembered the bundle tied to the key. She pulled it out and unfolded it, squinting to read in the dim light. The handwriting was elegant yet rushed.

Regealth is missing. Your horse has been stabled at the Mountain Fiddler Inn. Ride for Morning Hill. I trust you.

Amarynn's heart pounded in her chest, and her breath came faster. Her escape was the work of the Prince. And now Regealth was *gone*?

I won't let you lose your head, he'd told her. Amarynn's eyes narrowed as she drew herself up, suddenly unconcerned about being seen. Regealth was missing. She would find and kill whoever was responsible — and enjoy doing it. The Prince had given her a second chance to find her release, and no one in the Kingdom of Karth could stop her.

CHAPTER 8

"**G**et him up!"

Regealth was yanked up by the back of his robes from the wooden box he was crouching in. The crate had bounced about in the back of a wagon all night as it rolled over a rough and rocky road. His legs were stiff, and his back screamed in agony.

"Let's go, old man," said the burly, unshaven man who held his robes. He smelled like stale beer and dirt, and his breath was putrid.

Regealth, Gatekeeper and long-time advisor to the King of Karth, blinked his pale grey eyes, unseeing, in the bright sun. He could sense the light, and though he could hardly see anything, he smelled the sea and heard the crackle of gulls overhead.

"Ah, the ocean?" he muttered to no one.

"Gren! Bring him to me!"

Regealth turned his head toward the voice. It was familiar, he thought. He stumbled a few steps across a wooden surface. But when he hesitated, someone hooked him under the arm and half-dragged him toward the man shouting the orders. Finally, they stopped moving, and it was then he could feel the gentle tell-tale swaying of a ship's deck.

If he were stronger, he could use magic to spy on his captors from anywhere, but the mage had been through so much these last hours that he felt lucky his heart was still beating. He raised a shaky hand to try and reach out and touch whoever was in front of him. Tired or not, he was confident he would be able to gain identity through a simple touching bond.

As the Gatekeeper's trembling hand rose, the man jumped back as if it were a snake.

"Oh no, old man!" he hissed. "You'll not put one cursed finger on me. I know your tricks!"

Regealth dropped his hand to his side and made a show of sighing in defeat. His hand snaked upward to grasp the heavy jewel hanging around his neck. He fluttered his fingers around for a moment before panic struck.

"The Gate!" he gasped. "What have you done with it!"

His captor chuckled and turned toward the ship's bow, surveying the sky: slate-grey clouds were blowing in from the south with the rising wind, and they needed to get underway. His employer did not like to be kept waiting, and he was already behind schedule. He shouted to the crew to shove off and set sail. But a feeble cry from behind made him whirl around to see the aged Gatekeeper crumple to the deck.

"Get him below!" the man shouted to his men. "And feed him! I can't have him dying unless we all want to die with him!"

The men hoisted Regealth up and carried him below deck. His wispy grey hair disappeared down the stairs; a voice purred from behind.

"Ah, yes. Let's not kill the poor old thing."

He turned to see a tall, willowy woman gliding toward him from the ship's bow. She was dressed in a deep rich velvet gown, a fitting contrast to her pale skin. The dress hugged her curves, cascading to the deck. She locked her dark, brown eyes with his, and he was certain she could see straight into his soul. She idly twisted a section of her chestnut hair in her slim fingers before pointing them directly at him.

"You, Markan," she said, "are as clumsy as a cow."

She moved past him to lean on the railing, watching as the ship slipped from the wooden dock and into the bay. Venalise turned toward

Markan, leaning back against the rail. "You must be more careful. That old relic may be blind and frail, but do not mistake his outward appearance for weakness. Regealth is as powerful a mage as any that has lived. I would know." She smiled a sly and dangerous smile.

"Do not make him too comfortable," she continued. "The stronger his body becomes, the faster he will kill you." She leaned close to Markan. "And he *will* kill you if he gets a chance."

Markan waved her off and stood beside her at the rail. Leaning out over the water, he chuckled, "With what? His charm and good looks?" He reached into his pocket and pulled out a silver and leather thong. He held it up, reveling in the look on her face as a large, blue, and green crystalline stone fell from his palm to dangle in front of her. Its weight pulled the leather taut. "I'd like to see how powerful he is without this!"

"Fool!" she spat. In the blink of an eye, she snatched it from the trader's grasp. "This stone is more powerful than anything you could imagine, and you have it tucked away in your grimy little pocket?" She cradled the crystal in her hands and stepped past him. Without looking back, she hissed, "Keep him below."

She gazed at it for a moment more, then placed the stone in a pouch belted to her waist. She turned to Markan and dismissed him with a wave of her hand. He left, but not before glancing back over his shoulder to see Venalise caressing the pouch with a smile of satisfaction on her face.

Regealth wrung his hands as he was led down the rocking hallway. His mind raced. *The Gate.* He had worn the stone for so long; it had played an integral role in what made him who he was — the very thing that kept him alive these many hundred years since its creation. Everything depended on its safe return — his life, the safety of their world, and the very existence of the Travelers.

He heard a door open. "In you go, old man," a gravelly voice said, and rough hands shoved him inside. He was alone, with only the sound of the turning lock behind him to keep him company. Regealth took a step forward, but as he did, the boat lurched, and he went to his knees. The impact jarred him, and he fell forward onto his chest, his weakened arms useless to break his fall. He lay there, too drained from trying to rise. He took a moment to appreciate the opportunity to rest and allowed his legs to straighten. His captors had kept him in the cramped wooden crate with little opportunity to move. Thus, his body was wracked with cramps and aches.

He did not know how long he lay there on the deck, rolling and swaying as the boat sailed along. He pressed his ear to the wooden boards and noticed the pitch of the waves seeming to deepen — the ship was gliding over deeper water. He closed his cloudy eyes and slowed his breathing, moving his consciousness to its center. He sought to settle his thoughts, to try to find his sight. Drifting through his mind, he gently beckoned for the magic to come forth. It had been so long since he had drawn power from himself that he was unsure if it would still be there or if it had long since atrophied.

He searched for a memory of himself as a young man, drawing upon magical energy. He chose a simple task, like lighting a candle or lifting a spoon. Though, the images were fleeting and always just out of his reach. The effort drained him, and he stifled the urge to give up and sleep; however, there was little choice for him in the matter. His body, old and frail and now without food, rest, and the sustaining power of the Gate, could go no further. He felt himself dissolving into a wash of falling stars as he lost consciousness, rocking into a dreamless sleep.

Venalise sat down at the captain's desk, still mesmerized by her treasure. The fabled Gate, here in her hands — hands that trembled in anticipation. She turned the stone repeatedly, watching the lantern light shine in the blue-green facets.

"Wrought from the sea and stars," she whispered, transfixed. She closed her eyes now and clutched the stone to her breast. For a brief moment, she considered attempting to reach out to the power of the Gate, but she pulled it from her chest, withdrawing her efforts. She must be careful. Regealth created this talisman, and she was unsure which element Regealth was affiliated with. Should she not share his affinity, the incongruence alone could permanently dampen her abilities.

Venalise hesitantly opened her hand and lay the Gate in a heavy silver locket on the desk, lined with rowan bark. She closed the locket and gently placed its silver chain around her neck. She sat back in her chair, resting her hand on the ornament's decoration — a little jeweled acorn over her heart. It would take time, but her patience was a small investment that would yield such significant and glorious results if she were successful and her employer got what he desired.

A knock at the door snapped her from her reverie.

"Who is it?" she snapped crossly.

"Ma'am, your tea?" A tiny, thin voice came from behind the door.

"Come!" Venalise barked. She heard the shuffling of feet, and the door creaked open. A youth who looked no older than seven entered the room awkwardly, carrying a tray that held a broken teapot, mismatched cup, saucer, and biscuit. The woman gestured to the child to put the tray on the table. Venalise glanced back at the tray and noticed a small paper flower lying on the saucer. The mage looked back to the child, who wore a hopeful expression. "What is your name, child?" Venalise asked.

"S-Sam."

"Well, Sam, do you have so much free time that you can play with paper dolls?" She smiled at the child, whose faint smile slowly melted away. The child said nothing but began to back toward the door.

"Because *you* are idle," Venalise continued, her sweetness tinged with venom, "you can clean the floors of all the cabins. I want them done by dark!"

The ragged youth stifled a gasp, nodded once in understanding, and ran into a figure who appeared at the open doorway in their haste to flee the room. Venalise chuckled.

"And how can I help you, Master Omman?" She turned her attention to the man at her door, her feigned amusement fading.

The ship's captain, Omman Ehia, was a tiny man, but he made up for what he lacked in stature with presence. An Eztradian ship captain by trade, his time on the sea had made him hard and demanding. He was not an unintelligent man, either. The child darted past him and out of the cabin.

"You know, he's just a child—"

"Do *not,*" Venalise chided, "proceed to lecture me!"

The captain smirked at her, unafraid.

"My Lady," he said, "I merely suggested you not waste your time on such a small thing." He did not break eye contact with the powerful mage.

Venalise, unused to challenge, felt her temper flare but thought better of herself and calmed. She rose gracefully and took the few steps that led her just to Omman.

"My good Captain," her tone resonated with a haughty air, "I would advise you not meddle in my affairs."

The captain smiled again. He studied the woman for a moment. "My Lady." His smile did not fade, but there was a steely strength beneath his mask of civility. He continued. "I would advise you to remember that we ride upon the water, and I am the only one fit to guide this vessel where she has been paid to go. I am sure you understand the importance of hierarchy, and on this ship, when we are at sea, my word is law."

He tilted his head and smirked again, "That is, unless you are a water mage."

Venalise seethed inside. She was powerless on the water, and he knew it. Her strength came from the rocks and the metal of the land; without it, she was just a mage with little more than parlor tricks. The route over the water was an unfortunate necessity, and Captain Ehia was well aware of his unique position. She gathered her composure and strode back to the desk.

"You have matters well in hand, good captain," she said through clenched teeth.

He smiled at her and bowed. "Then I shall return to my post and allow you to rest."

Venalise slammed her fists on the wooden tabletop as he shut the door. *Idiot!* She mustn't allow her temper to get the better of her. Not here. Not where she was cut off from the source of her power. She sat and toyed with the locket. They should be on the water for no more than three days. Three days, and she would be back on solid ground — where there would be no doubt as to who was in charge.

CHAPTER 9

The galleon rocked back and forth as sunlight streamed through a small porthole high on the wall, cutting through the dust motes like a glowing sword. The old mage lay on the floor, as still as death, but with a color in his cheeks that had not been there earlier. A fine spray from the open porthole seemed drawn to him, hovering over his form like a cloud of tiny fireflies. Regealth's breathing was slower and less labored, and he seemed more at peace than at death's door. His right hand was outstretched, lying flat on the wood floor, a thin puddle of seawater pooled around it.

Outside, in the passageway, the child set the bucket down to turn the handle of the small cabin. It didn't budge, but one could never tell if a door was indeed locked or just frozen by rust from the sea spray on this vessel. Another hard twist, and the lock gave way. The child pulled it open, picked up the bucket, and stepped inside.

Inside the hatch lay the old man, who showed no apparent signs of life until he released a small shuddering breath. After a few more seconds of consideration, the child concluded that he was not dead. He was a prisoner, but the reason was not apparent — he just looked like a frail old man. Surely, he was no danger; otherwise, why would he just be lying on the floor? The task was to clean all the cabins, but that could not be completed with a body lying there like a pile of rags. Even after setting the bucket down and nudging him, he did not stir.

The child nudged again, higher, near his heart. Still, the old man didn't move, so any cleaning would have to be done around him, then he'd have to be rolled over to finish where he lay.

The small figure hauled the bucket to the corner and knelt to scrub the deck. The boat began to sway more and more. Minutes passed as the cleaned area progressed closer to the old mage. A giant wave caused the galleon to heave to the left, and the bucket tipped, sending a wave of water across the floor. It ran over the old man's hand and arm and then pooled around his head. The child jumped and righted the bucket, nervously watching to see if he would wake. Regealth's breathing deepened, and his fingers curled in the spilled water against the planks. He rolled over and reached toward the puddle, weakly splashing it over his skin. Once the pool was gone, the man lay back. He rubbed his face with his damp hands and opened his cloudy eyes. The child quietly stepped back against the wall and tried to tiptoe away from him.

"Thank you, girl," he croaked. "I can breathe again."

She froze. He knew.

"Come, and help an old man to sit." He raised one trembling hand, beckoning.

The girl hesitated but then moved to his side. She bent down and tentatively took his hands, pulling him to sit. He pitched upward, grasping at her to gain his balance, and she steadied him by his shoulders. He took her face in his hands. His cloudy grey eyes searched her face earnestly.

"What is your name, child?"

She stiffened, fighting the urge to pull away. "Sa—," she started out of habit, then ducked her head. "Sia, sir."

"Sia, can you bring me more water?"

"Yes, but don't you want some food?" she asked, her voice barely a whisper.

"No, just water," he said, "for now."

She nodded, her head still in his grasp. "Yes," she said.

"That's a good girl." He patted her cheek.

She stood and picked up her bucket. "I have to scrub this deck first," she said, looking at the water that was splashed all over the little cabin. "Or I'll be beaten again."

The old man let his fingers trail in the puddles around him. His smile was kind as he insisted, "I will help you."

She started to protest but stopped as a ripple of mist undulated across the floor. In the time it took for her to blink, the deck was clean. The old man sat in the middle, a soft and knowing smile on his lips.

The girl stared in disbelief. "You're a mage," she breathed.

"I am," he replied. "In fact, on this day, I am a mage that needs your help."

"That's how you knew I was a girl? You're magical, right?" She thought for a moment, then her face brightened. A mage could help her get off this ship. "I will help you, sir, if you take me with you when you leave."

The old man maintained his somber composure.

"My dear," he whispered, "if you help me, I will make you a queen." Her eyes widened.

"I'm no queen, sir, but I would like to go home to my brothers."

The mage lay back down. "We'll see where this path leads us, eh?" He folded his hands on his chest and inhaled deeply. "Bring more water when you can, and I will get both of us off this ship."

The girl gave a clumsy half-curtsey and hurried out of the room with her bucket, closing the door carefully behind her. *Free!* What dumb luck she had, finding a mage that could help her! Her heart beat faster at the thought of seeing her brothers again and not worrying about maintaining her façade as a boy. A wide grin spread across her face.

Suddenly, the hatch across from her began to open, and she ran down the passageway to the ladder, expertly keeping her balance in the rocking waves. Taking the steps two at a time, she cleared the top just before Venalise stepped out of her cabin.

"Ho there! Boy!"

Sia pushed through the gaggle of deckhands. She turned at the sound of Master Omman's call. The sea was rough — the boat crashed through the waves, and she had difficulty maintaining her balance. Master Omman beckoned to her. Sighing, she pushed back through the men toward the wheel. She reached the captain, steadying herself on the short railing.

"Did you finish the floors?" he growled.

"Yessir."

"Good. That'll keep the snake quiet," he grumbled, his brow furrowed.

"Pardon, sir?"

"Nothing."

He looked down at her, and his expression softened. Sia always did her best to follow his orders, knowing that she owed him her life. She had come to him dressed as a boy, just seven summers old. She knew the tear stains on her cheeks and the way her chin quivered had given her away to Master Omman, but still, the sea captain had taken her under his wing and maintained her façade, no doubt protecting her from the perils of a long voyage with a ship full of men.

Sia fidgeted in front of him, waiting to hear his orders.

"Tell Boosey that he is to take care of our lady guest from now on. I don't want you to talk to her again."

"Y-yes, sir." Sia opened her mouth, then snapped it closed and looked away.

"What is it, boy?" Omman barked, making her jump.

"The sick old man... can I see to him, still?" She knew it was an odd request, but it seemed reasonable that she should. He was old and feeble, or so everyone thought, and she was such a small thing that no one would think she could help him escape. Master Omman seemed to share her sentiment.

"Yes," he shrugged. "I suppose there's no harm in that, is there?"

Another rare surge of hope bloomed inside her, and she turned, elbowing her way through the men on the deck. A few deckhands watched her incredulously as she confidently crossed the ship's deck, her short brown hair fluttering as she disappeared through the galley hatch.

The sun was high by the time Sia was able to return to the tiny cabin. The old man remained prone on the rough wooden planks, still ringed by a puddle of water. He'd said not to bring him food, but Sia didn't believe he wasn't hungry. She had slipped a biscuit and a withered apple into her pocket from the galley while Cook was distracted. Sia cleared her throat and set the bucket of seawater on the floor. The old man had asked for water, but he hadn't specified what kind, and Sia had worried over the choice a long while before plunging her bucket over the ship's side. Seawater seemed more magical than stale drinking water from the barrels. Besides, someone might have noticed if she pulled a bucketful of water from the fresh stores.

Regealth stirred and opened his eyes, staring straight up at the overhead planks. "Ah, you're back."

"I brought the water. It's salty."

He lay there, quiet as death, while he continued to stare, unblinking. Unsure of what to do, Sia broke the awkward silence. "Do you want me to pour it on you?"

Regealth chuckled. "No, no. Not this time. Help me sit." He lifted his arms for her to pull. Together, they worked him back into an upright position. Sia placed the bucket in front of him and situated herself cross-legged on the other side of the container. She couldn't help but peer at his cloudy eyes, wondering how much he could actually see.

"The bucket is in front of you," she said solemnly, then hastily added, "My Lord, sir."

"Regealth, child, not sir. Certainly not 'lord.'" Regealth chuckled softly to himself. "And I know where the bucket is. Even blind as a bat, I could find the smallest drop of water perched on a butterfly's wing."

Sia's eyes widened.

"When I was at my best, that is."

Regealth squared his shoulders and extended his hands toward the bucket. He held them over the water, just above its surface. For a while, nothing happened. Then Sia saw it — the faintest mist streaming from the water toward the mage's palms. The mist caressed his hands and crept up his arms like vines winding around a tree. Sia stole a glance at his face. His cheeks were pinker than when he first arrived, and his cloudy eyes had cleared to an almost mirror-like grey.

They sat together in silence for several minutes until Sia spoke.

"My Lord, I'd be careful."

Regealth raised his eyebrows and sat back, letting his hands fall away from the bucket.

"What do you mean?'

She hesitated.

"Well, if you make yourself better, that lady keeping you prisoner will notice."

"You are a clever little mouse, aren't you?" Regealth wiped his hands on his robes. "However, that lady hasn't yet realized I am a water mage, or she wouldn't have put us on a boat, eh?"

Sia grinned.

"Not very astute, is she?" he laughed.

"No, sir. Not 'stute at all," Sia answered, smiling shyly.

"This will do, for now, little one." He pushed the bucket toward Sia. "And I think, from now on, you should bring the water in something less conspicuous."

Sia wrinkled her brow. "What's that?"

"What?"

"Con-scip… us?"

Regealth snickered. "Conspicuous?"

Sia shrugged.

"It means obvious. Bring the water in something less big, less noticeable."

She stood, brushing against Regealth, who grasped her hand for a moment. He let her go, and she moved to open the door. She hesitated as she released the latch and turned back to him. "I'll be back while everyone's having their supper." She stepped out and closed the door softly behind her.

Regealth watched the door close and considered the girl. She was bright, and to his surprise, he sensed magical aptitude. She was small for her age; children with gifts were often the littlest. The power inside them drew on their energy from birth, stunting their growth. He could not sense what element she was bound to, but magic was most definitely there. With a sigh, he leaned forward onto his hands and knees. He reached out for the narrow bunk beneath the porthole and pulled his way up and onto the mildewed blanket.

He closed his eyes and began to consider his escape. He would most definitely bring the girl. If she possessed any amount of magical ability at all, it would not be long before she was discovered. He could not risk any power, weak or not, falling into dark hands.

CHAPTER 10

The band of riders — Jael, Bent, and ten Legion men — pressed hard overnight and through the next day. By nightfall, they reached Karth's foothills and the small village of Morning Hill. As they thundered into the square, many townsfolk stepped out of their homes to see who had arrived — in the outer lands of Karth, visits from the Legion were rare. The Prince reined his horse to the front of the inn and dismounted, followed by Bent and one of the other men. He strode inside. The innkeeper recognized the sigil on his cloak and bowed hastily.

"Kevar!" Jael laughed, signaling for him to rise, "None of that! We require two rooms and provisions for my men outside."

The way Jael spoke as if he were anyone from the forest and not the son of the King was not surprising to the few townsfolk in the great room. By rights, he could have simply demanded or even taken what he needed without so much as a word, as most nobility did, yet he did not. He never had.

"My Lord!" The innkeeper said, "A pleasure! And an honor to see you here again, to be sure!"

He waved his hands at his serving girl and boy, who trotted over. "See to the two rooms upstairs. Fresh linens and hot water! Boy — get to the stable with water for the horses and pull down fresh hay." The two nodded and darted off to do their master's bidding.

Jael smiled warmly at the innkeeper. "You have the finest inn in all of Karth, my man!" He placed his hand on his shoulder and then handed him a small pouch of coins. "We thank you for your hospitality."

The innkeeper bowed again, and Jael turned toward the hearth. He scanned the room until his eyes locked onto a figure in the corner, the deep hood of its cloak pulled forward. He made his way to the table. "Surprisingly quick! I was fairly certain *we* would be waiting for *you*."

Amarynn looked at Jael and pulled her hood from her braided auburn hair. She opened her hand, allowing the crumpled note to fall to the table. "You don't know me very well, do you?"

Jael pulled a chair out to sit. "Clearly, not."

Amarynn stood as Bent and the other Legion man hastily made their way to the table.

"Lass!" Bent clasped her hand in greeting. "Oh! It does my eyes good to see you out of that blasted dungeon!" He gestured to the Prince. "When his Highness came to me and told me Regealth had gone missing, I told him we needed you. I don't know how he convinced his father to free you, but I am glad he did."

Amarynn cast a glance at the Prince and arched her eyebrow.

Jael's signal was nearly imperceptible, but she took his meaning by the way he lifted his chin and worked his jaw muscles. No one but the two of them — and whoever had delivered that key — knew of her escape. Until the dungeon guards discovered her disappearance, all of Karth still believed she was safely locked away.

"I should have known you'd beat us here!" Bent laughed heartily as he and Amarynn took a seat at the table.

A serving girl dropped a large loaf of aromatic brown bread and four tankards of ale in front of them. "Compliments of the house," she said, with a grin and a wink.

Jael smiled at the girl, then turned to the soldier standing beside the table. "We'll sleep here tonight and continue in the morning. Tell the men outside they will return to Calliway tonight once they are reprovisioned." He handed a satchel to him. "Have Osmir change into this. He looks most like me." The man gave a quick salute, took the bag, and exited the inn.

Confused, Amarynn asked, "You're sending them back? Why?"

Jael shifted closer to her. "I cannot take a small army out of Karth undetected, can I? This needs to look like I've made my usual rounds and returned home."

He was so close now that their shoulders touched, and she turned her head to glance at him. His face was strong but was softened by kindness in his expression. He smelled of new leather and spice.

Goddess! What was she thinking?

Amarynn sat back and snatched the crumpled paper from the table, studying the Prince in the flickering firelight. Jael had orchestrated her escape and would take the fall when the King inevitably discovered she was missing. But why? All these years, Prince Jael had maintained the appearance of being ruthless, just like his father. This sudden about-face, and the turn of events leading to her escape, made little sense.

Jael rested his elbows on the table. "I'm glad you were able to join us."

Their eyes met. Hers narrowed while she tried to understand what he was playing at. Obviously, he wanted to conceal that he was responsible for her escape. He perpetuated the façade that he was returning to Calliway with the men. She replayed the events leading to her arrival at Morning Hill, working out what she could have missed in his subterfuge.

When she had reached the Mountain Fiddler Inn after her dungeon escape, she headed straight for the stables in search of Dax. An impatient stamping of hooves had led her to a dark corner stall, where he was already saddled and ready to ride, a bag of provisions lashed to his pommel. Absently, she reached for the handle of her short sword, forgetting she was still unarmed. She ground her teeth in agitation until she noticed a canvas-wrapped bundle in the corner. She unwrapped it with a mischievous chuckle, pulling out all her blades.

Frost, her broadsword, was still in Bent's possession. She frowned as she replaced the six weapons in their sheaths, one by one. Buckling her swordbelt and slinging it safely onto her back, she grabbed Dax's reins and led him from the stall.

Three secret gates were known only to the Legion elite. She turned Dax onto the rarely used western road that wound upward through the foothills, surprised to see no evidence of recent use. She had considered that this might be a trap, just like her audience with the King. A Legion squadron could have been around every corner but wasn't — she pushed on and made good time. As the sun took its position directly overhead, they galloped undetected into the small forest village.

"Lass?"

Amarynn snapped her attention to Bent, who was looking at her expectantly. He frowned. "Where's that mind of yours, eh?"

By his expression, she guessed that Bent was oblivious to Jael's role in her release; this made her wary. She dismissed Bent with a shake of her head and turned back to the Prince. His Legion man had returned, and the two were in deep, quiet conversation. The soldier took notice of her focus, and as his eyes shifted in her direction, the Prince followed his gaze. Jael tilted his head in the soldier's direction. "This is Nioll."

Amarynn acknowledged him with a glance. Nioll pulled a piece of bread from the loaf.

Jael continued. "Nioll, you are in the presence of myth and legend. This is—"

"Amarynn," Nioll finished. "I know you're a Traveler." He pointed at her with his bread.

Amarynn gave Nioll a quick smirk. "My reputation precedes me."

Nioll scoffed, ripping off another chunk of hearty bread. "I thought you were locked up," he said between bites.

Jael looked to Amarynn, interested in her response.

"Well, obviously I'm not," she scoffed, adding nothing else. To change the subject, she shifted to face Bent. "Regealth. Who took him? What do you know?"

Bent grimaced. "He's missing, lass." He paused and tilted his head. "What makes you think he was taken?"

"If Regealth is missing," she said, "I cannot imagine his absence was of his own volition. He's as much a part of Karth's court as the King. A mage like him has no reason to just disappear."

Bent jerked his thumb toward Jael. "The Prince is the one with the most knowledge."

Jael scanned the tables around them to ensure no one was eavesdropping on their conversation. "From what we can tell, there was no struggle. I'm the one who discovered his absence."

"When?" Amarynn asked.

"Right after we spoke, I went to see him, to return the torc."

Because of me, she thought. Her breath caught in her throat. The memory of Jael removing the torc from her neck flashed through her mind.

Jael ran a hand through his dark blonde hair and shifted in his seat. "Regealth was in council early that morning. He and my father disagreed. It's possible their exchange drove him to leave."

"Not surprising," Nioll muttered around a swallow of ale.

Amarynn sat back, a troubled expression on her face. Jael took notice but continued. "It's safe to assume he hasn't been gone very long."

"Did he leave all his belongings?" she asked Jael, not looking up.

"His chamber was untouched."

"And the Gate Stone?" Amarynn's voice wavered slightly.

"What?" Jael furrowed his brow.

"Did he take the Gate Stone with him?"

Bent lay a hand on Amarynn's shoulder. "His Grace said the mage's chamber was untouched, lass."

She looked up, her eyes dark. She repeated the question. "Is it gone?"

75

Jael's silence was her answer.

"Then he didn't just leave." Amarynn did not break eye contact with Jael. She had known Regealth for twenty years, and she was sure he never left the castle, much less the city of Calliway.

Now all eyes were on her.

"I'm telling you. He was taken."

Bent held his breath while Nioll stopped chewing.

Jael tilted his head slightly, studying her. "I cannot fathom how that is even a possibility."

Bent slapped a hand down on the table. "Who could possibly have managed to kidnap one of the most powerful mages alive?"

A sinking feeling dropped Amarynn's gut like a stone in water. She scowled and closed her eyes. "Another mage."

Taking a deep breath, she considered her last statement carefully. She had been very busy in the previous few months and too careless in her quest to find release from immortality. Regealth had been unable to help her. When she'd heard whispers of an earth mage claiming to have the strength of Regealth, she sought her out. The woman had asked a ridiculous number of questions. Questions she had claimed she needed answers to craft a reversal. In the end, all Amarynn had been left with was a poison that proved useless. Amarynn's emotions had blinded her — in her self-centered anger and despair. She had traded Regealth's secrets for absolutely nothing at all. Because of her, Regealth and the Gate, the very sum of her existence, were gone. Her heart sank and settled in the lowest part of her being.

"Another mage?" Jael's voice was laced with disbelief. "Who?"

"Venalise Korr," Amarynn said. "The right hand to King Lors of the Darklands."

CHAPTER 11

"How do you know this?" Jael's voice was soft.

Having to face the three men that surrounded her was the hardest thing Amarynn had ever done. Harder than facing an angry horde alone on a battlefield, harder than coming back from the dead repeatedly, even harder than waking up every day with no end in sight.

"I told her," Amarynn whispered. "I told her everything." She dropped her gaze to the floor. She could feel the men's stares, so she continued without looking up. "She wanted to know how I was made and brought here. I didn't know everything, but I told her what I did know, what I remembered from my crossing. I told her where to find his aethertorium in the castle — where he kept the Gate."

Amarynn raised her head and held her breath. She looked hard at each of them, acknowledging her shame. Jael's furrowed brow and Nioll's surprised countenance stung, but what was left of her heart crumbled at the incredulous *"Why?"* she read in Bent's pained expression.

"I was looking for a way to die," was all she could offer.

"Did you mind that your information would help her create Travelers? You might well be taking the lot of us with you into death when she arrives at our borders with an immortal army?" Bent's voice was a whisper, but it pierced her soul as quickly as the flaming sword of Balan might. "Goddess, lass!" Her old mentor dropped his head into his hands.

She could find no words. There was nothing she could say to excuse her blatant disregard for her people, for the suffering she might have caused. When she walked through the gates of King Lor's keep and demanded to speak to the mage called Venalise, her only thoughts were of her herself. Her desperation had been so great, her despair so deep that she'd bleated every scrap of information she possessed, stringing together all the pieces of knowledge she'd gathered about her crossing. She had recklessly delivered the truth about the magic she had felt, the magic she knew was responsible for bringing her and the other Travelers into the world. Amarynn was certain she had given away the keys to their very existence.

She blinked. The inn was emptying in the late evening hours, and as the darkness deepened, she felt a black hole threatening to swallow her completely.

She wished it would.

Jael broke the suffocating silence. "There is no time for blame. Every second we sit here, we are closer to our destruction if another mage has possession of the Gate," he continued. "You must remember everything you told her." Jael leveled a penetrating stare.

"I told her *everything*," Amarynn began. "I told her what it felt like, what I heard when I woke, what I saw… everything."

"You do know many things," Jael nodded in agreement. "But crossing Travelers takes time. Each one is the result of almost a year of preparation. The moment of your arrival does not give away all the secrets."

"What do you mean?" Amarynn could not hide her apprehension.

"You know a great deal about Regealth's magic concerning Travelers." The corners of his mouth turned up ever so slightly. "But there is more to the creation to Travelers than his powers alone."

"I know there is. That's the reason we are bound to your father. I know he is a source of power, one that Regealth draws on to complete the crossing, and now, so does she. I told her about what happened to me, about the Gate stone." Amarynn shook her head, not understanding.

"You did, and if this mage is as powerful as you claim, we'll need to be vigilant. I've only ever known one mage, so none of us can anticipate what she can do." He grinned conspiratorially. "But she certainly does not have access to my father and his power. Remember, crossing Travelers is a complicated and lengthy process. We have time concerning the risk this mage poses. You'll just have to trust me on that." Jael sat back in his seat and took a long pull from his tankard of ale. "But the longer we wait, Regealth and the Gate become further and further away. Our true urgency is his safety."

Amarynn thought for a moment, then pushed herself to her feet. Jael did not seem to appreciate the full gravity of her deeds, but she felt no desire to waste any more time debating. "Whatever damage I have done or not done, you are right. We are wasting our time here. I could ride for days without sleep, but you three cannot. We have rooms. Let's use them and be off at dawn."

"Aye, lass." Bent agreed as he pushed back in his chair. Nioll took his cue from the aging Blademaster, though he hastily tucked the remainder of the dark bread under his arm as he rose.

The four made for the stairwell near the kitchen, Amarynn hanging back a few paces. She turned away at the last second and quietly slipped out the side door, but not before she glanced back over her shoulder to find the Prince watching her. She hesitated for an instant, then turned from him and slipped into the night.

Amarynn crossed the yard and ducked into the stable. Inside, sweet-smelling warmth combined with the soft glow of lanterns. A familiar whicker floated from the stall to her left, and she joined her horse, closing the gate behind her. Slowly and deliberately, she removed her weapons and set them in the corner. Her mind drifted back to the King's son. She tried to think back to her first days in the practice yard once she had recovered from Traveling.

She remembered a worried-looking blond boy, always in the shadows, watching her as she took blow after blow from the men. Maybe, because he was a blatant contradiction to how a child of Lasten's should behave, Jael confused her — and she did not like to be confused. When he'd reached an age to train, the young Prince had stopped lurking about. Amarynn had always believed Jael had fallen prey to his father's influence. She was sure his heart had begun to harden, that he was learning how to be just as ruthless as Lasten.

Her training had been brutal, with no sensitivity to what she had endured. The method was immersion — the idea that overwhelming a Traveler with the primal need to survive would drive away whatever emotional trauma they suffered in the crossing. This was King Lasten's directive. After two costly invasions, he wanted an army of unstoppable killers. This was why he'd conspired with his mage to bring off-worlders into his realm. He wanted "fresh blood, with no ties or loyalties to hinder them" in the Legion's ranks. Only two women were brought over, and Amarynn was painfully aware that Lasten never intended for either of them to join the Travelers.

An icy chill had crept through her bones. The memory of her crossing always imposed a shocking effect. She exhaled slowly, pushing the old images away, and returned to the present. A crunch of footsteps in the straw behind her made her jump.

"Who—"

She spun around to see Jael leaning against the stall gate. He studied her with a mixture of curiosity and sympathy. For a moment, he was that seven-year-old boy, watching her as she broke over and over again.

"Is there something you need?" she asked, lifting her chin in an unconvincing act of indifference.

He did not smile, but his eyes shone with understanding. "I know it has been tough for you."

Amarynn cleared her throat and gathered herself. She grabbed a brush from a bucket that hung on the wall and ran it over her Dax's back.

"Yes," she replied briskly, not looking back at Jael.

"I can only imagine what it has been like for the last twenty years, being who you are. The famous Traveler warrior, the stuff of legends." He paused, then began to walk around the edge of the stall. "I remember when you arrived. I must have thought about it a thousand times. You seemed unreal to me, like some fallen god."

Her eyes followed him as he stepped around Dax to stand behind her.

"I don't pretend to know what it is like to be you, but I know that you must feel alone. And that is something I understand more than you'd think."

She stopped brushing abruptly. He was the future ruler of the largest and most powerful Kingdom as far as the light of the sun and moons could touch. What would he know of loneliness? "Alone? You?"

She waited a long moment for his reply, but when he said nothing, she turned and found him gone. Hurling the brush against the wall in frustration, she returned her attention to the horse and finished settling him for the night. The boy from the inn darted in and heaped fresh hay into the stall's feed boxes. Without another word, Amarynn made space in the corner of the stall and sat down hard, leaning back against the wall. She'd be damned if she returned to the inn now.

She should leave tonight, she thought. Now that she knew where Regealth was most likely destined, she should just go straight to Venalise and retrieve him. What was one mage if she could take down an entire raging army on her own? The vile woman did not actually know how to end Amarynn's life, so she would be in no real danger. This was all her fault anyway, and she could set it right on her own — there was no need to drag Bent into any of this. She and

Dax could do this as they had done all the other impossible things a thousand times before.

She needed no one.

There was no one for her, anyway.

Amarynn quickly saddled the warhorse with a surge of stubborn determination and belted her weapons around her waist. Then, once again, Amarynn and Dax set out alone under cover of night toward the north and the cold, dark Kingdom ruled by Lors and his trickster witch, Venalise.

CHAPTER 12

Sia squeezed her eyes shut, holding her hands over the chipped bowl of seawater that sloshed back and forth with the ship's motion. The small cabin was dimly lit by one high porthole, and rays of light streamed across the cabin to light up the dark brown tangles of the girl's roughly cropped hair.

The old mage had suspected she was hiding a gift and, over the next two days at sea, was shocked to discover her affinity was to water. The gift of magic was rare, and the gift of the water element, even more so — in fact, in this age, he knew of no other save himself — so he thought to begin her training now while they were at sea. It would be easier on the child, surrounded by her element. He knew his days might be numbered — the sooner she was given some instruction, the better. She may never have the opportunity to learn from another.

"I think I feel something," she whispered.

Regealth looked to her hands and drew in a sharp breath. The delicate tendrils of mist she drew from the bowl coalesced into a dense fog beneath her hands. *She shouldn't be able to call the mist so soon!* He placed his hands above hers and was surprised to sense her strength.

She was proving to be more than extraordinary.

"That's very good, my dear," he said, "But I think we've done enough this morning."

Sia opened her eyes and drew her hands away from the bowl, water droplets clinging to her skin. She snuck a grin at Regealth. "I did good, didn't I?"

Regealth composed his face into a mask of seriousness. "One must never be content with their practice. 'Good' suggests you are moving toward mastery, and my dear, you have only just begun." He paused, ever so serious, then gave her a little wink. She giggled and winked back.

He chuckled, then broke into a fit of dry coughs. He took a moment to settle, then attempted an unconvincing smile.

"You need that pretty blue stone they took from you, don't you?" Sia said, concerned.

The mage waved her off. "As long as I am near the water, I'll be fine."

She pursed her lips and shook her head. "I don't think so, sir."

Regealth smiled to himself. *Nothing escapes her*, he thought.

"That is not for you to worry on. Now get your things and be on your way. I don't want you getting into trouble, especially with this crew." He worried that Venalise might pick up on the child's blossoming gift. Then, he knew the child would be lost. Most importantly, because only a water mage could wield the power of the Gate, Sia was now incredibly valuable... and at significant risk. He caught her hand in both of his, his thumbs tracing a quick pattern on her palm.

"Remember, child, tell no one of what you are learning here. Some would hurt you for what you can do. Best that we keep it between us, yes?"

She nodded solemnly, then flashed a grin and jumped to her feet.

Just as she gathered the bowl and her other cleaning supplies, the pair heard footsteps approaching. Sia hoisted her things and moved to open the door, but the handle turned, and she found herself facing Markan, the man who had overseen the kidnapping of her new mentor. Quickly ducking her head, she squeezed past him and skittered away down the narrow hallway.

"Ho!" Markan laughed, "You've scared the little darlin' away, old man!" Markan stepped inside the cabin, bringing with him the unwashed stench of stale smoke and ale.

"Hmph!" Regealth groaned and fell back against the wooden planks of the deck and closed his eyes, only partly feigning exhaustion.

"We're putting into port, mage, and I'm gonna need to know if you can walk off this ship or if we're gonna have to make… other *arrangements.*" Markan halfheartedly kicked Regealth's foot.

Regealth opened his watery eyes and stared at Markan. He remained stoic, focused on the shield he had created around Sia before she left. He tied it off subtly, ensuring it could not be detected, but it took great concentration now that he was solely reliant upon his power alone.

"Walk it is, then, old man!" Markan declared as he reached out to hoist the mage up by his arms and unceremoniously shove him through the narrow door.

Regealth stumbled, catching himself against the doorframe. As he stepped forward into the hall, he saw a glimpse of Sia peering at him from around the corner. She was nearing Venalise's cabin, where the Gate Stone was kept. He recognized her look of determination and tried to warn her away with a gesture and a hard stare. As the old mage was dragged down the hall and past Sia's hiding spot, he whispered urgently, "Sia — no!" She didn't respond — he knew she was fixated on retrieving the Gate.

Markan forced Regealth up the stairs to the deck, where he could hear Venalise's voice calling orders out from above. If Sia were reckless enough to try for the stone, at least she'd have a moment or two of safety. He couldn't help but hope the child was successful, though he would have never willingly risked her. Seeing her determination, he knew there was no way to stop her.

But he could help her.

He slowed his steps and then purposefully stumbled backward, falling on the stairs, pinning Markan behind him.

"Oh dear!" he exclaimed, exaggerating his feebleness, "I don't suppose I'll ever have sea legs!" Regealth did his best to become dead weight against his captor.

Markan issued a guttural response and jerked forward and up the short stairwell, pushing the old mage with him. Regealth was clumsily deposited on the deck, his ancient form sprawled out on the planks. He lay there for a moment until a shadow fell across his face.

"Markan," Venalise's voice almost purred. "I hope you have not damaged our guest." She stooped near Regealth's head, her deep burgundy skirts pooling around her. "King Lors will be quite put out if you have."

She quickly ran her eyes over the old man's still form in a halfhearted inspection. Satisfied he was intact, she rose and tossed a disdainful look at Markan.

"I trust you can get him off the ship without additional assistance. I need to gather my belongings from my quarters. The sooner I can get back on solid ground, the better!"

Markan grimaced, reaching down to haul Regealth up to his feet. Venalise swept past them and vanished down the stairs toward her cabin. As he stumbled forward through the bustling deckhands, Regealth said a silent prayer to the Goddess that Sia was long gone from Venalise's room.

Sia heard the old mage's warning, but she knew she must retrieve the stone, or he would not make it much longer. She could feel his life draining every time she entered his cabin. She would be quick — in and out — and she would have what he needed to spirit them both out of here.

She heard a clatter and, guessing Regealth had created a diversion, used the commotion to her advantage. No one noticed when the cabin door's handle twisted in her grasp, and she slipped through the hatch as quickly as she could, closing it behind her. When she turned to face the cabin, her heart sank. The captain's quarters were the largest on the ship and full of boxes and bags. Scarves tumbled over shelves of books, scrolls —both rolled and open — were stacked in the corners, and half-open loads of herbs were scattered on the table in the center of the room.

"Did you think the thing was just gonna be to be layin' out on the table?" she muttered. "Oh, you wanted to steal a 'spensive jewel? Why," she gestured grandly to the table with one hand, "here ya go!" Still, the table seemed as good as any spot to begin searching.

She was only halfway through her rapid inspection of the table when the door suddenly swung open. Sia froze — her breath catching in her throat.

"I thought I heard a little mouse!"

Venalise Korr towered in the doorway, one hand casually toying with the locket that hung from her neck. Sia frantically cast about with her eyes, not knowing what she was looking for but desperate to disappear. Her heart pounded, and she felt a rush of warmth from her toes, creeping quickly up to her belly.

"Oh, now...!" The elegant earth mage's eyes widened suddenly. She glided over to the small girl and grasped her face in her hands. "What have we here?"

Heat surged upward in Sia's tiny body, and she stiffened; her fear intensified. The heat licked upward toward her face, filling her with a burning sensation like a fever. What would the mage do to her? She became frantic.

Sia moaned as the last wave of burning pain washed over her before plummeting into cool, quiet darkness.

Outside on the deck, Regealth felt a cold hiss as the shield he'd worked so hard to maintain sizzled away. Shock seized him as he felt a sputter — and then the little girl's magic simply disappeared. She had been there earlier, an ever-present ripple of magic onboard the ship

87

since his arrival, and then she was not. Fearing the worst, he cried out, reaching toward the small hatch that led below.

Confirmation came as Venalise's dark head emerged from the opening, slowly climbing the steps to the deck. She clutched the limp child in her arms, stroking her hair possessively. Sia's skin was pale, and her breathing shallow.

"My, my, dear Regealth. We've been keeping secrets, haven't we?" Venalise frowned melodramatically. She gestured to Markan and his men. "Bring him!" she barked. "Keep him away from the girl and me."

"And Markan." Venalise's voice was a cold snarl as she added, "I only need him breathing by the time we get to the keep. Do what you wish."

CHAPTER 13

Amarynn crouched behind a large oak tree, the watery light of dawn filtering through the dense canopy above. A rider had been following her for the last two hours, and she was ready to put a stop to it now. Dax was several hundred feet away, hidden by the dense underbrush. The horse and rider came into view.

Jael reined his mount in between the trees toward her position. Amarynn contemplated her options: reveal herself and deal with the intrusion or remain hidden and let him wander on. She sighed deeply.

"Why are you following me?" She stepped from behind the tree as Jael pulled his horse to a stop.

"I was under the impression we were *all* going after Regealth and the stone."

Amarynn whistled for Dax. He emerged from the brush to ease up behind her and butt his head against her back. "I decided to handle this myself, considering I'm the reason we are in this mess to begin with." She swung herself up into the saddle and urged her horse into a walk.

"*You* decided?"

She looked back over her shoulder at the Prince. He was attractive — even with that irritated look. "I've always heard rumors the royalty in Karth had issues with defects... deformities and whatnot." She guided Dax around a stand of trees. "I suppose you could be hard of hearing," she pondered, adding, "from the inbreeding."

She continued, not looking back.

Jael scoffed and frowned but said nothing as they continued to weave in and out of the trees. She wanted to ask about Bent — how Jael managed to leave without her old master and Nioll — but she held her tongue. After they cleared the dense thicket, the Prince and his mount drew up beside her. She cast a sideways glance at him. His stamina was strange; he did not seem fatigued at all. He had ridden all night, but still, he sat tall in his saddle, and his eyes were bright, not bleary. His eyes. She looked just a little longer. They were the color of a stormy sky in the mountains.

Amarynn shook her head and grimaced. *Why do I care?* She pushed her heels into Dax's side, and he jumped forward, surprised.

The morning wore on. They stopped briefly to water their horses at a meandering stream. Amarynn leaned against a tree and waited for them to drink their fill while Jael crouched to fill his waterskin.

"They'll follow, regardless," Jael finally said, breaking the hours-long silence.

Bent. Of course, he would.

"I know," she bit back.

"They'll be slower." He looked around. They were at the base of a heavily forested hillside. "I'm sure they'll do something ridiculous and follow a road or a trail."

"That was the idea." She pushed off the tree and whistled again for Dax. "There's a long road to the pass. Could take them a week, easily." She swung into the saddle and chirped for Dax to break into a trot. The Prince grabbed his horse's reins and followed her back up the hillside.

They continued up and over the rough, wooded terrain until the sun had started its descent toward the horizon. A breeze had picked up, the trees blowing and bending above them. Amarynn reined her horse from beneath the boughs and branches into a clearing, with Jael following behind.

She dismounted and, with one hand resting on Dax's neck to settle him, she surveyed the edge of the clearing. The woods had gone quiet, save for the breeze. Something — an agitated sensation, like spiders crawling on the back of her neck — tugged at her. The air felt off somehow. She raised her hand, signaling Jael to stop.

Amarynn continued her survey of the area when something caught her eye. Moving across the clearing carefully but quickly, she eyed a patch of disturbed grass near a trail of bent branches and flattened plant life. The unsettled foliage continued as far as she could see into the darkened woods beyond the clearing. She carefully stepped onto the trail and squatted down to look for any evidence that might tell her what had come this way. Nothing. She crept forward into the shadows, all her senses alert. Breathing in deeply, she tried to fully assess her surroundings. The forest was vast, full of different scents and sounds. She could sense there were elements out of place when a strange, distant sound halted her in her tracks. It rang out like a bird call but with the deep throatiness of a bear.

She snapped her head to the right and glanced back over her shoulder toward the clearing. Jael crouched behind two fallen trees, his longbow and quiver slung across his back. He raised his hand in a signal, telling her to wait.

She complied, her warrior instincts kicking in. Amarynn carefully picked her way back to the Prince until she reached the spot where he was concealed. The two huddled together, and Jael whispered, "I've never seen anything like it!"

"What are you talking about?"

"When you started down the trail, I saw something flying above the tree line. I thought it might be a young greall, but I couldn't be sure," Jael's tone was hushed, his tension clear.

"Greall don't come this far north."

"Exactly," Jael agreed. "I tried to track where it went, but it dove into the woods. I thought you saw it. I followed you to get a better look."

Another wild shriek tore through the quiet forest. The two looked in the direction it had come from. Jael's countenance hardened with the focus of a soldier. He pulled a leather arm brace over his right forearm and jerked the straps tight with his teeth. Finished, he said, "I'm going."

Amarynn, broadsword already drawn, nodded. "I'm coming with you."

Not waiting for Jael to take the lead, she rose to a half-crouch and moved toward the sound. Jael followed, drawing and nocking an arrow.

Another shriek rang out, followed by a higher-pitched cry of a similar timbre. Amarynn didn't hesitate; she broke into a low run toward the source of the sound. Jael followed, quickly catching up to her pace. The sounds became louder, mixed with the thrashing and breaking of tree limbs. They stopped just short of a break in the brush.

Without warning, a greall — little more than a blur of brown and grey — crashed through the branches and into Jael, hurling him against a nearby tree. His bow clattered into the undergrowth, and Amarynn jumped back, sword at the ready. The beast landed on its back but quickly twisted to its feet. It squared itself on four heavily scaled legs and swung its thick-jawed head back and forth between Amarynn and Jael.

Another cry resonated from the clearing behind them. Jael, stunned, stayed down as Amarynn bolted to put herself between the horse-sized greall and the Prince. It sidestepped, keeping her in its field of view, and edged itself back toward the clearing. Amarynn adjusted her grip on her blade and took a step forward, ready to engage.

The beast swayed back and forth, its muscled neck moving like a bear. Large, black bird-like eyes focused on Amarynn. It took a step forward and shrieked, closing the gap between them. With a grunt, Amarynn swung her sword.

Metal and scales connected, neither succumbing to the other's force. Her blade bounced back as if she'd hit the dummy in the practice yard.

The greall spun around, whipping its thick, leathery tail at Amarynn. It was low enough that she could jump to avoid it, but Jael was not so lucky. The end of the tail was rigid, with scales pointed outward, and they slashed across his right thigh. She heard him cry out, and without understanding why, a different kind of rage flowed through her.

She advanced. The creature snapped and bit while Amarynn, dodging, countered with strikes to its head and neck. She spun, using the extra force to strike at its jaw. The satisfaction of the resounding crack and shriek from the greall emboldened her. It reared back, and she saw her target at the base of its neck. Too small a mark for her broadsword, she dropped Frost, reached for the dagger on her belt, and charged. A dart to the left at the last moment and her whirling dagger found its mark.

The animal cried out, and as it came down, both front legs buckled. It fell to its side while Amarynn sidestepped back to where Jael lay. She crouched beside him, keeping the creature in her sight.

"Can you sit?"

He frowned and nodded. "I'm fine. It's nothing."

She hooked one arm under his and pulled him to a sitting position. He pushed himself around to lean back on a tree. Amarynn reached for his leg. "Let me see."

"No."

"Don't be an ass; let me see if I need to stitch it up."

She reached again, and he grabbed her hand.

"Why won't you let me look?"

He didn't answer. She noticed he wasn't looking at her — his eyes were fixed above her head.

She followed his stare.

Two reptilian eyes met hers. The head, crisscrossed with ridges of scars, remained motionless while its neck swung as it gathered its legs beneath it. Amarynn's right hand drifted to the hilt of her short sword. "As soon as I move, get behind this tree," she murmured. She didn't wait for Jael to respond. Before she could take a step, the creature shifted its attention to the smaller beast on the ground, stretching its neck in the dead greall's direction. This beast was twice as large as the animal Amarynn had just taken down. Black scales shimmered with an iridescent green hue from its long, triangular head to its tail. Nostrils flaring, the creature adjusted its stance and leaped. The ground shook with the force of its weight.

Amarynn staggered back and watched, transfixed, as it raised its clawed front foot, then gouged it into the felled creature's chest, ripping scales and fur in one slicing motion. It reared back onto its hind legs, balanced by its large, muscled tail, and screamed. As the echo of the deafening cry faded, the creature settled on all four clawed feet, sniffing. It found the greall's heart and bit down, swallowing it in one smooth motion. A black, forked tongue darted over its snout as it turned to level its green-gold eyes directly on Amarynn and Jael.

There were no beasts as massive as the one in front of them in this world. Greall were the closest, and they were only the size of an over-large horse. The monstrous black reptile they now faced towered over them. Jael had recovered enough to stand and regain his bow — now drawn and ready.

"Wait," Amarynn hissed. The monster crept closer, its eyes never wavering from theirs.

Her sword was drawn, but she kept it low, tightening her grip. She stepped back with one foot to ready herself. It was three sword-lengths away but suddenly stopped its forward progression. For one frozen moment, all three were fixed in place with uncertainty. Amarynn's skin crawled with electric ripples that wove from her spine to her scalp. The black creature's eyes changed, pupils dilating to pinpoints, then it snorted and blew out, shook its head, and reared back. Amarynn drew her sword up and prepared to strike, but the creature turned and retreated to the clearing. She followed and watched it unfurl its wings and beat them in hard, fast strokes. It lifted from the clearing, scattering branches and dust in the air. It skirted the treetops, then banked back over them as it flew toward the northern mountains.

Jael limped up behind her and lowered his bow. Amarynn relaxed her grip, still scanning the sky as the animal disappeared. Dark clouds dotted the sky to the east, and a strong wind bent the treetops above them.

"Rain is coming." Amarynn's voice was quiet. She glanced back at the bleeding gash on Jael's thigh. "We need to clean that up, or we'll have wolves after us."

The stinging static dissipated from Amarynn's skin. She could almost feel the electricity disappearing into the air. Sheathing her sword, she turned back toward their horses, still in the clearing. Deep in thought, she absently signaled for Jael to follow.

Both horses were quivering when they returned. Dax, sensing the danger, was alert and ready for battle, but the mare was fearful, stamping her forelegs frantically. Amarynn reached out and grabbed her bridle, soothing her until she calmed. She handed the reins to Jael and then turned to Dax, who welcomed her with a nicker. Amarynn patted his neck, then pulled a small leather pouch from her saddlebags. "Have a seat, Highness." She gestured to his injured leg.

"Here?"

"I don't want you tracking blood from here to wherever we camp. Might as well invite the wolves and bears to dinner." She snorted and pointed to the ground. "Sit."

Jael complied, letting Amarynn examine the injury. She poured water over the wound, frowning at what was revealed. The gashes were not as severe as the amount of blood would suggest. In fact, the edges of the lacerations looked hours old, not minutes. She hesitated, then hastily grabbed a long cloth strip from her pack and wrapped his leg tightly. She poured water over his boot to wash away any residual blood.

"That will do for now." She tied up her pack and swung into Dax's saddle. "Let's go before we attract company."

Jael winced and lifted his leg up and over his horse's back. Once he was settled, they both urged their horses into the woods. Light continued to fade, so they rode in silence a short way into the forest. Amarynn wanted to put more than just a little distance between them and where their encounter had taken place. She stopped when it was fully dark; they hastily threw a camp together.

Around the small fire, Amarynn had built, they made a quick dinner of jerky and cheese. Jael chewed slowly, lost in thought.

"Why didn't it attack?"

"What?"

"The big one. The black... greall?"

"That was no greall," Amarynn huffed. "I have never seen one of those in my life.

It was a big bastard, though."

Jael fidgeted and looked at the ground for a long moment. "I'm serious. It should have come after us by all rights like it did that greall." He looked up. "But then, it only took the greall's heart, so it wasn't hunting for food." He scowled and shook his head. "I don't understand."

Amarynn stared into the feeble, hissing flames. She was unsure. "It was me. I... confused it, I think."

"Confused it? What do you mean?"

Amarynn shook her head and stood, heading to her bedroll. She sat down and leaned back against the nearest tree, and pulled the blanket up over her legs. She knew what she was thinking was ridiculous, but the connection she felt was undeniable. Leveling her eyes at Jael, she explained. "I'm not sure, but I think that thing, whatever it is, is a Traveler just like me."

CHAPTER 14

"Goddess damn that girl!" Bent tossed his pack onto the empty cot next to his.

Nioll appeared in the doorway.

"The Prince is gone as well."

For a moment, Bent stood there with his hands on his hips, staring at the cot as if Amarynn might simply materialize. Finally, he turned to Nioll. "You know she's gone off to deal with this on her own, don't you?"

The Legionnaire sighed, then said, "Aye, and it seems the Prince is having none of that."

Bent nodded absently.

"You'd think he'd bother to say something before he took off after her," he mumbled, running a hand through his greying hair.

Nioll scrubbed his face with his hands and stepped back into the hall, gesturing for Bent to follow. "You know her better than anyone. If she's to be tracked, you're the one to do it."

Bent shook his head in grim agreement and shouldered his pack. The two men secured provisions from the kitchen and then retrieved their horses. They stood outside, Bent surveying the road leading to the north, then to the rough terrain of the heavily wooded forest.

"She didn't take the road, did she?" Nioll asked.

"Not likely," Bent answered.

Nioll swung up and into his saddle.

"Of course she didn't," he muttered. Both horses pranced, eager to be off. Bent held back for a moment.

"That road leads to the same place," Nioll reasoned, pointing toward the well-worn road. "There's shelter along the way. If we follow her immortal arse through the forest of despair there," he noted to the tree line, "we risk becoming lost."

"Aye, we'll move faster on the road," Bent agreed. The first drops of rain were beginning to fall from the grey sky. Bent kicked his horse into a trot and turned him toward the worn dirt track, Nioll following. The two broke into a gallop and disappeared around the bend.

Morning came with hesitant light cutting through low, misty clouds. As Jael saddled up and secured his bedroll, Amarynn watched, noticing he no longer favored his injured leg. She also noticed that, while his clothing was damp from the mist, as hers was, his skin and hair remained dry. He caught her staring.

"Do I have something on me?" He hastily glanced down at himself.

Amarynn ignored him and finished her preparations. With the horses saddled and packed, she offered Jael a leg up, but he refused, earning another long look from Amarynn. After she mounted, they kicked their horses into a trot, winding through trees and ever-steepening ground.

They traveled up and through the hills for several more hours, then crested a rise where the trees were sparse, allowing a look ahead. Both horses slowed to a stop. The Dark Mountains loomed to their right, and on the left were the first, low peaks of the jagged Stone Giants, the impassable frozen crests that guarded the Stone Reaches.

"Well," Jael said, looking toward the vast landscape. "That's not completely terrifying."

Amarynn snorted. "Lor's keep is on the other side of the Darks."

"I gathered as much. But we aren't on the road to the pass, so how do you propose we get to the other side without doubling back?"

She leveled a hard look at the Prince. He winced.

"I don't want to know, do I?"

"Probably not. Maybe you should head back to Calliway, highness?" She smiled sweetly.

"Nice try."

She closed her eyes for a moment. Then, gesturing to the shadowy base of one of the northernmost peaks, she reluctantly explained, "There's a cavern entrance there. It goes through the mountain."

"And you know this because..."

"It's how I got there the first time. Legion deserters don't typically take the open road to get somewhere," she retorted.

"What about the horses?"

"Dax has excellent night vision," Amarynn gave the war horse a gentle nudge, and he picked his way down the steep hillside. Jael hesitated and watched the two of them make their way down. He considered his horse — a fine, chestnut mare from the King's stables. He'd elected to leave his horse, Rhyssa, behind.

"Horse," Jael patted his mount's neck. "No pressure, but you're going to have to keep up." The mare tossed her head as if in understanding and stepped out onto the slope in pursuit of Amarynn. Jael leaned over her neck and held on as they descended.

"This is it?" Jael stood next to Amarynn and pondered the narrow opening.

"We'll need firewood," she said and wandered around the clearing, gathering small branches and sticks. Jael took her cue and did the same. They bundled the dry wood and lashed it to their saddles. Digging through her pack, she produced two short torches and a fat tin. She handed Jael one of the torches and then popped open the container, letting the lid fall with a clatter. They scooped out globs and smeared the linen-wrapped ends of their torches. When the tin was empty, Amarynn tossed it aside and produced a flint and steel. She struck twice. Sparks caught the linen, and the torch ignited.

Jael stretched his arm out and touched his torch to hers. While he waited for the flame to catch, his gaze drifted from her hand to the scars and tattoos twisting up her lean, muscled arm. Amarynn, noticing his interest, stepped back and said, "Do exactly as I do. The way isn't as long as you might think."

"Long enough to need firewood, though?"

She ignored him and picked up her horse's dangling reins as she slipped through the entrance, Dax following obediently.

Jael drew a breath and did the same, letting the shadows draw him into the fissure as he began his trek through the mountain.

Amarynn led them down a steep incline, her horse as sure-footed as she until the path eventually narrowed. A soaring granite wall anchored the course to the left, the top undetectable in the cavern's darkness. On the right, the trail dropped off into nothing. Jael stumbled, and a stone skittered over the side, vanishing into blackness as it fell. There were no noises indicating it ever hit bottom.

Amarynn stopped when she heard Jael's unsteady footsteps.

"You good, Highness?" she called without looking back.

Jael reached out and steadied himself on the wall. He took several deep breaths before he answered. "Perfect."

Dax snorted, and Amarynn continued. Finally, the path gradient leveled out. They traveled across a flat area illuminated within the circle of light cast by the torches. Their cavernous trail wound through an endless field of stalactites and stalagmites, some dainty and delicate, while others rose like stone giants guarding the inside of the mountain. Occasionally, they passed evidence of others who had crossed through there: an empty canteen, discarded torches.

Jael estimated it must have been nightfall by the time they stopped. It seemed as if hours had passed since they had started their descent.

They were in a larger cavern now, large enough that torchlight couldn't illuminate the entire soaring granite wall.

She wedged her torch between several large rocks and untied the bundle of sticks and branches, then looked over her shoulder.

"Give me yours as well."

Jael obliged, and in minutes, she had built a roaring fire. Orange and yellow light danced on the cavern walls, still not reaching the ceiling. Though the spot Amarynn chose to stop was dry, Jael could hear water dripping in other areas, the hollow sound of droplets on stone reverberating in the silence of the cave.

They sat opposite one another. Jael pulled out a large strip of jerky and a round of hard bread. He ripped off a chunk of the dried meat and offered it to Amarynn. She reluctantly took it, and they sat in silence.

She stole a glance at Jael, at the way he studied her in the firelight. Was he seeing her scars, the tattoos, the way her auburn braids tumbled over her shoulders? She looked away. She knew she always put up such a solid and hardened front. Everyone she encountered was surprised that a girl who appeared to be nineteen or twenty was a seasoned warrior. In her battle gear, with her weapons and armor, she was death incarnate, but what would she be without all that steel? Who might she be if she were given the time and freedom to just be more than a Traveler warrior?

She could feel the Prince's eyes still on her and looked up. He grinned.

"What?" she snapped.

"Nothing," he said, raising his eyebrows at her tone.

"Liar."

"All right, then, I was curious about your markings." He pointed to his temple. "That one there."

Without breaking eye contact, she said, "I earned that one for killing the King of Ardwyn."

Jael touched his jaw, "And this one?"

101

"For taking the life of Imira, Queen of the Handaals... and her guard. All ten of them."

"Don't you feel powerful? You are *immortal*."

Amarynn let loose a halfhearted chuckle.

"Think about it! Never dying — seeing the world grow and unfold?" Jael sat back against the cavern wall and laced his fingers behind his head. "I mean, we all want to live forever—"

"Until we don't." The vast cavern and dim firelight magnified her dark expression. Jael had no idea what it was like for her. He knew why she deserted the Legion, about the events that led up to her flight. The three Travelers, Matteus and his two cronies attacked her and slit her throat — one of the most brutal mortal wounds to recover from for an immortal warrior of the Legion, yet she had. And he still felt that immortality was a privilege? She looked away.

Jael broke the silence. "So, why commemorate all of those wounds like that?"

"I do it for all of them."

"Not all the tiny ones." Jael's eyes ranged all over the visible parts of her body. "You must have thousands!"

"Hmm," was all she said.

His hand moved down and rested on his neck, the same place where she bore the signs of a new, fresh tattoo. The design was intricate, reaching up toward her jaw on one end. On the other, three delicate tendrils wrapped around her throat, intertwining with a thick, braided scar.

"And that one?" He looked at her expectantly.

For a moment, she didn't say anything, then she whispered, "Oh, I think you know."

Jael said nothing as she unsheathed one of her ornate daggers and sharpened it, signaling the conversation was over. Jael didn't push her further.

She finished her piece of jerky and stood, offering her unwanted bread to her horse. She mumbled something unintelligible to Dax, patting his side. Amarynn took her time spreading her bedroll on the cavern floor. Still facing away from Jael, she thought about the Prince. He was nice — kind, even. He'd saved her from the dungeons and followed her through the forested mountains and into this cave. The Prince was proving time and again that he was not like his father, but still, she didn't trust him.

Amarynn knelt, then lay down, her back to the Prince. She waited for him to settle into his bedroll, then she answered him in the smallest of whispers. "I had that one made to remind me I will always be alone."

CHAPTER 15

Sia felt herself swaying back and forth. The boat must be back out to sea, she thought. She was so warm as she snuggled into the blankets, just on the edge of sleep. But despite her reverie, something felt off. A prickling started on her scalp, and as she breathed in, she could taste an earthy mist in the air. Rustling leaves and crunching sounds beneath her confused her ears and made no sense. Then, everything came back in a rush.

"Regealth!"

Sia bolted upright but was stopped. Two strong arms were wrapped around her as a woman's voice clucked tenderly, "Now, now, my sweet."

Sia's eyes were pasty and difficult to pry open. But when she finally did, she was horrified to find the pleasant softness and the soothing voice belonged to Venalise. She was wrapped in a down blanket secured firmly in the mage's arms, and they were on horseback, not on a ship at all. Venalise allowed her to readjust, and she sat up, peering over the mage's shoulder at the caravan behind them. Three carts back, she saw a small wagon fitted with what appeared to be a cage. Inside, she could make out the tattered, grey robes and fine, wispy hair of a man who could only be Regealth.

She struggled against Venalise's grip, becoming frantic as she tried to remember the events on the ship. How could she have come to be riding with the earth mage that frightened her so?

"Calm yourself, child," Venalise chided. Sia looked up at Venalise's face. Her smile was laced with venom. "There's nowhere to run."

Memories flooded back in greater detail — the table in the cabin, the burning fever racing through her body, the fear as she remembered how frightened she was, that same warmth kindled in her legs. She felt the heat radiate into the air around her like a blazing fire.

"Oh, no, you don't!" Venalise cooed — a warning. She reined her horse to a stop, then spread her hands wide over the blanket shrouding the girl and clutched her close. The mage quietly chanted as tendrils of energy wound around the child. Sia lost control of her limbs until they hung limp like a doll's. The girl's eyes widened as Venalise's magic rendered her helpless.

The magical bonds writhed against her — she could feel them through the fabric — slipping over and under her like silk ribbons. Somehow her instinct told her that the bonds were weak, but she could not discover how or where. Just out of reach, a whisper urged her to whisk the bindings away, but it was gone just when she thought she could hear the voice clearly. Frustrated, she recalled her brief lessons from Regealth and how it felt to touch the power she had only recently discovered. All she could muster was a strained whimper. Her head lolled to the side, and she could see the rear cart more clearly as they rounded a bend. Regealth was trapped there, for sure. She could sense his life force was draining — almost see it leaving his body in a fine, shadowy mist. He leaned back on the rough-hewn cart slats, chin to his chest. His skin was waxy, and his chest rose in halting breaths. She thought she saw him lift his head. Once again, Sia strained against the magical bonds that held her, but it was useless. Her secret training on the boat with Regealth had been too new, too brief, for her to understand what she was doing.

The boat!

Master Omman would not have allowed Venalise to take her from The Blackfly. He was like a father to her. With trepidation, Sia realized the mage would have to have done something terrible to him, or he wouldn't have allowed it. Another heavy stone of dread added weight to her already sinking heart.

She felt drowsy, her eyelids slipping closed. She struggled to keep them open and understand where she was being taken. Through slitted eyes, she watched the road wind through soaring, ancient trees, their spread of foliage broken by glimpses of looming, jagged peaks of black rock.

Venalise shifted. Sia's head fell forward, and she could see those dark peaks grow taller in the direction they were headed. The small caravan continued underneath twisted boughs dripping with crone's hair moss. Mist rose from the mossy forest floor. If she weren't terrified of her present company, Sia would have been enchanted by her surroundings. She felt a tug as if the mountains were trying to speak to her. It seemed the trees were reaching toward her, and the heavy air wanted to hide her. She couldn't help but feel as if everything around her wanted to be with her, but the thin, impervious layer of Venalise's magic cut her off.

Venalise looked down at her, frowning. Perhaps she sensed it, too.

Sia thought she could hear the swaying boughs in the gentle breeze whisper, *Rest. Regain your strength. We will not leave you.* With fear still nibbling at her heart, she breathed in. Unable to glance over her shoulder toward her friend, she decided to trust the trees. Maybe she imagined it, but the idea that the forest wanted to protect her made her feel safe, so she closed her eyes, and she slept.

Regealth could see Sia's head bobbing just above Venalise's shoulders at the front of the line of carts and horses. The woman hadn't let go of the child since she appeared from below deck with Sia in her arms. Regealth could draw on the mist that rose from the ground just enough to stay awake as they made their way down the road through the oldest part of the Dark Mountains. Since they began the trek, he could sense Sia's magic again — not as he felt it earlier, but he could feel it nonetheless. No doubt, Venalise muted her with a spell. Now, he only hoped Sia was sharp-witted enough to keep her gifts as hidden as she could. If she were as bright as he assumed, she would know to pretend that she knew nothing about them. If Venalise thought the child was merely a source, it could buy them some time.

He groaned as he tried to adjust his back against the rough planks. His treatment had been harsh, and the fall he had faked on the ship had taken its toll. And, despite his best efforts, Venalise had still discovered the child. This was a conundrum, and he furrowed his brows in thought. A weak voice cried out from the front of the caravan.

"Regealth!"

His eyes snapped to the source.

He could hardly lift his head, but he could see the child as she struggled against Venalise. He sensed the now-familiar hum of the child's magic, but quickly, Venalise subdued her with shimmering ribbons of elemental earth magic that she wove over and around her. He knew her magic had been quelled and shielded when he could no longer feel her.

Though, he could still feel something as if the forest's energy around them had changed its resonance. Foreboding gave way to acceptance like symbiosis had been achieved. Regealth inhaled sharply as the implication registered. The child exhibited a water affinity. If she was resonating with the life force of living things, she possessed an affinity to more than one element.

There had never been a wielder who could touch more than one. In fact, until now, it was believed only a handful of wielders could exist for each of the four. The discovery of someone who could touch and control more than one element was unprecedented.

There had never been one in all recorded time.

He had held the water for over a hundred years. Elemental magic prolonged a wielder's life force if they had access to it. This was the reason for his chambers deep beneath the castle at Calliway.

Venalise could sense it, too, he noticed. She eyed the dark green expanse around them warily. She was an earth mage; her senses were more finely tuned to the magic of the mountains and the forest than his. There was no doubt she sensed Sia's blossoming talent. There was no way of knowing if Venalise was aware of the child's water affinity, but something had caused the mage to snatch her up and hold her close. Regealth decided there were two possibilities.

His deepest hope was that Venalise believed Sia to be a rare kind of source — strong, but nothing more than that. However, if she realized the child was a wielder, it would only be a matter of time until she discovered Sia was able to touch more than just one element. If Venalise uncovered the full extent of her abilities, then no other source would be necessary. Venalise would have everything she needed to use the Gate. She would have positioned herself to assume control of the most powerful magic known. Dyaneth died for the magic of the Gate, and her death would be for nothing if it were lost. Venalise, with Sia by her side, could Travel anything she wanted — and ultimately, the world would be hers.

CHAPTER 16

Amarynn's words played over and over in Jael's mind. *I had that one made to remind me that I will always be alone.* Jael couldn't grasp how a mighty, legendary warrior could feel as isolated as she did. He thought back over the last few years and realized that he could not recall her presence in or around the palace at Calliway. He'd never seen her at any war council, nor could he remember her at any of the grand celebrations held in the capitol. He didn't recall seeing her anywhere save the battlefield or in the training yard. She wasn't much of a talker, but most of the other Travelers seamlessly fit into Calliway society. And despite her strength and prowess in battle, she wasn't brutish. Amarynn was quiet. She was stoic and carried herself with a grace that reminded him of his mother's people.

He was acutely aware that her crossing had been exceptionally traumatic — more so than any of the others. Even the other female Traveler, Ehrinell, had fared better. She was frequently seen around Calliway with the other Travelers and Legion men in the pubs, battle councils, and brawling in the streets for fun. He recalled seeing Ehrinell at the Evenfall gala just this past year. She was resplendent, dressed in a gauzy, ethereal gown, her blonde braids abandoned for a cascade of curls. And happy. She laughed and danced the night away.

111

He had no such memory of Amarynn — she hadn't made an appearance.

Besides watching her in the training yard as a child, he only had one other real memory of her and had never shared it with anyone. He had just celebrated his fifth year when Regealth whispered for him to slip away from his caretakers on a bright, crisp morning. He had briefly visited the mage's chambers but had never seen the inner sanctum where the greatest of all magical castings took place. That dark, forbidding room was where the Gate stone was kept — the blue stone that held the key to Regealth's power. The cold, damp aethertorium was where new life was conjured from the echoes of other lives somewhere else in the aether. He knew his father disappeared into that room once a year, but he was never allowed. Jael nearly lost himself gazing into the facets of the delicate gem perched on a pedestal of alabaster while he waited for Regealth to prepare.

He recalled that Regealth led him to a stool just beneath the stone altar where the Gate was displayed. The old man patted him on the head and cautioned him to be still as a mouse, no matter what. And he did exactly as he was told. Jael stayed frozen on the edge of that cold basin. Regealth told him he would attempt something new, and he wanted the future King of Karth to bear witness. He said this was to be the birth of the warrior who would "win him the world." And when she appeared from within the shower of stars and light in the vast stone basin, the wonderous hum of electricity that enveloped him was something he'd never felt. It would be the only time he would personally witness a Traveler as they crossed from their world to his.

"Watch your step here."

Amarynn's sudden remark startled Jael back to the present. They were beginning their ascent out of the cavern. She was hiking up a steep incline, the shadows from her torch flickering off the narrowing cavern walls. He let his gaze linger on her longer than he intended before she disappeared into the darkness ahead.

The second part of their journey was shorter than the first. By the time they reached the last stretch of the tunnel, their torches had utterly sputtered out. Fortunately, pale light was streaming in from the cave's far end. Jael sought out the source, studying the rays as they filtered through the heavy air, illuminating dust and mist. He mused; the air almost looked like the underwater view from one of the sea caves at Banmorrow.

They approached the cave's exit, and Amarynn dropped her horse's reins.

"Wait here," she said, her voice low, "and be quiet." She slipped away without a noise, exiting the cavern.

Jael complied, taking a moment to rub his mount's neck. "I think I'll call you Mole," he said. "Because you are as comfortable underground as on top of it."

At the sound of the Prince's voice, Dax swung his head toward Jael and blew out a quiet, disapproving huff.

"I've been scolded!" Jael whispered dramatically. He turned toward his newly named mount, which shifted just as Amarynn returned from the mouth of the cave.

"It's safe to leave, but we must be quick and quiet," she said intensely. Jael gathered his horse's reins, and they made their way to the opening.

Amarynn was well outside the mouth of the cavern when Jael stepped onto the mountainside. The low, wide opening was on a higher face than where they had entered on the other side. He stood on a wide ledge that afforded a view of the keep nestled between the Dark Mountains and the ominous Stone Giants.

Although Jael had traveled extensively as a Prince of Karth, he had never needed to visit this particular corner of the world. He heard rumors and even descriptions of the dark and formidable Athtull Keep but had dismissed them as hyperbole. Now, he understood. With the Dark Mountains as a backdrop and the ancient oldwood forests surrounding it, Athtull Keep rose like a monument to darkness itself.

113

The towering structure stood in the middle of a rise and was crafted from the black stone of the Dark Mountains that surrounded it. It backed up to the face of one of the mountain peaks, its base as wide as a small mountain and surrounded from mountainside to mountainside by a tall and formidable stone wall. Further down the hill, another enormous structure spanned the width of the rise from one side of the mountain to the other. The walls ran down the bank, and at the bottom, a fortified rampart stretched from one side to the other, enclosing the entire structure. Each corner supported its stone tower, while the front gate's arching portcullis was made of banded iron and dark, blue-black oldwood.

"If you'd like, I can signal to have King Lors' archers use you for target practice," Amarynn hissed from the tree line. Jael blinked and hastily made for the trees, pulling his horse behind him.

Once under cover of the forest, Amarynn began to strip her horse of the riding gear. "You'd best do as I do," she said over her shoulder to Jael. "We'll be leaving them here for now."

"Leaving them?" Jael asked.

"Aye," she returned, still unbuckling the saddle.

"I'm no idiot, Amarynn," he said, "but when we have retrieved Regealth, how will we get away without them? They aren't just going to wait here for us, and we can't leave them tethered for a predator to pick off."

"Dax will stay here. He is trained, and I doubt that mare of yours will wander too far from him," Amarynn answered, shouldering a small pack and sliding another blade into her boot.

Jael rummaged through his things for supplies, but Amarynn stopped him short with a hand on his shoulder. "There's nothing you'll need, Highness," she said. Then, stepping away quickly, she added, "I don't plan on being there very long."

He gave his mare one last pat on the neck and then followed Amarynn down the mountainside.

They carefully picked their way down the steeper parts of the mountain. The sun was crossing the middle of the sky as the land changed from a treacherous slope to a gentle hill. Amarynn picked up the pace, and before long, the black sides of the fortress could be seen through the trees. Jael and Amarynn crept along the forest's edge, following the length of the immense wall. He began to feel the barest flutter of anxiety as the corner tower came closer and closer. Soldiers on the ramparts surveyed the tree line. The Prince flagged, staying well behind Amarynn, who was expertly creeping through the undergrowth.

He felt a measure of shame at his hesitation. He had spent very little time on the front lines with the Legion and had only actually fought in two minor battles. As the Crown Prince, he was forbidden from taking a position that put him at risk. Several years ago, he would have welcomed the idea of a daring mission fraught with danger, but so many years of being protected made him doubt his courage. So, he hesitated while Amarynn, who appeared to be but a maiden, boldly put herself in such positions without a second thought. He studied the ground, taking a deep breath to bolster his resolve. Leaves crunched, signaling Amarynn's return.

"I've felt the same way, you know." Amarynn stood just a few steps away. She studied the Prince.

There was an uncomfortable silence.

"I'll lead. If we get into any trouble, you do whatever is necessary to get away. I'll make sure you can. But for now, I just want to scout and find our way in."

Jael nodded, and Amarynn started to turn back toward the Keep. Jael blew out a long breath. He knew he did not exude confidence. "A Crown Prince doesn't usually find himself doing this sort of thing," he said in her direction as a half-hearted explanation.

She stopped and looked back at him, her expression unreadable. Finally, one corner of her mouth turned up, hinting at a smile, and her eyes sparkled. "Well, I've never been one to follow tradition. Why start now?"

CHAPTER 17

They crawled through the undergrowth for hours. Jael complained about his knees and back aching, but Amarynn felt no signs of fatigue. She shimmied under fallen trees, crept through thorny bushes, and even scaled four enormous trees in their quest for information about how to enter the Athtull Keep undetected. The light had faded into an ominous orange and red haze when she stopped, head tilted slightly to the side.

Jael, watching her from just a few paces behind, followed the direction of her head. There was a road, not well-worn, winding down from the lower hills and mountains to the east. At first, he saw nothing, but then a shadow flickered through the trees. Soon two horses came lumbering around the bend, pulling a heavily laden cart. More horses and carts followed.

Jael crept up beside her as she watched. They were both crouched behind a dense stand of shrubs, and Amarynn leaned forward onto one knee, muttering a hushed curse. His eyes darted between the caravan and the Traveler's face. Her stare was locked on the rider of a regal grey horse — a statuesque woman dressed in deep red velvet. Holding her head high, as if royalty, she held a bundle in her arms. He couldn't be sure what was inside for a moment, but as they marched closer, he could see the top of a child's head resting against the woman's chest.

Amarynn watched the woman in red as they rode past into the Keep. She scanned the line of wagons and horses until the final cart in the convoy made its way around the bend. They both glanced in its direction. Amarynn's breathing quickened.

"Regealth."

She tensed, the urge to lunge forward nearly overtaking her. Her hands gripped the ground, knuckles white, and she steadied herself. Calculating the odds, immortal or not, she knew better than to rush forward without a plan. Jael, sensing her urgency, nudged her.

"You are a legend, yes," he said quietly at her ear, "but no one wins if you go out there right now."

"I know," she bit back as she pushed him away. Her agitation confirmed an emotional reaction to seeing the old mage, and she loathed to show such a personal response. Her surveillance never strayed from neither the cart nor the old man inside the makeshift cage, clenching her hands open and closed over and over as she assessed the situation. The cart rolled through the grand archway of the keep, and the black portcullis slowly lowered behind it.

Jael stood and stepped back one pace, giving Amarynn room. She waited a moment, then stood as well. She studied the Prince for a moment.

"After nightfall, when the guard is on night rotation, we'll watch their pattern," Jael said. He pointed in the direction of the nearest corner tower. "I assume you mean to climb the wall at that junction there, where the wall meets the tower?"

She glanced over her shoulder, then back to Jael. "No."

She angled herself halfway, facing the wall. Gesturing, she indicated the bottom where it met the rounded tower. Just as they both turned in that direction, a well-hidden door eased open, and a soldier and servant girl hastily slipped out, sliding along the wall. Shadows elongated in the fading light, giving the pair a patchwork of cover to sneak away. Looking up every few seconds toward the rampart, the two quickly made their way into the woods, only a few hundred paces from where she and Jael were standing. She smiled at Jael. "Are you up for a hunt?"

"Quintas?"

Amarynn pressed the soldier against a large tree, one of her daggers at his exposed throat. She looked him over a second time.

His eyes widened when he realized who had snatched him up from his secret lover's tryst. Jael held the servant girl, covering her mouth with his hand.

"A-Am-a-rynn," the soldier stammered. "Why—"

"Ah! Well, hello there, Quin!" she smiled, and he shuddered. "How has desertion treated you?"

The soldier's ebony skin glistened with nervous sweat as his eyes darted between Amarynn and the girl. He paid no attention to the man holding her.

Amarynn jerked her head in the direction of the Prince. "He'd like to know."

Jael leveled his gaze on the man in Amarynn's grasp. Quintas stared, then paled as he realized who stood before him. Jael, playing his part, tightened his hold on the girl and frowned.

Amarynn twisted her head around toward Jael. "Desertion's a hanging offense, no?"

Jael did not acknowledge her question but remained quiet, not breaking eye contact with the young man. Amarynn turned back and leaned in to whisper in his ear. "That's Prince Jael, Quin." She grinned, continuing, "He could order me to run you through right now, and I'd have no choice." Her dagger left his throat and pressed into his belly. "You can save yourself and your pretty little girl and cooperate, or..." She arched an eyebrow suggestively, applying more pressure to the ornate dagger that cut through the man's shirt, drawing a rivulet of blood.

Quintas squeaked.

"Are you interested in what I have to offer?" she asked, serious again.

The soldier nodded vigorously.

"You and your lady friend have been liberated from the service of King Lors. You will strip yourselves of your uniforms and go up the mountain. If you are careful—" she patted him on the chest "—and use the training I know you received in the Legion, you should be able to locate our horses. That is where you'll find supplies. Are you with me so far?"

"You will stay there and wait until we return. Then, you'll both accompany us back to Karth—" The soldier's eyes grew wide, and he glanced at the Prince.

She grasped his chin and pulled his face back in her direction. "—Where the Prince will pardon you and restore you to the Legion ranks." She searched the soldier's face for a moment. "You've been given an opportunity, Quin. Will you take it?"

The Traveler gestured to the girl. "If not for your sake, then for hers?" Amarynn stepped closer to Quintas and lowered her voice, "What's her name?"

Quintas hesitated, then shrugged and smiled sheepishly.

"Goddess!" Amarynn exclaimed. "Maybe I *should* kill you!"

"What's your name, girl?" Jael asked his captive. The girl glared at Quintas, then twisted her head around to look at the Prince.

"Mina, your grace."

He turned her, still gripping her by the shoulders. He scanned her face, noticing faded bruises in different stages of healing. "Something tells me I don't have to convince you that leaving this keep is in your best interests." The hard line of his mouth softened just a bit. She bit her lip.

Amarynn sheathed her dagger and stepped back. She gestured to her captive. "Go on, now. Off with your clothes!"

Quintas did not hesitate. While he began to remove his boots, Amarynn paced in front of him. "I knew your father, you know," she said casually.

He paused.

"Borland was one of the best archers I have ever known," she continued. "How did his son end up in the enemy's service?"

Quintas dropped his head and continued untying the laces. Amarynn dismissed him with a snort. "You, too, girl. Get busy!"

Jael looked at Mina reassuringly. "No, she'll do no such thing," he said quietly.

Louder, he called to Amarynn, "We don't need her clothes." Amarynn spun around, her expression dark. "We only need to get into the keep. We'll get what we need once we are inside."

Quintas and Mina were dispatched, hastily on their way in the evening dusk. The sun had fully set, replaced by the twin moons peeking just above the mountaintops in the distance. Amarynn sat, stretched on the ground, her back against a tree. Quintas' uniform lay next to her. "You should go with them, you know. Waiting out here might be boring."

Jael stood in front of her, hands on his hips. "Waiting?"

Amarynn didn't respond; instead, she pulled one knee up and began to tighten the laces of Quintas' boot. Jael leaned over and picked up one of the pieces of armor, trying the fit on his arm.

"What are you doing?" she mumbled, pulling her other leg up and working on the other boot.

"It makes the most sense for me to wear this," he offered.

She sighed heavily and reached for the breastplate next to her, then buckled it over her leather vest. Jael reached out a hand to stop her. Ignoring his touch, she kept tightening the straps. She stood and grabbed the vambrace from Jael's hand as he protested. "Rynn, be reasonable."

She slipped both vambraces on her forearms and settled the pauldron over her shoulders.

121

"I haven't seen any female gate guards, you know," he said, stepping closer to her to make his case.

Close enough to feel his breath on her cheek, Amarynn looked up at him, locking eyes. She pulled her dagger from its sheath; in one fluid motion, she wrapped her braid around her hand, reached up with the blade, and sliced. The long braid fell to the ground. Waves of now-short auburn hair tumbled over her eyes, and she ran her hand through it. "I told you I was going to handle this. You've followed me here, and that's on you. Now." She broke the gaze and looked toward the dark structure, "You are staying right here, and I am going into that keep."

She slid Frost into the scabbard down the middle of her back, her face a mask of grim determination.

"I am getting Regealth back. And I am doing it alone."

CHAPTER 18

"Alone?" Jael paced back and forth in front of Amarynn.

"As I recall, I tried to do this alone from the beginning, but someone followed me," Amarynn retorted.

Jael ran both hands through his hair.

"This is not your problem, highness."

"How is this not my problem? Hmm?" Jael was nearly shouting. "Regealth is my Kingdom's mage. You are my Kingdom's warrior—"

"I am no one's *anything*!" Amarynn was on him in an instant, nose to nose. She was breathing hard. Her hazel eyes danced with agitation, new shorter locks of hair curling across the side of her face.

He stepped back, lowering his voice. "You are not the only one who has an interest in what happens here."

"But I am the *only* reason we are in this mess, to begin with, and I will be the one to end it! I will not have anyone else risking themselves for my stupid mistake!"

She was shaking, and Jael was unnerved by her emotion and intensity. He stared for a long moment, unable to think of anything to say. His silence allowed her to turn away.

"Go. Just go back to the horses and wait. If I am not back by sunset tomorrow, you must return to Karth and prepare for whatever Venalise can and will unleash." She turned back to Jael. "She is dangerous, Jael, I promise you. She and Lors will come for Karth, I know it. And if I don't get Regealth and the Gate Stone back, they may just be able to take it."

She didn't give him a chance to argue. In seconds, she had ducked out of the undergrowth and was jogging toward the keep.

Amarynn tried not to think about the Prince left standing behind her as she made her way across the clearing. She knew he was watching when she reached the wall. She only hoped he wasn't foolish enough to try and follow her, though she doubted he would just sit and wait. She wished he would do as she asked, go back to the horses, Quintas, and the girl.

His earlier behavior, when they watched the caravan pass, confused her. She sensed an urgency in him — some strange possessiveness. And even now, she felt odd leaving his presence. It was especially strange because they had never spent any time near each other, neither in Calliway nor on the battlefield. Amarynn shook her head. She absently reached up to touch the crudely shorn ends of her hair. When Jael offered to wear the soldier's uniform, her instinctive desire to protect him at any cost was not something she had never been prone to do for anyone — not even for Bent. *Why now?*

Nightfall deepened, and the two moons were just a sliver of light in the sky. In good time, she made the wall and sidestepped toward the hidden door. She glanced back over her shoulder and could just make out Jael's from among the shadows. *Damn him!* He should be gone — if he stayed longer, she knew he would get it in his head to follow her again. With one last look back, she quietly lifted the latch, opened the door, and slipped inside.

The room on the other side of the hidden door led into a storage chamber—barrels and grain sacks and piles of broken weapons against the wall. She crouched in the shadows for nearly an hour, waiting patiently for the keep's bustling activity to die down as later evening fell. She could hear the guards in the room above her clattering and shouting from outside. The movement in the yard outside gave no indication of slowing, so she unbuckled Frost and slid the broadsword and scabbard beneath a bundle of broken longbows. She'd stand out with it strapped to her back.

She wished she had been telling the truth about learning stealth when she was in the north. She grimaced. Hiding in the shadows had never been her strong suit — she much preferred an open field, blades swinging. Finally satisfied there was nothing too obvious to single her out, she steadied herself and opened the door to the bailey.

Evening had turned to night, but the yard was still bustling and crowded; carts and wagons still being unloaded by servants while guardsmen oversaw their work. Amarynn turned her head just in time to see the last cart with the makeshift cage roll past. It was alone and empty, but just as she turned away, a flash of grey robes between two guards caught her eye as they disappeared into a doorway in the inner curtain wall. They'd left Regealth in that filthy cage for hours like no more than livestock. She bristled.

She had been in this keep once, groveling at the feet of Venalise. Her stomach turned, thinking about it, but she knew exactly where she needed to go.

Jael watched her cross the treeless expanse between the forest and the keep wall. Something tugged at him to follow. Not because she might need his help, which was a laughable idea at best, but because he knew that somehow, they were more formidable together. He couldn't explain why. In the forest, when she stood between him and that giant black beast, sword at the ready, there was more happening than a soldier defending her liege. No sense of duty could explain her ferocity or determination. He had seen her fight for his father and the legion commanders, but what he saw in that forest was different.

Jael checked her progress. She was already across the grassy expanse and inside the tower. He sat for a few more moments, unsure what he was expecting. Finally, he decided. He was going to help whether she wanted it or not.

Jael felt as if he was outside of his body, observing, watching himself do the most dangerous thing he could do, as if he'd given up hope of talking reason to himself and was resigned to accept his fate. He was no battle-hardened warrior, nor was he an assassin, but there was one thing he did well. He had spent his entire life being groomed to command attention. He smoothed his rumpled clothing, took the heavy gold sigil ring from the leather thong around his neck, and seated it firmly on the fourth finger of his left hand. The bear and thunderbolt sat just above his knuckle and gleamed in the faint moonlight.

Karth had endured two invasions and had prevailed both times. His grandfather had fought the first and his father, the second that nearly ended them. Because of that war, he had lost his father's only sister — his Aunt Dyaneth — and two cousins. If another invasion was imminent, it was time to prove his worth as heir. He would be the first to stop a war before it began. Jael hesitated only a moment more, then stepped out of the trees, calling forth every ounce of courage he had. He channeled a little of his father as he strode forward to the dark and formidable gates of Athtull Keep. No longer hiding and waiting in the shadows, he was Jael, First Son of Lasten, Crown Prince of the High Kingdom of Karth.

"Hold!"

The guard atop the tower bellowed, his voice echoing along the ramparts. Amarynn froze, then followed the sound from the direction of the portcullis towers. Something below, outside the gates, had caught their attention. There was more shouting, and then a runner from the tower made his way into the inner bailey toward the Keep.

Amarynn heard voices calling back and forth, and then the great gate groaned as the chains began to lift the heavy wood and iron. Servants and guards alike stopped their work, turning their attention to the commotion at the front tower and gate. Amarynn returned her attention to where she thought she last saw Regealth, but now all she saw was an empty doorway.

With all eyes diverted, this was the opportunity she needed.

She ducked her head and crossed to the doorway Regealth and his escorts had disappeared into. No sooner had she slipped into the shadows of a passageway just off the vast hall than the fall of heavy footsteps echoed off the stone, getting closer. She pressed herself into the shadows of an alcove as six well-armored high guardsmen strode past her, headed for the bailey yard. She felt a strange feeling in the pit of her stomach as if she had left something behind, but she dismissed it and continued.

The hall split. She chose the left side, noticing the curve of steps leading downward. She remembered that Venalise kept her chambers in the underbelly of the Keep — only fitting for an earth mage to want to be underground, surrounded by rock. The stairwell curved along the wall, winding into shadowy darkness. She waited for a moment, listening. The only sounds were faint, coming from the bailey yard above.

The steps continued downward. Just when the light faded to complete darkness, another step revealed the glow of another torch. The curve of the stairs broadened as she descended. Confident she was alone, she padded lightly around the broad, sweeping bend to judge the space and calculate her move. The wooden door was slightly ajar, so she nudged it open with her toe.

Venalise's chambers were vast. They were also exceedingly dark and shadowy. An alcove alight with several torches stood out against the gloom, revealing a wide worktable strewn with vials and crystals. She remembered the middle of the large chamber was fitted with several types of chains — incredible lengths anchored to the walls and smaller versions scattered across the floor. The best-case scenario would be that Regealth would be somewhere here, Venalise would be gone, and Amarynn could use whatever distraction was still going on outside to get him out.

She had no such luck.

Amarynn had just stepped around the open door at the bottom of the stairwell when, from behind, a woman's voice slithered down her spine, chilling her to her core.

"How nice of you to come back for a visit, Traveler!"

CHAPTER 19

Amarynn dropped back into a crouch and lowered her head. Perhaps if she played the part of the disgruntled deserter, she could talk her way out of this and regroup. She steadied herself and slowly rotated on her heels, then stood to face the mage.

Venalise approached, appraising her. Amarynn stood still, controlling hands that itched to reach for any of her blades. The two women locked eyes and held each other's stare while noises from above indicated guards were on their way. Three uniformed men and one woman came around the bend and stopped behind Venalise. Silently, they drew their swords and stood ready.

Amarynn smirked and went for her short sword.

Venalise raised her hand, and Amarynn's sword clattered to the floor with a flick of her wrist, the metal responding immediately to Venalise's power. So it was to be a fistfight, Amarynn thought. A slower method, but she was still more powerful than the four. The mage stepped back as the guards encircled her.

"Do not resist, Traveler." Venalise's warning was almost amusing.

Amarynn waited to see who would strike first.

"Did you know he followed you?"

Jael? Idiot!

The guard in front of her swung hard. Amarynn met his fist with her hand and twisted till she heard an audible pop. He screamed.

129

"He's with Lors now, actually," the mage continued her commentary as if nothing was amiss. The guard to Amarynn's left swung his sword, the blade finding purchase in the space between her breastplate and backplate. The slice stung, and she turned, driving the guard against the wall, her back to the other two guards and Venalise. She pried the sword from his hand, and it clattered to the floor, the bones of his hand cracking under the pressure.

"They are discussing terms of some sort, I believe."

Terms?

In that distraction, the remaining two guards grabbed her arms from behind as the other fell to the ground, clutching his hand. She felt a heavy cuff clamp around her right arm and was wracked with a blinding pain that began at her wrist and tore like fire through her body. She stumbled backward and doubled over, unable to breathe. Stars exploded behind her eyes, and she fell to the stone floor; painful convulsions wracked her body. She saw the guards reaching for her, and then she saw nothing as darkness closed around her.

The gate rose before him.

Jael dug deep into all the years he'd lived in his father's shadow. He arranged his face into the mask of ruthlessness that was so familiar and stood with a confidence he knew he did not possess. He knew his arrival alone would be suspicious, but he had no choice but to try. After all, he *was* the Crown Prince of the largest Kingdom in the land.

The gate cleared the arching portcullis, and he took in the scene. Servants scurried back and forth across the torch-lit square, unloading wagons while guards watched. He scanned the yard but did not see Amarynn.

Good.

A little fox-faced man hurried toward him. He was slight and dressed in robes that indicated he maintained a court position.

"My Lord!" he exclaimed, a little too eagerly. "You are…?"

"I am Jael, Crown Prince of Karth, and I will see your King—" Jael barely inclined his head to make eye contact with the man. "Immediately."

"We were not expecting such an honored visit! Have you no horse? I'll have the stable boys…" His voice trailed off as he looked around Jael and saw no mount. An awkward silence ensued until the little man shrugged and gestured for Jael to follow him as he scurried back through the gate.

They crossed the yard and entered a nondescript doorway, no one giving them a second look. He followed the man through a maze of corridors and down a long flight of stairs, torches creating pools of light at scattered and uneven intervals. He trailed him without speaking, surprised that such a lack of decorum was afforded a visitor of his stature, even for such a small holding. Granted, he was unexpected.

Athtull Keep was in a state of ruin, as far as Jael had thought. Once, this had been the southern stronghold of the people of the Stone Reaches. A secretive, but powerful people, they populated the massive expanse of unexplored land beyond the Stone Giant mountains. Now Athtull seemed to have fallen under the control of a noble of questionable origin. This "King" was unheard of, as was the mage who served him. Fitting, he thought, that Lors would have chosen an earth mage. Who better to breathe life back into the mountain-carved keep?

After several more twists and turns, they reached what served as a receiving hall. Jael was confident they were inside the mountain itself. The underground room seemed almost the entire width and depth of the keep, dimly lit, with a dais and throne on one end and along one of the long walls, a great hearth blazing. At the other end was a large table scattered with maps and scrolls, where a man bent over, poring over one of the larger maps. He held a quill in one hand, apparently making notes on the map in front of him.

The fox-faced man cleared his throat. "My Lord?"

The man straightened, turning toward them abruptly. He seemed irritated at the intrusion. He was dressed in tall black boots, a finely tailored black linen tunic over supple leather pants, and a heavy black and grey cloak that swept the ground. His face was undeniably handsome beneath his dark, wavy hair.

"My Lord, King Lors, I present Jael, Crown Prince of Karth!" The attendant waited to be sure he had been heard. He gestured to Jael's sword. "Your weapon, My Lord." Jael reluctantly pulled his sword from its sheath and handed it to the little man, who hurriedly bowed then darted out of the room.

The King set the quill down and picked up a handkerchief. He walked across the room, wiping his ink-stained hands as he eyed Jael from head to toe. Now face to face, Jael could see lines at the corners of his eyes and creases on his brow.

"So, your father sent you?"

"I wasn't sent," Jael replied with as much indignation as he could muster.

"Interesting," Lors said, still studying the Prince.

"I believe you have something that belongs to my father," Jael began, "and my Kingdom. I'd like it back." He cocked his head slightly to the side. "Actually, I'd like both of them back."

Just as he finished speaking, a woman swept into the room. She glanced at him briefly but made straight for the King's ear. She leaned in and whispered so Jael could not hear the exchange. This was the same woman Amarynn had identified as Venalise earlier that day when they had watched the caravan enter the Keep. She was younger than he first thought and quite beautiful. Rich, dark hair tumbled across her shoulders, and her pale skin was creamy against the deep red velvet of her gown. She slid her gaze to Jael as she stepped away from the King.

Lors addressed Jael, a smirk appearing on his lips, "Oh, it seems I have acquired more than you think I have, my young lord."

Jael tried not to let his confusion show. He kept his face blank as his mind worked to decipher Lors' meaning, but his stomach dropped when he realized what the King implied. Surely, he couldn't mean Amarynn. If that were true, Jael knew he couldn't let on that it mattered. He feigned indifference, though it killed him to do so. "I don't believe there is anything else that matters to me," he said, hating the taste of every word that crossed his lips.

Lors adjusted his stance and crossed his arms in front of his chest. He chewed his lip for a moment, then spoke. "Prince Jael. I'll be succinct. I have the mage, and I have the stone. I intend to keep both. Well," he chuckled to himself. "At least the stone. I don't know if the mage will survive much longer." He glanced over at the woman, who smiled like a beautiful, deadly predator. He and Venalise shared a menacing smirk.

"Apparently, now I also have Karth's deadliest warrior on the way to my dungeon as we speak. She was caught trying to locate your mage. So," Lors said, pacing in a circle around Jael. "Shall we begin again?"

Jael said nothing. He fixed his eyes on the table across the room, fighting to suppress the pounding in his chest. She had been captured. This was precisely what he feared when she'd left him outside the keep. The ability to subdue Amarynn so quickly only confirmed Venalise's power as a mage, and the thought of her trapped in her hands shook him to his core for reasons he could not explain. He was on his own now, and even if Bent and Nioll were smart enough to return to Karth and tell his father, it would be days until anyone arrived. Between the Travelers and the Legion, Karth could take the keep, but now that Venalise possessed the stone and Regealth, they could be gone within the hour — and both would be lost once again.

"I have to ask myself why you are here," Lors continued. "Without your Legion. Without anyone at all!" He laughed. "Well, except for your Traveler. I believe you are either very brave or foolish."

Jael held his ground. "You have what belongs to Karth, and what belongs to Karth belongs to me. I want them back."

Lors laughed out loud. "After all the trouble we went through to infiltrate your castle and steal your mage and his pretty necklace, do you think I would just hand them back to you?"

"Perhaps you forget who I am." Jael grew bolder with every word. "In a few days, my father will arrive with his Travelers and the Legion. This is nothing more than a courtesy. You can give them to me now or wait for Karth to take them back while you watch in chains."

"You do know I have a mage, too." Venalise stepped forward. "And soon enough, I will have Travelers, just like your father's."

"I will not repeat myself. Return Regealth, Amarynn, and the stone." Jael's thoughts were racing now, but he maintained his authoritative tone. "Do this and spare the slaughter of your men." He only hoped his father would come as quickly as he claimed he would. But he wasn't even sure Bent had gone back to Karth.

"I think we could strike a deal, Prince." Lors stepped directly in front of Jael. "I know I can't kill your Traveler, but *you* are mortal, as is your mage, no?"

Jael swallowed hard but kept his face stoic, refusing eye contact with Lors.

"I will admit, you are brave for thinking you could waltz in and retrieve them on your own. Brave, indeed." Lors moved behind Jael, and the Prince could feel the King's breath at his ear. He spoke in a whisper. "Let me ask, how long does it take a Traveler to heal from a sword to the gut? A broken back? A knife to the throat?"

Jael stiffened, then immediately regretted his reaction.

Lors turned on his heel and strode over to the table where he had been working earlier. "You see, I have had my eye on Karth for quite some time. The people of the Reaches nearly took it twenty-something years ago, but they were messy, disorganized."

Jael turned his head towards Lors.

"I am no warrior, I will admit." Lors held his hands up in mock surprise. He dropped into the ornate chair next to him and picked up a stack of papers. "But I study, you see. I have been studying since well before Karth took The Handaals, and I know you must fight fire with fire. Therefore, I stole the ember that will give me the same strength as your father."

Jael took a step toward the table. "You don't know what you are doing. The Gate is magic you cannot wield."

"And why is that?" Venalise asked from behind, feigning ignorance.

"The Gate is not a magical gem you make a wish on or whisper over to make Travelers appear from thin air. It is delicate and intricate magic. Your studies didn't reveal that, did they?" Jael sneered.

"Oh, they did," Lors chuckled. "And now I have the mage and the stone. I even have a Traveler! What else do I need, Lise?"

"Nothing, Lord," Venalise purred. "If there is something we missed, we have this one to guide us." Her satisfied smile was poisonous.

"I won't help you!"

"No?" Lors stood. "I think I can inspire your cooperation." He meandered around the table, letting his fingers trail along the smooth edge. "She's a pretty thing," he said, almost to himself. "Stubborn, too. I recall seeing her just as she arrived, looking for Venalise."

Jael's heartbeat quickened.

"Your Traveler is quite a specimen. I can see why you'd want her back."

"I will not help you."

"My boy," Lors nodded, "you will help me. Because if you do not, the consequences will be unpleasant."

"Do what you will," Jael challenged, his heart pounding. The words left his mouth before he could think. He was inviting disaster.

"Oh?"

Jael's eyes glittered with defiance.

Lors smiled and called over his shoulder, "Bring her!"

135

Amarynn awoke to a heavy numbness in her limbs. She cracked open one eye and saw her sword leaning against a nearby stone wall. Her arm, heavy with the weight of the cuff wrapped tightly around her wrist, inched toward the blade. Her hand crept closer to the hilt but stopped just as the iron chain reached its full length, keeping the grip just out of reach. She opened her other eye and fixed her stare on the cuff, then followed the chain to a stone wall where it was attached to a thick, metal hook. Laughter assaulted her ears, and she bristled with rage. She heard footsteps cross the floor; then, a guard held her arms while another gathered the chain and unhooked it from the wall.

"Let's go, girl!"

The guards hauled Amarynn up by the arms. Venalise must have used the iron to spell her, to keep her slow and subdued. The sensation was similar to the torc Lasten used to disarm Travelers, but this magic felt dirty and rough. Not only did it drain her strength, but it also hurt. Her muscles and bones ached against the enchantment attached to her wrist.

The two guards were familiar; they were the ones she had not injured. They kept her chained as they dragged her across the stone chamber and then through the arched doorway on the other side. Amarynn could barely lift her head to look for any sign of Regealth as they passed through. They hoisted her roughly up an endless flight of stairs, and when they finally stopped, she was confident it would be at a cell. She was surprised to see large, iron-banded doors. They were ajar, and she could hear low voices from within.

"Bring her!" The command reverberated out into the hallway.

The guards yanked on her arms again as they elbowed the doors open and pulled her into the room. She pushed herself to stand a little taller and walk more than be dragged as they entered the room. Her pride was too tricky to completely contain, even as she was incapacitated by magic beyond her control. She refused to appear weak.

As they entered the chambers, she kept her gaze on the floor. When the guards stopped, she raised her head, prepared to see Lors at his council table. She was not ready to see Jael.

Her heart plummeted. She had hoped Venalise had lied to her, but there he was. Jael had made the worst kind of mistake following her. Now they had leverage. Lors and Venalise would hurt her or Regealth repeatedly until the Prince revealed whatever knowledge they sought. Jael was strong, she knew, but eventually, he would break. She channeled every ounce of her rage away from her body and into her glare, focused solely on Lors.

"Ah!" King Lors exclaimed, making sure to gauge Jael's reaction. "Here she is!"

Jael raised his head, and his eyes fixed miserably on Amarynn. She saw him wince for a moment, and she shook her head almost imperceptibly. She could not allow him to be broken by Lors, using her as bait. The King gestured to the guards to bring her forward. He ran one finger along her cheek.

"So beautiful."

Amarynn tore her eyes away from Jael to glare at the King again.

"And so damn mean!" he chuckled. He pulled his dagger from its sheath and set it at the hollow of her throat, just between her collarbones. He turned back to Jael. "You know her, Jael. Does she even have a heart?"

Lors turned back to Amarynn and plunged his dagger into her chest without warning.

Amarynn grunted as the blade pierced through the muscle and bone near her throat. Pain blossomed through her, but she refused to scream. Her eyes widened, and she instinctively sought Jael with wide eyes. His horrified expression was telling. She was sure he'd break, and sooner than she had thought. The Traveler struggled, but only briefly. She felt her lungs fill with the blood pumping from the open vessels in her neck and settled into the inevitability of her heart slowing to a stop.

Lors stood with his arms crossed as he watched her, observed her with a sick fascination.

Ever defiant, Amarynn stayed on her feet as long as she could. Lors turned back to Jael, smiling sadistically. Her breathing became quick and shallow, gurgling as fluid continued to fill her lungs. She willed herself not to fight it as she mouthed two words at the Prince.

Don't break.

Finally, her legs gave out, and she fell to her knees.

Conserving whatever breath she had left, she held on to consciousness as long as she could until black spots crowded her vision. Her eyes never left Jael's until the darkness claimed her, blood pooling on the stone at her feet as she sagged between the two guards.

"Get her out of here!" Lors bellowed.

Amarynn's feet left a bloody trail out the door as Lor's men dragged her limp form from the chamber. Jael stared at the pool of her congealing blood while Lors strode back to the table, wiping his blade on his ink-stained handkerchief. Eyeing Jael, he sat down, placing his elbows on the table.

"I'm fascinated by the immortal human Travelers," he began. Lors rested his chin in his hand. He reached across the table with the other and snatched a blank piece of parchment. "Do you know how long it will take for her to heal?"

Jael's right hand clenched so hard at his side that his fingernails drew blood in his palm. His presence of mind had left the room Amarynn's limp body.

"How long?"

Jael broke his stare and looked towards Lors, dumbfounded. He had never imagined it would come to this. He knew that walking into the keep was a mistake, but he was unprepared for Amarynn to become Lors' captive. The thought had never even crossed his mind. She was legendary, unbeatable, yet he just witnessed her being cut down like any other soldier. Travelers survived wounds like the one she just endured, but at a significant cost. He knew that if the blade had penetrated her heart, it would take her many painful weeks to recover.

"I... don't know," Jael whispered.

"How could you not..." Lors shook his head in exasperation. "Never mind. That's a shame," the King said as he scribbled notes. "I will document each injury so we can be certain." He stopped, quill feathers brushing his chin. "If a Traveler is already injured, would other injuries take longer than usual to heal?" Lors shook his head, admonishing himself. "I should have wounded her with a sword first. I have such a terrible habit of rushing things!"

Venalise, who had remained in the background throughout the entire ordeal, glided past them. She stopped for a moment at the chamber door.

"Lors, while your fascination with Traveler healing time is riveting," she announced, "I have more pressing matters to attend to."

Lors looked up from his paper quizzically.

"It won't matter how long their healing takes if I cannot summon one."

CHAPTER 20

Dolls. There were dolls scattered throughout the daintily decorated room. Sia sat in the middle of the four-poster bed, her hands toying with the doll in her lap. She had never owned a doll in her life. Her parents said there was no time or money for something as frivolous as a toy. She turned it over in her hands. The doll was finely made — porcelain, with intricately embroidered clothes.

The fire crackled in the hearth, throwing dark shadows against the stone walls. She was dressed in an ankle-length gown of blue velvet, and the leather slippers on her feet were the softest she'd ever felt. She didn't remember how she came to be wearing these things or when she came to be in this room. She only recalled a small part of the ride after leaving the ship and nothing else.

She scanned the walls. Thick tapestries hung around the room, but there were no windows, and there was only one door. No one opened it — at least she hadn't seen anyone open it — but there was a tray of soup and crusty bread on a table by the hearth. Sia couldn't help but feel small and trapped in this dark, stone room.

She instantly thought of Regealth lying in the wagon. She wondered where he was. Pushing the doll out of her lap, she raised her hands in front of her. Maybe she could summon some of her magic to try and find him. But without water, she didn't know how. Scanning the room, she searched for a washbasin. She slid her legs from the bed and went to the food tray. A yip of excitement escaped her lips; a cup filled with cold, clear water was on the tray.

Holding her hands over the cup, she closed her eyes and tried to call the mist. At first, nothing happened. She could feel the water, sense it, but she couldn't make it obey. She stepped back, shook out her hands, then tried again. Tension and worry crawled over her skin, her knees shook, and her hands trembled.

This time the mist rose, just a wisp at first, then a steady stream as she focused more. She tried to pull harder on the water than she ever did for Regealth.

Splash!

Water was everywhere — on her, all over the tray, and dripping onto the floor. Gasping from the cold shock, she couldn't help but grin at her success. Emboldened, she tried to move the puddles of water from the floor back to the tray. She began with the smallest one, closest to the hearth. It rose quickly, and vapor coalesced around her tiny hands. She was very near the hearth as she marveled at the tiny droplets that clung to her fingers. The shimmering water vapor distracted her as she moved, her hands inches away from the fire.

It all happened so fast; she did not realize that her hands were burning. The sparkling water became tiny flames that danced along her fingers.

Sia stared. There was no pain.

Fascinated, she turned her hands over, watching the fire crawl over her skin. The flames chased themselves around and around her fingers, ending in graceful arcs at her fingertips. Her chest burned and she let loose her breath.

Unsure what to do with the fire, she held her hands back to the larger flames within the hearth. She tried to give a gentle mental nudge, and at first, the tiny flames resisted. Finally, after trying several times, they seemed to fly from her hands into the hearth, rejoining their brethren.

Sia sat down cross-legged between the hearth and the table. How could she have managed to call fire? Regealth said each mage only manifested one affinity, and like him, hers was most definitely water. While she contemplated what just happened, the finger of her left hand drew shapes in a puddle of water next to her knee. The other drew little circles of sparks in the air, just above the fire.

She sat there for a while until she heard the door's latch clanking as a key turned the tumblers in the lock. Sia snatched her hands back to her lap. She grabbed a linen napkin from the tray and dropped it over the largest puddle.

No sooner had the napkin settled to the floor than her chamber door slowly opened. Sia peered around the table to find Venalise frowning as she looked at her, one hand still resting on the doorknob.

"I— I— fell," Sia offered as an excuse.

"That's all right, dear," she cooed. "Are you hurt?" A forced expression of concern settled on her face.

Sia looked down at her hands in her lap, quickly bunching up the singed edges of her dress sleeves in her fists.

"I'm fine," she whispered.

Venalise, satisfied, glided into the room toward Sia. She offered her one outstretched hand. "Come with me."

Sia complied and stood to grasp it. Her skin was cold yet soft. The child felt a slight repulsion but willed herself not to let go. She looked up at the beautiful, frightening woman.

"Where are we going?"

"I would like to show you something." Venalise tugged lightly on Sia's hand and smiled at her. Sia did not want to admit it, but she was afraid. Venalise, sensing her fear, knelt in front of her. "Have you ever had a pet, little one?"

"A pet?" Sia furrowed her brows. "Like a cat?"

"Well, that all depends on you." Venalise gave Sia's hand a little squeeze and stood.

143

"First, I will show you where I do my work. We can try a few things that might be fun." She arched an eyebrow conspiratorially. "Maybe even exciting! Who knows what will happen?"

"And after that?" Sia was cautiously intrigued. They walked out her door into the hallway.

"Then, we are going to meet the King."

The door slammed, metal and stone grating against one another as Amarynn was unceremoniously deposited on the stone floor of a dungeon cell. The blade had missed her heart, and the freezing pain of healing was tearing through her even as she was pulled from the throne room. Had her heart been struck, the injury would have been as difficult to recover from as Matteus' slice of her throat. Amarynn's breath gurgled, and she coughed up clotted blood. Her thoughts came slow and foggy, but the blood vessels in her neck were coming back together and feeding much-needed oxygen to her brain.

Little breaths.

Tiny shards of bone eased back into place above her breastplate, each piece like a needle slicing through the tissue sending shocks of pain across her chest. As the pressure in her vessels began to return, her heart gained strength; she could feel its pulse through to her spine. Amarynn went through the healing routine in her head as air trickled into her lungs like rivulets of water.

Just sip at the air. You are fine.

Whenever battle wounds made her feel like she was asphyxiating and panic began to rise, she soothed herself with the steady beat of her heart returning to life. It might have been easier to sleep through the healing process, but vigilance required she stay alert. Opportunities usually presented themselves when she played dead, and she was sure this was no exception.

Hours passed while she faded in and out of consciousness, but her breathing became less labored as the suffocating heat in the cell heat dried out her mouth and nose. She could feel the stone floor beneath her, against her cheek, and when she ventured to open her eyes, only dim light greeted her. At least in Venalise's chambers, there had been a healthy glow from her hearth. Now, the light was so scarce that shadows were difficult to discern. As her eyes adjusted to the dark, she made out the iron bars looming on either side of the cell. She lifted her head as far as she could and saw stone lining the back wall, but with that movement tore a ragged cough through her lungs, and she was instantly overcome with the memory of Lors pushing his dagger into her chest. He had aimed high to miss her heart on purpose, no doubt.

She coughed again, then experimentally opened and closed her hands, rubbing them against the stone to combat the prickling sensation that permeated her limbs. They felt better — not strong, but at least she could make a fist. She lay there for several minutes letting the magic finish its work. Finally, she felt like she could move.

Rolling over to her back, she swallowed hard as a wave of dizziness hit her full force. For a moment, all she could do was close her eyes and try not to vomit.

Images replayed in her mind.

Flashes of the throne room.

Lors' poisonous smile.

Another coughing fit wracked her body, and another before she could breathe without gagging. She reached up to feel the spot where the blade had penetrated. The wound wasn't completely closed, but it was getting close, which was strange. She had never healed so quickly. She still wore the magically-imbued cuff around her wrist, sapping her strength, making her rapid recovery even more unusual.

A cry broke the quiet, sounding eerily like the dragon-greall she and Jael had encountered in the forest. The echoes resonated off the stone, making it impossible to discern if they had come from above or below. Amarynn tried to push the Prince from her mind, tried to

145

forget his face when he looked into her eyes. He had admitted his lack of battle experience to her while they scouted the keep. She feared the shock of seeing her cut down like that would significantly weaken his resolve.

A noise close beside her caught her attention.

"I wondered when you would make an appearance." A voice, dry and thin like parchment, drifted through the bars from the cell on her left.

Amarynn's eyes snapped open.

She turned her head and, despite the dim light, recognized the tattered robes belonging to Regealth.

She eased up to a sitting position, catching herself on the partition as the cell spun. She leaned against the cool metal and pressed her forehead against the bars. With one eye open, she could see the old mage leaning against the back wall. He looked nearly dead — pale, thin, his breath rattling.

"Regealth," she breathed.

He let his head roll in the direction of her voice.

"Ah, Amarynn," he mumbled. His eyebrow raised as if he were listening to someone in his mind. Then a smile played upon his lips. "Did you know," he said. "Your name means 'shining star' in the old tongue?"

Amarynn closed her eyes for a moment. The old mage was delusional—probably from lack of food and water.

"Yes," she answered softly. He continued to smile.

"Regealth?" she questioned.

"Yes, my star?"

"I will free you," she said, her voice laced with determination.

"Oh, I believe you will try." The corners of his mouth turned up, attempting a smile.

She worked to reposition herself to stand, but her limbs felt heavy. Whatever spell Venalise had placed upon the metal cuff was not

146

dissipating. There was no chance she would be able to rescue herself in this condition, much less an elderly mage who could hardly walk.

"I was badly injured. I don't know why, but I heal quickly, even with Venalise's magic. Can you remove the spell on this damn cuff? It's dampening my strength."

He didn't answer. His breathing was ragged. Amarynn gripped the bars as best she could and pressed herself close. "Regealth?"

A long moment passed. Screams and strange noises from the passages and chambers around them filtered through the darkness. Finally, he inhaled and said, "Hmm. Perhaps."

"What do you mean, perhaps?"

"Ah, now, that's the problem. I have no water in here to draw power from." He plucked at his robes. "I am already weak, and my magic is drained." He opened his pale blue eyes and looked at her with regret.

Water. There was none with her, and the guards had not provided any to either of them. She scanned the cell, looking for drips or even condensation—anything. There was nothing.

Deep in thought, she chewed at her lip. She tasted iron and touched a finger to where she had bitten down. A single drop of blood glistened like a bright ruby against her skin when she pulled her hand away. It began to trickle down toward the palm of her hand. She touched her lip again, and another drop clung there before sliding down to join the other. Amarynn stared at the tiny pool of blood collecting in her palm, an idea forming.

If water was what the old mage needed, she knew exactly how to get it.

147

CHAPTER 21

The hall fell quiet after Venalise exited, save for Jael's heart, pounding furiously in his chest.

"You made a grave mistake coming here. Lucky for us, not so much for you." Lors shrugged. "I don't know if you are aware, but Venalise has already conquered the magic of Traveling. Not humans, of course."

Though he tried, Jael could not hide his shock.

Lors tapped his temple. "Remember, boy, I study. I observe. I know it takes two to create a portal between worlds, and I know your father's sister was the key to creating the Gate."

This was true.

His Aunt Dyaneth and Regealth had studied for years to unlock and harness the magic of the Gate Stone, and it ultimately cost her life. While the intricacies of sky and water magic had culminated in a portal between worlds, the draw on both powers was great — so much so that his father's sister did not recover. Regealth had yet to understand where the Travelers' bodies were wrenched from, but these immortal warriors were the crown jewel of his accomplishments. Dyaneth, the only sky mage ever known, had relinquished her life, and whatever power she had left passed to her brother, Lasten, though he could never wield it.

"If you think I possess the power of my father, you are wrong." Jael's voice was cold.

"We shall see."

Lors searched the table for a document, and when he found it, he turned back to Jael, brandishing it excitedly. "You must possess even an inkling of the sky magic your family holds. If not you, then there is a bastard running around Karth who can."

"You don't understand. My father cannot *wield*. He is only a source. And he did not acquire that power until after my birth. If all Dyaneth passed to my father was source magic, I am no use to you." Jael paused and thought for a moment. He could not let them know only one wielder was necessary to draw from the Gate. "If Venalise already has a portal stone and another mage, why do you need the Gate? Why do you need Regealth?"

Lors waggled his finger in front of Jael. "No, no. You get no information from me. You *provide* information."

"No."

"That's what I thought you'd say. Guards!" Lors called over Jael's shoulder. Two burly uniformed men, much like the two that had dragged Amarynn away, came through the door and were at Jael's sides in an instant. "Take him to one of the chambers near the dungeon. I want him to hear what happens to people who do not cooperate."

The men seized Jael by the arms and proceeded to haul him forward, but he jerked his arms free and walked on his own accord.

"Plinus!" Lors barked toward the door.

The little man who had brought Jael through the keep scuttled forward; his head lowered.

"Accompany the guards and educate our new guest on how business is handled here in the Darklands. He still seems a bit confused."

Plinus bowed again and beckoned for Jael to follow him. The Prince willed his feet to move as Plinus disappeared through the double doors. The little man waited for Jael and the two guards to catch up, then together, they walked down a long hall to where the passageway narrowed abruptly. They turned sharply to the right.

"My apologies, but we must pass through the dungeons to take the stairs up. Most of the quarters are carved in the mountain, and the fastest way is a direct route," Plinus explained. "King Lors prefers it, though," he added, "because he likes the prisoners to see him regularly."

Plinus stopped, Jael nearly stumbling into him. He took a hasty step backward and cast a sideways glance. "He thinks it keeps them afraid," he whispered, "but it only makes them angrier if you ask me." The little man shrugged his shoulders. "But, who asks me?"

Jael, sensing an opportunity, said quietly, "I would."

Plinus looked at him in surprise. He raised his eyebrows, then turned and resumed his rapid pace through the dark hallways.

Jael followed, but his pace began to flag. He was still reeling from what he had witnessed in the throne room. Amarynn had been struck down just as she had been by Matteus, and he had been powerless to stop it. At the moment of Lors' assault, her face was etched in his memory: fierce but with undeniable panic in her expression. Heavy helplessness weighed on him, and breathing became more difficult until he felt like he was suffocating. His feet became lead weights, refusing to take another step. The guards gave him a shove, and he stumbled.

"Plinus," he whispered.

The little man did not hear him and instead kept moving forward into the darkness.

"Plinus!" Jael rasped.

Plinus stopped and turned, concern growing in his eyes. He shuffled back to Jael just as the Prince slumped against the wall. At an imperious gesture, the guards stepped away, and the little man placed a hand on Jael's arm.

"The cruelty of Lors knows no bounds," he whispered.

Jael nodded mutely.

"We must continue, My Lord. It would do you no good to be seen here in your state."

Jael watched Plinus. A pearl of odd, unnerving wisdom glinting in the small man's eyes led Jael to wonder whether his loyalties truly lay with Lors. Plinus stepped back, allowing him room to push off the wall. They resumed their journey through the dark passageways at a slower pace.

Soon enough, they entered what could only be the dungeons. He scanned the area, hoping to catch a glimpse of Amarynn. He hoped they were not keeping her with Venalise. As he looked through the iron bars, he only saw men in various states of decline. But just as they were nearing the edge of the narrowest hallway, he heard a scream that sounded like the greall they encountered in the forest.

Plinus waved it off. "That's just one of the winged wyverns Venalise has been able to call. I know she wanted humans, but when it arrived in her chamber, my goodness, was she surprised!" He tried to hide his smile. "The Stone calls what it is attuned to."

Jael cast a sideways glance at Plinus. "How long has she been crossing Travelers?"

"For years. Ever since the fall of the Handaals, but that—" he gestured to the darkness and the wails and screams that wafted from below, "—has been all that the stone has produced. She calls them atranoch. Earth and fire magic are less nuanced than water and sky, which would account for…" He trailed off.

"For?" Jael prompted.

"I know no more, My Lord. I've said too much." Plinus bowed his head and shuffled on.

They continued, and Jael scanned the darkness for signs of Amarynn. His eyes roamed from cell to cell, but still, he saw no trace of her.

They were about to turn down another hallway when he finally saw a pair of familiar leather boots and raggedly shorn auburn hair. Through the dim, he saw Amarynn leaning against the side of her cell, her gaze on the floor as she bit at her lip. He watched her touch her mouth and examine her fingers. He was just about to shout her name when he felt a rough tug on his sleeve as the guards pulled him back to the main hallway and gave him a shove. Jael stumbled blindly forward, keeping his eyes on her, his mind in a million places. This was not supposed to happen this way. They had both gambled, risked everything, and now they were trapped. He wanted to call her name, but he knew that would not bode well for either of them. Only after they turned the corner did Jael stop looking over his shoulder.

The journey ended after climbing a long, curved flight of stairs. The guards hoisted him by his arms, dragged him up when he faltered near the top, and then dropped him to his knees in front of an uncomplicated door. Plinus offered a hand to help him to his feet, then opened the door. Just as Jael was about to step through behind him, he saw Venalise out of the corner of his eye. She was leaving another chamber further down the corridor with a small child in tow. The little one looked frightened, but she still clung to the mage's hand.

Jael watched them go, then stepped into his chambers.

Plinus wandered through the room, pointing out this and that, but Jael only feigned his interest. He hadn't heard a word the little man said. As Plinus was leaving, the Prince watched him reach for the key from a thong around his neck. The man's sleeve fell back, and Jael saw torchlight flicker on a metal cuff attached to his forearm. Plinus made quick work of covering his arm, then closed the door behind him. There was a click of a lock, then Plinus' footsteps faded away down the hall.

Jael sat on the edge of his bed to gather his thoughts. A metal cuff was wrapped around Plinus' arm, a cuff just like the one he'd seen Lors place on Amarynn. Immortal Travelers could only be subdued by the magic that created them or when constrained by an infused object. This was not usually a liability for a Traveler — most people with ill intent never got close enough to a Traveler to attach such a thing. But Plinus? He was no warrior. Why would he be wearing a similar device?

Jael closed his eyes. He breathed deeply and dug back through the memory of Amarynn behind those iron bars. It had been only a handful of days since they had come to know one another, yet he could think of nothing else but her safety. He snorted. *Her safety?* She was immortal, and he was not. He needed to consider his own skin, for the moment at least.

He stood and went to the door. He knew it was locked, but he tried it anyway. He shook the handle halfheartedly, then placed both hands on either side of the door and leaned in, resting his forehead on the heavy black wood. How was he going to get out of this mess?

Jael's head swam with regret, worry, and the sickening feeling of failure. Amarynn's face hovered in his mind, and a wave of nausea rolled over him. He was questioning everything now. Perhaps escape was the best option. He could make a run for Karth and return with his father and the Legion and...

And it would most likely be too late to recover the Gate or help Regealth and Amarynn.

Running was not an option.

A sudden shriek startled him: the atranoch, no doubt. A memory of the great black beast they had encountered in the forest surged to life in his mind. Amarynn had stepped between both beasts and him without a second thought. Yes, she was Legion and trained to protect her sovereign, but there was an urgency to her movements that did not seem likely only days into this journey — their first time spent near one another.

Amarynn had kept him at arm's length their entire expedition, but he could not deny the sense of familiarity blossoming between them. Her sense of loyalty to Regealth — the very man who had pulled her into the life she loathed — fascinated him. Her reaction to seeing him on the road outside the keep hovered in his mind. She had been reckless and ready to strike as the caravan passed with the old mage. If Venalise hadn't been sitting at the head of the line, she would have, most assuredly, recovered Regealth, and they would be on their way home by now.

Venalise. What did she know of Travelers? Plinus claimed she had unlocked the power to travel, but how?

He gave a fleeting thought to the little girl he saw with Venalise. All the puzzle pieces hovered close together in his head, though he could not visualize the picture they had created. Was she the child they had seen in Venalise's arms when the procession entered the Keep?

Amarynn, Regealth, the girl — so many variables were at play. Jael knew he must stay the course. At the very least, he needed to find a way to get to Amarynn, free her, and get out of Athtull Keep alive.

CHAPTER 22

The darkness of the dungeons was almost palpable. Only red and orange flickers from the depths below offered any light. Amarynn sucked the bone-dry air through her nostrils, the heat stifling her healing throat and lungs. Venalise's spell of weakness shrouded her like a heavy blanket.

Regealth needed water, and any liquid contained just that — water he could use to try and access his magic. Then he would be able to remove Venalise's spell. There was no hope of finding any water in either of their dungeon cells, but that snake of a mage forgot that Amarynn had an unending supply of blood. As an immortal, she could bleed herself out completely and trust her body to heal repeatedly.

Amarynn leaned her head back against the stone wall.

"Regealth, you have to try and get closer to me," she rasped.

There was no response. The old mage had grown quieter and quieter in the past few hours. Amarynn turned her head to assess his condition. He was nearly grey, and his chest barely rose and fell. She swallowed, her tongue dry and swollen in her mouth. There was no time to waste. He needed access to her blood now, or he would die, and she would never be free.

Amarynn contemplated how to draw her blood so it flowed freely. Certainly, she could bite her wrist, but she doubted her teeth could inflict enough damage to fully open a vein. She reached up and felt along the iron bars for an uneven edge she might use but found none. Her hand dropped to the floor, her fingers brushing a loose piece of stone. She allowed herself a hint of hope.

Amarynn closed her hand around the stone piece and was pleased to find one edge thin and sharp. It would do nicely, she thought to herself. Now, she needed to make sure she could position herself so that the blood pooled near Regealth's form. Oas soon as she lost a sufficient volume of blood, she would be incapacitated until her body healed itself. If there weren't enough within his reach, Regealth would not be able to recover; he didn't have that kind of time.

"Regealth," she tried one last time. No response.

She gripped the stone in her right hand and raised it to her left wrist, nudging the iron cuff up her forearm as far as possible. She drew in a breath and steeled herself, pulling the thin edge against her skin with as much force as she could muster, the cuff's magic reducing her strength. A few beads of blood welled up, and Amarynn sighed. This would take more time than she wanted — more time than Regealth had. Without her blades, she needed to channel her rage, to call on her battle fury and make this happen with sheer force of will.

Easy, she thought.

Lors' face and his venomous smile flashed in her mind. She felt her blood begin to rise. He was somewhere in this very keep, and she needed to get free of this cell and get her hands around his neck.

She clenched her jaw and pressed the stone against her wrist again. This time, she dug deep and pulled. The brutish force sent pain spikes singing up through her arm, but the cut was still not deep enough. Without thinking it through, she sawed back and forth at the skin and ligaments, grunting through gritted teeth.

With one last pull, she felt the warm gush of blood flow from the wound and into her hand. She placed the sharp stone in her bloody hand, then pushed and strained to twist her hips so that she could angle her shoulder through the bars. Finally, she thrust her arm into the adjacent cell, reaching as far as possible to allow the blood to flow in Regealth's direction. The sharp stone tumbled from her grasp but lay close enough to her hand that he would see. He would need more blood to recover, and he would have to use the stone to open her vein himself.

She smiled weakly in relief when the old mage slid his hand toward her, his eyes still closed. Her blood ran in tiny rivulets toward his outstretched fingers. She leaned into the bars, willing the precious fluid to find its way to the mage's hand. Now, all she could do was watch and hope it was enough.

Thick rivers of her blood slid across the warm floor of the dungeon toward Regealth's hand. With no cold stone to cause the blood to pool and clot, it stayed fluid in the heat of the dungeon. Several small streams followed different paths across the uneven floor, but one finally reached its destination. Amarynn's blood caressed and then pooled around Regealth's outstretched fingers. The digits twitched, a faint movement, but it didn't escape Amarynn's keen vision even in the dim light.

She strained her legs to make her heart pump harder. More blood poured from her wrist, and she began to feel lightheaded. She hoped she had provided enough to rouse him before she bled out entirely or the wound closed on its own. The old man lifted his hand and then placed his palm flat in the growing pool of blood. His fingers moved back and forth hungrily; then, he raised his hand ever so slightly from the darkening fluid.

The other rivulets arrived at his body. One small stream began to soak into his robes near his thigh, and the other ran behind his back. More and more of her blood found its way to the mage, and the more that reached him, the more it seemed to be pulled from her body and in his direction.

Amarynn could feel she was starting to weaken. She had been supporting herself against the iron bars, but she sagged as her blood left her body. Her feet lost their purchase against the floor, and her legs went slack while her heart slowed. Her breathing became more and more shallow, but a smile formed on her lips —she was confident she could see delicate tendrils of steam rise from her blood to Regealth's hand. Stars danced in her vision, and she saw his eyes flutter open before her own went dark.

Sia placed one tiny foot in front of the other down the dark stairwell. She fixed her eyes on the back of Venalise's red dress and wondered how many steps they had taken. When they reached the bottom, she felt sure they had arrived at the mountain's base. Venalise produced an iron key from the folds of her skirt and opened the heavy door in front of them. As they entered the chamber, the child could not help but stare in awe. It was massive — rounded at the top and more immense than at least three ships. The air was cold, but the glow of torches illuminated an alcove that beckoned with warmth and light across from them.

A squeeze on her shoulder caught her by surprise, and she jumped. "Overwhelming, I'm sure."

Sia looked up at the mage, then back at the chamber.

"Did you make this?" she whispered.

The corner of the witch's mouth turned up. "Yes."

Sia's face shone with wonder.

Venalise shrugged. "Well, not all of it. This was a cave in the mountain that I... embellished." She flashed a quick smile, then stepped toward the alcove, pulling Sia along by the hand to the cramped little room, where scrolls overflowed from crude shelves carved into the stone. Pages and pages of paper lay strewn across the table in the center. Venalise dropped Sia's hand and busied herself at a stone outcropping that jutted from the back wall.

Sia scanned the room. Nothing too frightening in here. She supposed she expected to see skulls or strange talismans, even dead animals, but there was nothing of the sort. The alcove reminded her of

Master Omman's quarters aboard the Blackfly, one of the only places she had ever felt safe on that ship.

The sound of groaning rocks brought her attention back to Venalise. A thrum of energy tickled Sia's skin, and she turned just in time to see the stone in front of the mage shudder and tear apart. With one hand, Venalise held the split in the rock open; with the other, she reached through and produced a small wooden box.

Clutching the box to her chest, she turned, leaving the wall to rumble back together behind her.

"What's that?" Sia climbed up onto the bench near the table, unable to resist the urge to lean in for a better look.

Venalise set the box down and toyed with it for a moment, her fingers tracing an intricate pattern across the wood. "When I was a girl, my mother told me that magic was forbidden, but I could feel it tugging at me all the time. She wanted me to ignore it." She leaned closer to Sia. "I couldn't. Could you?"

Sia pursed her lips and looked away, Regealth's warning repeatedly playing in her mind. Some would *hurt you for what you can do.* She dropped her gaze to the box. Venalise opened the lid, and in an instant, the contents were singing with an energy Sia had never felt. As the mage lifted the sparkling blue Gate Stone from its rowan bed, the tiny hairs on Sia's neck stood while a shiver washed over her. Venalise was watching her closely now.

"Magic is in your blood like it is in mine. You can feel it, can't you?"

Sia tore her gaze from the stone and glanced up at Venalise. "Like Regealth feels water?"

"Yes, my sweet." Venalise set the gem back in the box and closed it. "He is the one who made this." Sia wanted to reach for it, to hold it, but she clenched her hands and resisted. Her eyebrows furrowed. "Where is he?"

"He is resting right now, so we won't bother him for a while. But I'll take you to see him soon." Venalise stood and returned the box to its hiding place inside the stone. She turned and lifted a gold chain from around her neck, producing a teardrop-shaped gem from the neckline of her dress. Facets of red and gold shone a blazing fire, with dark onyx at the center. It pulsed in the glow of the torches.

"Did you make that one?" Sia's voice was a whisper. The tang of metal filled her nostrils, and her limbs warmed. She began to feel feverish.

"It's pretty, isn't it?" Venalise held it out to Sia. The stone dangled from its chain, beckoning to her with a magnetism she couldn't deny. She held out her hand, and Venalise gently laid the gem in her palm. "Come with me, Sia." Venalise stepped out of the alcove and waited for Sia to follow.

They walked away from the warmth of the alcove to the center of the vast cavern, but Sia no longer felt the chill. Venalise knelt in front of her, guiding her hand to an indention in the floor shaped like the stone. Grooves, etched in the rock, radiated from the indention, connecting to others on the cavern floor, forming a circle. "Now, let it go," she murmured.

Sia hesitated, then let the stone settle into the teardrop-shaped hollow. The mage gave Sia's hand a quick squeeze, then stood and guided her to stand on one side of the pattern on the floor. The air was charged with a hum that felt like hot metal. Venalise crossed to the other side of the circle, then faced her.

"Sia."

The child looked up at the mage across from her.

"Call to the stone."

She didn't know what to do. She could feel magic pulsating around her. Even though she knew it must be coming from the stone, she could not find its center.

"Just call to it. I'll do the rest."

Frustrated, Sia closed her eyes like Regealth had taught her and let the room fall away from her senses. *Only the magic*, he had said. *Let the world disappear and exist only in the magic of the element.*

The mountain and the cavern began to drift and fall away from her conscience. Gentle warmth swelled into a wave of heat, undulating around her.

"There, now. I can feel you."

Venalise's voice was distant.

"Now, call to it. Call the magic from the stone."

She pulled from inside, like someone might take a deep breath, but without actually breathing. She trembled as she held it while thin, ghostly filaments stretched up from the floor at her feet. Heat surged around her, but it did not burn. Lines of fiery magic swirled around her, through her, tore from within her. She would have been frightened if she could sense her body, but there was nothing to feel except fire, and it was the most exhilarating thing she had ever felt.

And then it was gone.

In its place was a void of freezing cold. She hadn't wanted to let go, but she needed to breathe. The air had been stolen from her lungs, and she collapsed to her knees, gasping. She fell forward, catching herself with her hands as she hit the cold stone beneath her, her head bowed. Then her breath returned while hot tears streamed down her face.

Something soft nudged against her cheek, and she pulled back to sit on her knees. In front of her lay a bear cub, nearly white with tips of grey. Sia stared in wonder at the creature. She glanced nervously toward Venalise, who also seemed to be in shock. The young animal was crying, a mewling sound like a kitten.

Sia reached for the bear and picked it up, holding it close. It stopped crying and nuzzled at her neck, licking and snuffling the soft skin behind her ear. She stroked its fur, cradling it like a baby. She didn't notice Venalise's approach.

"You did it." Beside her, the woman's voice trembled. Sia hugged the cub tighter and buried her face in its fur when Venalise reached out to touch it. "A stone bear," she whispered.

Sia looked up at her. "How do you know?"

Venalise didn't answer her. She was fixated on the little creature in Sia's arms.

"How do you know what she is?"

Venalise tore her gaze from the bear. "I… I have seen them in books. They are from the Stone Reaches, not too far from here." Her voice trailed off, and then she lifted her chin, her fingers lingering on the animal. "He chose you."

"She," Sia mumbled without looking up.

"*She* is yours, child." Venalise stood, and Sia looked up. "That creature is connected to you now, and she will do anything to protect you."

"Anything?" Sia scrambled to her feet, holding the bear close.

"Yes," Venalise narrowed her eyes. "She is bonded to you now. You are her blood, and your magic flows through her."

The bear pushed its wet nose against Sia's chin.

"If I am correct, she will grow to be larger than an ox. You'll need to think about training her."

"She's just a baby." Sia frowned.

"That baby will become your greatest protector. She is just like a Karth Legion Traveler."

Sia's voice was a whisper. "She cannot be killed?"

"That remains to be seen, child. But I would think she is no different. You brought her here through the same kind of portal I Traveled the atranoch. And they are indestructible." Venalise held out her hand to Sia. "You must be tired from our little experiment here. I will take you back to your room, and you can rest. I will study what we have done today and when you are ready, we will try again."

Sia didn't feel tired, but her legs wobbled, and her breath came harder and faster as she stood. She clutched the bear that scrabbled against her, trying to find a comfortable position. The room spun, and she stumbled.

"Slowly…" Venalise steadied her by the shoulders.

"I suppose I am tired."

"Using your gifts will always take a toll, child. Never forget that." Venalise tapped her nose. "Your new little friend may be unbreakable, but *you* are not." She pulled back and appraised her in awe, wonder filling her eyes. The witch placed one hand on Sia's back and ushered her across the great stone floor to the chamber egress. Sia's feet felt like wood, and as she spied the long, dark staircase, she groaned. Before she could take a step, Venalise swept her up in her arms and began gliding upwards. An irresistible need to close her eyes overtook her. She nestled her head against the mage's shoulder, and the world fell away until there was nothing but darkness, the rustle of Venalise's skirts, and the tiny heartbeat of the bear who slept so softly in her arms.

CHAPTER 23

S ia picked at the bowl of berries that had been left for her while she slept. She pulled on the same blue gown from the night before and sat cross-legged on the floor in front of the hearth, studying the flames. The bear cub happily gnawed on a bone next to her.

Yesterday's discovery had left her both frightened and thrilled at the same time. Now, she would need to be careful if she wanted to explore her magic because of the King. What if he was a bad man? She wanted nothing to do with him, then. Not at all.

"Hrmph!" The cub growled.

Sia tossed it a berry.

She gathered her skirt in one hand and laid the bowl on the floor.

She got to her feet and faced the hearth and the flames that danced within. Holding her hands out as she had last time, she tried to focus when she called to the fire again. She thought about how she could call the mist from water so gently, so softly. She tried to coax the flames just like that. The fire seemed to dance higher when she centered herself, as Regealth taught her. The tiny flickers looked like they were dancing just for her, and the thought made her giggle. The red and orange fingers snapped and hissed with every nudge she gave.

Footsteps echoed from the hallway, and she froze, the fire dying back down to its gentle glow. They came closer to her door, but they continued, passing by her chamber instead of stopping.

She listened to be sure the footsteps had vanished. Satisfied, she turned back to the fire to give it one more nudge before hearing a click from the lock on her door. She quickly released the fire and scrambled over to sit in the chair by the table. When Venalise stepped inside, the girl took a bite out of a plump, golden beeberry.

"Oh good," she said with oversaturated sweetness, "you are already up and dressed."

Venalise glided over to stand behind Sia's chair, picking up a brush off the dresser as she passed. She brushed through Sia's unruly curls, then pulled her bangs away from her face, fastening them back with a delicate silver pin covered in tiny stars.

"Now, you look like a little lady," Venalise smiled. She took the bowl of berries from Sia's lap and set them down, holding out her hand.

Sia slid off the chair. She ignored Venalise's outstretched hand and gathered up the cub.

"Have you given her a name?"

"Yes," Sia whispered.

"Well?"

"Thera."

"Ah," Venalise smiled again. "The Huntress. A good choice. Now, we should go, child. It is time for you and Thera to appear at court."

"Little one," Venalise whispered into Sia's ear, "meet your King!"

Sia stared at the man who sat on the throne. His dark hair curled over one eye, and he wore all black. He wasn't old, but he wasn't a young man, either. His style and the cocky way he perched on his throne made him seem to only be pretending to be a King. He looked at her the same way the sailors on Master Omman's ship looked at her the first time she came on board. She immediately disliked him.

Venalise put her hand on her back and gave her a little push forward. Heavy iron sconces hung from the walls in the throne room, their firelight quivering like the fear that writhed in her belly. Her hands and feet tingled with warmth like she'd felt earlier, but she willed it to retreat. She dropped her chin to her chest and stared at her blue leather slippers. Her tiny feet made no noise as they carried her across the stone floor. She cradled the cub in one arm and, as she walked, gathered the fabric of her dress in the other, twisting it nervously. Finally, she stood just at the bottom step of the dais.

"How long have you had your magic?"

Sia looked up. The King's voice was low and warm, almost comforting. He leaned forward, his eyes narrowing as he studied her.

The young girl reluctantly lifted her chin to survey the room. There were no windows because they were deep within the Keep; however, thick, heavy tapestries hung over the cold stone walls in a weak attempt to soften the harsh rock. Rugs were scattered across the expansive floor in no particular pattern. It was clear that many had been once rich and elegant, but looking at the carpet beneath her feet, Sia could see they were becoming threadbare and faded. Even the throne appeared second-hand — one of the gilded, clawed feet was missing toes, and the throne's arms were covered in nicks and scratches.

"Well?" the King asked, the tiniest hint of impatience coloring his voice.

Sia closed her eyes for a moment, deciding how to respond. She clutched the little bear close to her chin. "What magic?" she mumbled into the cub's fur.

Sia's big silver eyes opened and locked on Lors in the quiet that followed. Her voice was small in the big room, but she lifted her chin a touch higher to punctuate her defiance. The King raised his eyebrows but said nothing, and the ongoing silence made Sia squirm. Then he laughed, throwing his head back and slapping the arms of his throne.

"Oh, my dear," he said, looking toward Venalise, "I believe you have found the perfect protégé to suit your personality!"

Venalise, pleased with the King's reaction, stepped forward to join Sia.

169

"I must tell you she is still quite the mystery to me. It seems she has an affinity for water, and I have ascertained she possesses fire as well. Interestingly, she also shows affinity to earth magic. She is precious, indeed!"

"Is that even possible?"

"It has never been recorded, but anything is possible, My Lord." Venalise stroked Sia's hair possessively.

Lors rose and descended from the dais to where Sia stood. He pointed to the bear. "Did she do that?"

Venalise nodded.

Squatting down, he placed his hand on Sia's head, then ran it around to grip her neck a little too forcefully. The girl winced, and the little cub shook with a tiny growl.

"You are going to serve me well, little one. Mark my words." Lors voice had a chill that made Sia scrunch her eyes and nose in distaste.

"I don't think I want to," she whispered, lowering her chin and leveling a menacing glare. "I want Regealth back."

Lors feigned shock, then clutched his chest as he straightened up.

"Oh, what a frightening little thing!" He raised one finger and tapped her on the nose, a wicked smile spreading across his face. "You are like a little starling falcon, aren't you!"

Lors chuckled as he walked around her, Venalise stepping aside. He leaned over from behind and gripped her thin shoulders, bringing his head down by her ear. His voice lowered. "You are in no position to make any demands, my dear. Now," he turned her to face him, "go with Venalise."

He spun on his heel and climbed the short steps of the dais. "You *will* do as Venalise says," he commanded without turning to face them.

He twisted and sat on the edge of his throne in one graceful motion, a dazzling smile on his lips. "Or, my pretty little falcon, you will stay locked in a cage until you grow old and rot."

The soft shuffle of feet by the hearth roused Jael from his fitful slumber. He was sprawled sideways across the bed, one arm thrown over his face. A slit of a window high on the wall allowed a sliver of morning light to filter into the room, and it fell across his eyes as he pulled his arm away and squinted against the brightness.

Rustling sounds caught his attention, and he turned his head toward the hearth where Plinus crouched, hunched over, unsuccessfully attempting to stoke the dying fire. Jael started to speak, but before making a sound, Plinus slowly raised one hand and directed it toward the embers. His fingers trembled, and Jael could see the muscles in his neck straining.

Jael leaned forward in anticipation of what Plinus was trying to do. The fire in the hearth had nearly sputtered out, but just as the light had almost disappeared, a glow began to emanate from under the coals. Plinus angled himself forward, one knee on the ground. The little man dropped his chin to his chest and inhaled deeply, bringing his left hand up to join the right. In seconds, the glow had undulated into flames that curled and danced along the fresh firewood.

Jael's sharp intake of breath startled the little man. He pulled his hands back quickly into the folds of his robe and looked at the Prince, eyes wide.

"I did not mean to wake you," he murmured, then dropped his gaze to the ground.

Jael pushed himself to a sitting position. He started to speak but stopped himself, suddenly registering the implications of what he had just witnessed. Images of Amarynn with Lors' dagger in her chest came flooding back, and Jael gasped. His heart was racing. He stood, wanting to leave but having nowhere to go.

"I won't tell anyone."

Jael stood and moved to sit in the old, tattered wingback chair by the hearth. Plinus hastened to set a plate of bread and cheese on the short table near him, and Jael began to pick over the offerings on the plate, "It will be our secret."

171

He stole a glance at Plinus. He was so slight, almost as if he had stopped growing at ten or eleven years old, yet he looked nearly older than his father. His rich, coppery-brown skin was wrinkled around his eyes and neck, but his hands were still smooth and graceful. And his hair was the strangest of all. The wiry curls were shorn close to his scalp, but the color was marbled in every hue possible — reds, blonds, browns, even deep, rich black.

"Where are you from, Plinus?"

Plinus looked around the room nervously.

"It's just you and me, friend," Jael said.

The little man cast his eyes to the ground. "The Far Handaals, sir."

Jael's brows rose in surprise. The Far Handaals were positioned in the southernmost region of the continent. While the people there were dark-skinned and somewhat slight, they were not nearly as small as Plinus.

Lasten had taken control of the coastal Kingdom when Jael was in his early teens. He suddenly remembered Amarynn explaining the part of her tattoo that ran along her jawline. *For killing the Queen of the Handaals.... and her personal guard. All of them.* She had played a role in his father's conquest.

"How did you come to be in the service of King Lors, if I might ask?" Jael lifted his plate and offered a pastry to him.

Plinus shook his head in polite refusal. Again he looked around the room nervously.

"Plinus," Jael said, "I only want to know who you are. I can imagine what kind of master Lors is to you, but in my Kingdom, I always know my servants and staff as best I can."

Plinus swallowed, looking only partially convinced of his safety. "I was recruited by Venalise many years ago. Just after your father invaded."

"Recruited. Why?" Jael leaned forward, offering his interest and sympathy.

"I am from the outer islands — the Fars we call them — and traveled by ship with my brother and his sons. They were bringing a shipment of mead and sea honey," he began. Jael smiled encouragingly. "I was transporting a small cache of blessed Lakrim pearls as a tithe for the Queen," Plinus began as he took a small step toward Jael, wringing his hands nervously.

"We put into port a day or two after Karth flew its sigil from the Queen's tower. We didn't know what had happened, so my brother and his boys left the ship to get information. I stayed behind."

"With the pearls?" Jael asked.

Plinus nodded. He looked at Jael for a long moment, then cleared his throat and dusted his hands on his pants.

"I must go now, Lord," he mumbled, adding with a bolder tone, "King Lors has provided you with new attire. You will find everything you need in the wardrobe. He wishes you to report to him within the hour. I'll be back to collect you."

Plinus turned and slipped out the door without another word, the lock softly clicking.

Jael sat for a while longer and picked at the food, lost in thought. Hearing that Plinus had been transporting Lakrim pearls, there was no doubt in his mind that the Handaalian was a priest. Priests possessed their own special kind of magic, but he did not believe that magic had anything to do with fire. While the arcane magic of priests was a boon, if Plinus were also a fire mage, that would make him a valuable ally. He knew that he needed to win him over, which could be difficult considering his father had killed Plinus' Queen. But there had to be a way. He vowed to find it.

The Prince stood and crossed to the wardrobe, pulled open the doors, and stared. Nothing but black fabric hung inside: black tunics, black pants, even two pairs of black boots. He pulled out a tunic, feeling a deep sinking in his chest as he saw the sigil of the Darklands emblazoned on its front: the blood-red crescent moon and dagger.

He bristled at Lors' unsubtle joke. He hoped Bent had gone back to his father, though Lasten was probably enraged that Jael had secretly left on his own. Not to mention, by now, his father had most likely discovered that Jael had been behind Amarynn's escape. He felt genuinely sorry for the court staff.

Though he would have preferred to have gone naked, Jael changed his clothing. He studied himself in the mirror, not expecting to feel how he did. All his life, he had been immersed in the deep blue and burgundy of Karth. The shining golden lightning bolt across the great tree bear was emblazoned in his soul. To see himself all in black, the red sigil of his enemy fastened to his shoulder broke something deep inside. He couldn't remember the last time he had shed real tears, but they threatened to fall just then.

I am doing this for Karth, he reminded himself, tugging the tunic's hem to lie straight. *I am doing this to save Amarynn and Regealth;* he repeated over and over in his head as he sat and pulled on a pair of elegant black boots. *I am doing what a good King would do*, he thought. He was making himself a willing sacrifice for the sake of the Kingdom, *his* Kingdom—the one thing he had never seen his father do.

He stood up and took a few deep breaths to steady himself. As difficult as yesterday was, he knew the real test had not yet begun. He could not break, no matter what.

There was a knock at his door. Plinus opened it and stepped inside the chamber, looking at Jael with an odd mix of surprise and sympathy. The little priest studied him up and down, then gave him a fortifying nod.

"His Majesty will see you now, Lord Jael."

CHAPTER 24

Lors hovered over the map of Karth for a full hour after Jael's arrival. He bombarded him with a barrage of questions about the roads and villages and the vulnerable areas of the palace in Calliway. He asked about the keep's layout in Banmorrow, but Jael refused to respond. Jael forced his mind to another place, focusing his attention on anything in the room but the King. Lors grew more agitated with every minute, yet Jael managed to tune him out completely — he was playing out exit strategies in his head.

Certainly, Plinus could be swayed to help if Jael guaranteed him sanctuary. Then, he just needed to convince Plinus to retrieve Regealth and bring him to his quarters to get him out of Athtull first. That part would be the easiest.

Facing Amarynn would be the hardest part.

He was ashamed that he had stood by and allowed her to suffer. A man of better mettle would not have done so, he thought.

"Are you going to continue to ignore me, Prince?" Lors rapped on the table with his knuckles. "You are in no position to refuse me. I don't see your father's banners on the horizon."

"Yet." Jael stared at the wall just behind Lors and clenched his jaw.

Lors scrutinized him, then pushed away from the table and stood. "I received a welcome surprise early this morning. Perhaps one that might persuade you to cooperate. Bring them in," Lors called over Jael's shoulder.

A commotion at the door made Jael turn to see four guards dragging two men in by the arms. They were dirty and bleeding. All the breath left Jael's body when he saw the colors they wore. Blue and burgundy — the colors of Karth. They were Legion soldiers, most likely on a remote border patrol near the Dark Mountains.

"My men caught them a few days ago, just off the road. They were on the wrong side of Karth's border." Lors moved to stand in front of the prisoners. They hung between the Darklands guards, exhausted and injured.

One of the men looked up and saw Jael. Hope flooded his expression, and he gasped, "My Lord, Prince Jael!" The other man did not attempt to move. A dark red stain covered the lower half of his tunic.

Lors studied both men. He ran his hand along the face of the soldier who spoke. "My soldiers brought them back for interrogation purposes, but that will not be necessary," he said, looking at Jael. "We have *you* now." He grasped a handful of the soldier's hair and forcefully pulled his head back, exposing his throat. Lors unsheathed his dagger, the same one he had used on Amarynn, and pressed it against the soldier's neck. "I'll ask you one more time, *Prince*. Will you give me the information I seek about your family's magic?"

The young soldier swallowed, straightened as best he could, and leaned into the blade. "Say nothing, My Lord," he snarled. "We stand with you. We stand with Karth."

Jael focused on the dagger in Lors' outstretched hand. He knew he had been a fool to think he could walk into this keep and demand Regealth and the Gate. Now, the soldiers would pay the ultimate price for his arrogance. How could he get out of this and save the two lives in front of him? His mind spun in a thousand directions until Lors broke the silence.

"Well?"

"You'll get nothing from me."

"You're sure about that?"

Jael remained silent.

Lors released the soldier and walked back to the table, tapping his dagger against the palm of his hand, stopping directly in front of Jael.

"Let's try this another way. Your refusal to cooperate has a consequence. But because I am generous, I'll let you choose your punishment. It's these two, or your precious mage." Lors glanced over his shoulder toward one of the guards. "You can kill a mage, am I right?"

The guard nodded curtly. "I believe so, My Lord."

"Yes, that's right." Lors turned back to Jael with a sinister smirk. "So, who will it be?"

Jael was second-in-command of the Legion, sworn to protect and lead his men to ensure their safety whenever possible. He knew these soldiers were destined to die, regardless of his choice, but at least he could guarantee them a swift death that would spare them hours of painful interrogation. He drew a shaky breath and rose from his chair. "What are your names, soldiers?"

"Aeric, My Lord," the one whispered, his voice shaking. He tilted his head toward the other man. "This is Barrim."

"Predictable choice, Prince. And too quick a decision. I don't think you are quite getting the message." He flipped the dagger in his palm and offered the hilt to Jael. "You will do it."

A vicious chill seized Jael's chest, and his insides turned and twisted at once. He had to force himself to breathe. Ending their lives was unthinkable, and his heart screamed in resistance as his hand closed around the dagger involuntarily, as if he were in a nightmare. Lors returned to the soldiers and positioned himself behind them. Every ounce of humanity in Jael's soul cried out as Lors placed one hand on the soldier's head. Jael beheld the young man, no older than twenty. *Rynn's age.* Aeric squared his jaw, unable to control the trembling in his face, but the young soldier nodded bravely. "Do it now, Lord. Before Barrim wakes," he whispered through gritted teeth.

Jael inhaled deeply as he whispered the prayer he knew no one else would say if these men were left alone in the hands of Lors.

"May the Evenfall wash over you and deliver you to the ever after. May the Goddess hold you close forever."

Knocking Lors' hand away, Jael pulled Aeric to his chest and drew the dagger across his throat. He held him tightly while the soldier strained for a moment — held him there until he was still. The warmth of Aeric's lifeblood seeped through the layers of Jael's tunic as the young man sagged against him. Jael lowered the man to the ground as gently as he could. When he stepped toward the second man, his heart was burning with a rage he could barely contain. He repeated the process, opening the chasm in his soul even wider. As he let the second man go, Jael silently vowed to avenge them. He swore an oath that their deaths would not be in vain.

Jael remained where he stood, even after the guards dragged the two soldiers' bodies from the room. He could not bring himself to face Lors for fear he would see the tears in his eyes. He took a moment to steady himself, then composed his face into his father's mask, cold and calculating.

"Impressive. I did not think the pampered first son of Karth would have the backbone to kill his own men."

Jael turned to face Lors. "You will pay the highest price for this."

Lors frowned, blinked, then burst into howling laughter. His mirth waned quickly, but he continued to chuckle to himself as he meandered toward the door. With a quick gesture, he summoned two other guards to enter the chamber. "Get this man a horse, and get ready to ride."

"You are a legend, yes."

Jael's breath was warm against her cheek. She felt his face in her hair while her ear hummed with his voice's soft vibrations. She could smell his heady scent — leather and spice mixed with sweat.

"No one wins if you go out there."

His hand tightened on her wrist. She looked back over her shoulder, expecting those storm-grey eyes but finding them an icy blue instead. King Lors' lips stretched into a sinister smile as her surprise registered.

He squeezed her wrist harder, and she felt her bones breaking like twigs. She closed her eyes and tried to struggle, and then a scream pierced the quiet.

"Amarynn," a new voice hissed.

She opened her eyes. Lors had become Matteus.

"Traveler bitch," he sneered and twisted her hand until it felt like it might tear away from her body.

"Amarynn!"

She couldn't breathe. She felt hot, and her mouth was bone dry. She tried to move, but nothing was responding.

"Amarynn." The voice again, but not Matteus. This time the voice was raspy, old.

Her eyes opened, and she strained to turn her head toward the sound. She moved just enough to make out Regealth's worried face peering through the bars. She managed a half-smile.

"It worked," she croaked.

"Oh yes, yes, my dear," he whispered. She felt him lightly pat her arm. "I'm sorry I needed to open your arm again," he apologized, then continued. "Twice, actually." He frowned, then smiled, "How clever of you to think of using your blood. Now," he said, "let's get you back to your old self, shall we?"

She could feel the mage place both his hands on her arm and a warmth spreading from his touch, up through her arm and into her body, like water spreading out on the shore. The prickly feeling in her arms and legs told her that her strength was returning. Her heartbeat, which was thready and weak, began to beat, a tribal drum pounding in her chest.

Regealth's magic removed the dampening spell and transformed the magic, turning it on itself, fortifying her. The cuff still hung heavy on her wrist, now no more than an unattractive piece of jewelry.

"Child, you must listen to me," Regealth said, his task accomplished. He sat and leaned in toward the barred wall they shared. "You and I must now play our parts."

179

Amarynn pushed herself to a sitting position beside him and looked at him quizzically.

"We must remain weak in their eyes. We cannot let them know of our recovery." He offered a small smile. "I've done this very thing, back on the ship."

Amarynn arched an eyebrow, "The ship?"

"That's how they brought me here."

Amarynn stifled a laugh, "The idiots put you on a ship?" She paused for a moment, then stared. "She doesn't know you are a water mage, does she?"

Regealth shook his head, "I'm sure she does now. She knew I was either attuned to water or sky. She must have assumed sky at first, but now that she has Sia, she surely knows. Which is why, I suppose, we are without water in here." He gestured to the barren cell.

"Sia?"

"A child. One of the young deckhands on the ship." Regealth chuckled to himself. "She was pretending to be a boy. She took a liking to me, and she helped me." He leaned his head to the bars and continued in a whisper, "I discovered she has magic."

"Like you?"

"Oh, and more. She is very gifted. Untrained but gifted." He pulled away from the bars to eye Amarynn. "Very much like you, too. Headstrong as a warhorse."

Amarynn looked down and smiled.

A piercing scream rang out, and Amarynn flinched.

"The atranoch," Regealth said.

"The what?" Amarynn rolled to her knees and stood.

"Atranoch. They look a bit like greall at first, but then you see they—"

"They are bigger," Amarynn said, staring at the cell door as another cry rang out. "I saw one of them in the forest on the other side of the pass. It was after a greall I killed. Jael and I—"

Regealth blanched at the mention of the Prince's name.

"Yes, he followed me here." Out in the hallway, footsteps approached. Amarynn scrambled and sat back against the wall, leaning near Regealth's position on the other side. The door to her cell groaned as it opened to three large, armored guardsmen.

"Play your part," Regealth breathed before letting his eyes flutter and close.

It took every ounce of restraint she could muster to keep from bolting for the first guard's sword and taking the three of them down. It would be so easy, she thought. She was explosive, full to bursting with anger.

"The King's mage has something in store for you."

She stood on her own, slowly. The guards stopped moving toward her, placing their hands on their sword hilts. "If I wanted to kill you, you'd already be dead," she smirked, keeping her voice low.

The leader of the three nodded to the others, and they moved to take Amarynn by the arms. As they left the cell, Amarynn did her best to shuffle her feet; however, her pride got the better of her, and she allowed herself to walk without stumbling. Infused with energy, most likely from Regealth's counter-spell, she was buzzing with a momentum that threatened to spiral beyond her control. She jerked her arms from the guards' grips, enjoying their fleeting panicked expressions.

She could only guess as to where they were taking her. There was no reason for Venalise or Lors to try and end her, though knife wounds still hurt, and no one in their right mind sought pain on purpose. The guards quickened their pace, quickly arriving at a set of unreliable-looking steps that jutted out from the walls of the mountain keep. The largest of the guards gripped her by the back of her shirt. "It's just you and me from here on," he rumbled by her ear, pushing her forward.

They climbed the stairs for what seemed to be hours. Amarynn slowed her pace for show, but she sensed the tiniest kernel of trepidation with each step. While she was an unbeatable force on the battlefield, she was still human. And humans, she had always reasoned, were not meant to occupy heights. She could face anything with a blade and her feet firmly planted on solid ground but always maintained that the mountains should be left to the mapmakers and expeditioners. If climbing were what she had to do, she would do it — but only if necessary. Otherwise, she wanted no part of it.

Finally, Amarynn and her captor reached the landing at the top of the stairwell. With one hand still on her back, the guard pulled a heavy ring of jangling keys from his belt and unlocked the heavy metal door. What lay beyond could be anything, Amarynn thought. Perhaps Jael had struck a bargain with the guards to help her escape, or maybe this was another of Lors' attempts to test her.

Leaving the keys in the lock, he pushed the door open. The light was near blinding, and before her eyes could adjust, he shoved her through, closing the door swiftly behind her. She could not see much, but she heard the click of the tumblers in the lock and then the guard's fading footsteps.

Amarynn stepped backward and leaned against the door, allowing her eyes a few moments to adjust, trying to process what had just happened. A gust of wind buffeted her, and as she flattened her palms against the door, the cuff on her wrist clanged against the metal. Her breath caught, and the corner of her mouth turned up in a smirk; this had to be Jael's work. She pulled the key from her pocket, and in seconds, the cuff fell to the stone by her feet.

Her eyes had adjusted to the brightness enough that she could step away from the door. She was in a vast, open-air cavern. In actuality, the space was more like a deep, sweeping ledge. The air felt thin. Quite high up the mountain, one whole half of the room was open to the sky, the ridge extending past the end of the walls.

The wind whipped her hair around her face while she scanned the area. In the middle of the floor, there were her scabbard, belt, and blades in a haphazard pile. She made for the weapons, fully expecting an ambush, but she no longer cared to sit idle.

The leather belt felt comfortable in her hands. She buckled it around her waist quickly, noting that she needed to use a different notch — she'd lost weight — the toll of all the healing she did after aiding Regealth. She hid the throwing knives in their places and slid her daggers into the sheaths she strapped to her thighs.

Amarynn stood and slid her short sword into the scabbard. The weight was right. It felt good to have her balance again. If Jael had managed to arrange this, perhaps it was the best escape opportunity he could find. He would know that if she hurt herself on the descent, she would be able to heal and continue on. If he had convinced the guards to bring her here, he was truly more gifted than she gave him credit for. "Silver-tongued bastard," she murmured with a smile.

Her curiosity got the best of her, and she crept toward the sunlit ledge. Gravel skittered off the rock as her feet neared the outcrop, so she knelt, her pulse quickening. Palms flat to the ground, she managed to peer over the edge but had to stifle a shudder. The face of the mountain plummeted straight down, a near-vertical drop of no less than several thousand feet before it disappeared into the forest canopy below. Amarynn's head spun, and her stomach dropped at the sight of the open space between the ledge and the trees below. She pushed back away from the cliff's edge but remained in a crouch, scanning the clear, bright sky. In the distance, she saw an atranoch, as large as the one they had encountered in the forest, circling near one of the closest Dark Mountain peaks, banking hard.

A series of muffled, metallic clangs and groans sounded somewhere nearby at the back of the cave. She glanced over her shoulder, but the space between her and the door remained empty. She stayed low, turning her attention to the sky as strong wind gusts buffeted her. The atranoch in the distance continued to circle, banking in her direction. Something seemed off.

A hiss from behind caught her attention, and she spun around. A lone atranoch was perched on an outcropping above the door she'd come through only minutes earlier. It was small compared to the one she had seen in the forest, but small meant nothing if it was quick.

Amarynn stepped sideways and turned, gauging the distance between herself and the cliff's edge. With one eye on the beast's perch, she backed up to the cavern wall, but just as her back hit the stone, the atranoch leaped. Amarynn instinctively reached for Frost, but her hand found nothing. The horse-sized creature was now within striking distance, and Amarynn drew her short sword, preparing for a fight at close range. With a shriek, the atranoch twisted at the last second and bolted off the ledge, unfurling its wings to catch an updraft. It glided in an arc, then dove out of sight.

Sheathing her sword, she sidestepped as far as she dared toward the ledge. The wind picked up, howling into the cavern behind her. She teetered against the gusts, her stomach fluttering as she caught another glimpse of the sheer face. Taking a quick look to the right, she saw that same vertical face end at a collection of tall, grassy slopes. Of all the possible escape methods, this was the worst kind of predicament. At the very least, a fall from this height would result in shattered legs or a broken back. She grimaced. Maybe Jael wasn't as bright as she thought.

Movement on one of the low hills drew her attention — horses. Each mount carried riders, and all were headed towards the tallest hilltop, turning toward the ledge where she stood. One horse carried a woman and child. Sitting astride a great black mount was the unmistakable form of King Lors, and next to him, trailing slightly behind, were Jael and two mounted guards. The woman was pointing towards the ledge. Lors raised his head to see, but the Prince's head remained down.

Pieces began to fall into place. Amarynn looked back to the sky. The atranoch that circled the distant peaks was now bearing down on the ledge. As it neared, it opened its mouth and let out a piercing scream, just like the one she heard inside the mountain, but thunderous enough to rattle her bones.

This was not an escape route for her. She turned back to look at the hilltop. Now, all six faces were looking in her direction.

The atranoch screamed again, and Amarynn's head snapped back to the ledge before it extended its clawed feet to land. No, this was most definitely not an escape plan.

This was an arena.

CHAPTER 25

Amarynn launched into a run to clear the cliff's edge. She slid into the covered portion just as the atranoch hit the stone, talons throwing sparks as it skidded to a stop. With one hand against the back wall, she turned to face the beast and calculate her strategy.

This atranoch looked precisely like the creature she and Jael had faced in the forest on the other side of the mountains. Its arrow-shaped head pulled back as it regarded her with gleaming eyes. It opened and closed its wide mouth, exposing a double row of teeth as it folded its leathery wings back and dropped down to all fours.

Slowly, carefully, Amarynn drew her short sword. It was as large as the one she had faced in the forest with Jael, and there was no way she would be able to effectively defend herself with a creature of this size in close combat — not without Frost. She would have to be smart about it and quick. Her movements must be precise if she planned to emerge from this in one piece.

The atranoch put one clawed foot in front of the other and stalked toward her, lowering its head. Sunlight caught its face, and she recognized the ridged scars that covered its hide. This *was* the creature from the forest! Adrenaline pumped through her body in such a rush that she didn't notice an electric ripple creeping up her spine until tendrils of an icy sensation crawled over her scalp.

Amarynn stayed near the edge of the wall, keeping her options open — she couldn't allow herself to get trapped inside the cave. Once the atranoch was confined with her, she'd have little room to maneuver. But if she stayed out on the ledge, should she make one poor choice, she'd be over the edge if she was unable to compensate. She grimaced. Neither location was ideal.

The beast prowled closer. Amarynn slowed her breathing enough to detect the peculiar tingling on the back of her neck. An uncomfortable buzzing sensation wrapped itself around her head, throbbing at her temples. She scowled.

Then she recalled the encounter in the forest.

Taking a risk, she carefully replaced her sword in its sheath. The atranoch stopped its forward motion. Its scaled chest heaved as it breathed heavily through its nostrils, scenting her. As she lifted her empty hands slowly to show the beast she was unarmed, the current in her head changed from an uncomfortable buzz to a hum. Maintaining eye contact, she took one tentative step forward. She wasn't sure how, but now she knew the atranoch was a Traveler, just like her.

The wind slowed around them, quieting enough for her to hear the heavy breaths of the atranoch. The two faced one another, bodies tensed and eyes locked. The beast lifted one heavy foot and edged forward without so much as a click of its talons on the stone. It wasn't stalking her but seemed to be testing her. Amarynn's fingers twitched, eager to hold a blade, but she maintained composure. She moved to lower her chin to her chest, but instead of dropping her eyes to the ground, she adjusted her position and held her gaze firm.

The wind picked up again, blowing dust whirls around them. The atranoch halted its approach, just an arm's length away. More than once, it swung its head to look out at the riders on the hill before turning back to her. Amarynn could sense its confusion, and, strangely, she sympathized. Neither one of them had asked to play a part in any of this. She braced herself and reached out with one slightly trembling hand.

The atranoch pulled back and snorted, stretching its head forward. Just as her hand settled on the gleaming scales of its snout, Amarynn's muscles contracted, and she arched her back, crying out as she fell to her knees. Two arrows quivered in her shoulder.

The beast reared back and bellowed, then swung its great head in the direction of the arrow's path. A shadow disappeared from another alcove high up in the cavern wall. The creature turned to face the riders on the hill and dropped low to the ground. It screamed, then launched itself off the ledge, unfurling its broad, leathery wings and hurtling directly for Venalise.

"You see, Lors," Venalise shielded her eyes against the late afternoon sun. "This is yet another reason why we should keep her."

Sia squirmed in front of Venalise in the saddle. She leaned forward to peer around Lors at the young man beside him. Jael had kept his gaze on the ground but looked up when the horses stopped. He noticed the little girl looking his way and gave her a quick wink. Sia grinned and winked back, continuing to stare at the Prince.

"There's no need to convince me to keep her," Lors replied. "I fully intend to study her healing abilities."

Jael stiffened at the King's words. They were discussing Amarynn. To study her abilities meant to hurt her, perhaps to deliver death blows repeatedly. He resolved that, by nightfall, he would have a plan in place to escape, with Amarynn and Regealth safely with him.

Venalise pointed toward a large, sweeping ledge jutting out from the side of the mountain. To his surprise, he saw Amarynn there. She wore her blades, all but her broadsword, Frost. When they rode out from the keep, Lors would not tell him where they were going. Jael had assumed they were going on some sort of hunt. He assumed wrong.

Venalise glanced in Jael's direction, but the piercing scream of an animal rang out, and she turned away. Jael's eyes followed the oddly familiar sound.

"What was that?" he breathed.

"That, my friend, is the crowning achievement of the Darklands' Travelers." There was no mistaking the pride in Lor's voice.

"Travelers?" Jael remembered how certain Amarynn had been that the atranoch were Traveled to their world, but he hadn't quite put all the pieces together. He turned toward Venalise. "I suppose they are yours?"

Venalise offered a half-smile then Jael returned his attention to Lors.

"Why do you keep me, then?"

The Prince waited for him to respond. When he didn't, Jael pressed on. "If she could already call beings through whatever magic she uses, why take what is rightfully Karth's?"

"Does that beast look human to you, fool?" Venalise cut in, her tone scathing. "There is only so much one can do with beasts in a battle."

Another shriek rang out, and all the riders turned back to the ledge. A creature leapt from the mountain and took flight, eventually disappearing around the other side of the craggy cliffs. Winged, scaled, and feathered, but with four thick, muscular legs, the beast he just saw very closely resembled what he and Amarynn had faced in the forest. Another shriek echoed, closer and louder this time.

"It is finally time to see what they can do," Venalise murmured, looking to the sky near a neighboring peak.

Jael followed her line of sight, eyes widening as a much larger beast came into view. Three times the size of the one he had just seen, there was no mistaking it now. This was the beast they encountered in the forest. Amarynn darted away from the ledge where he could no longer see her, his heartbeat quickening. "If they engage, they'll tear each other apart," Jael snarled. "And then you will see the insanity of pitting two immortals against each other. This ends in perpetual destruction. Call it off."

"No..." Lors breathed with the anticipation of a child.

The giant beast hurtled toward the aerie, crashing onto the stone ledge and skidding to a stop.

All eyes were fixed on the ledge in suspense of the inevitable battle. Jael, powerless, could do nothing but will his strength to Amarynn and pray it ended as it had in the woods, but he doubted that outcome when the beast dropped to the ground and began to stalk her. One heavily clawed foot at a time, it crept toward her until it reached within striking distance. He held his breath as it stopped its forward progression. Jael sat up in his saddle, trying to get a better view of the warrior. She was only partly in his sight, but he could see she had gone still. To his surprise, she replaced her sword in its scabbard and raised her hand as if to touch the creature. His eyes darted between them, not understanding what was happening.

"Why did she put her sword away? Are they friends?" Sia's innocent questions seemed to aggravate Lors, who whirled on Venalise.

"Yes, the child asks fair questions. Are they to become comrades or fight each other?"

Venalise ignored Sia and Lors, but she could not hide her fascination. Just before the two immortals touched, Venalise lifted one hand high, palm open — at that moment, Amarynn fell to the ground. Jael strained to see her, but the cliff edge was too high.

The atranoch screamed and hurled itself off the ledge. It became a projectile with its wings folded back, headed straight for the riders. Its cry echoed off the mountainside as it bore down on them, open-mouthed. The horses reared, but Venalise raised her arms and shouted an incantation. At the last second, the atranoch banked, barely missing the riders who nearly tumbled from their horses from the burst of air pumped from its wings. Venalise crouched over Sia protectively, but the child scrambled to see, her eyes fixed on the massive beast. Even the little bear she clutched had stopped squirming, sharing her interest. The horses scattered in confusion; riders were shouting as they worked to regain control of their mounts and turn them back toward Athtull.

The atranoch was now a speck in the distance, but Jael's gaze was engrossed on the ledge. He still couldn't see her, but he fixed his eyes where Amarynn had crumpled. When she didn't rise, he turned his horse and was surprised to see his two guards had not stayed behind. He looked to the dark forest in the west and considered making a run for Karth. His horse stamped the ground, impatient to follow the others. She was an older mare and would never survive a long, hard run through rough terrain. If he tried to escape, he'd be caught, and he didn't want to imagine how that would play out for Amarynn or Regealth. Discouraged, he spurred his horse to follow the others back to the Keep. He couldn't run, he decided, but the time had come for him to put a plan — any plan — in motion and end this once and for all.

Lors and Venalise were still shouting in the stables, their voices raised in anger when the guards led Jael back to his chamber. The room had a new stillness; the air was thick, weighted. Jael paused just inside the door until he noticed that the light wavered, like heat rising off stone, near the tall wingback chair.

Jael took a few cautious steps toward the disturbance, stopping when he noticed a shock of grey, wispy hair just over the back of the seat.

"Regealth?"

The mage stood, clutching a bowl of water in one hand, and turned toward Jael, smiling and nodding in greeting.

"How...?" Jael embraced the old man.

"It seems we have a mutual friend here in this keep."

Regealth sat back down and rested his hands in the bowl of water. "My old friend,

Plinus seems to have been pressed into the service of Venalise. I would assume it happened—"

"—When Karth invaded the Handaals. He and I spoke of this." Jael crouched in front of Regealth. "He wears a metal band on his wrist."

"Yes, it seems his service was forced."

"Why would Venalise put the same device on Plinus as she did on Amarynn?" Realization crept over Jael's face. "He's a mage, isn't he? He told me he was just a priest delivering Lakrim Pearls to the Queen when she fell."

"He is, in fact, a fire mage."

The door creaked open and shut. Jael and Regealth froze.

"Not a very good fire mage, I'm afraid."

Plinus appeared from the shadows, wringing his hands and picking at his robes. As he neared them, Regealth gestured, and he held up his wrist. "Are you ready, old friend?"

Regealth handed the water bowl to Jael, then rose to stand in front of the little priest. He placed his damp palms on the iron cuff and whispered to himself. For a moment, nothing seemed to change, then a faint glow began to grow, spreading from Plinus' wrist to his shoulder.

Plinus' nut-brown skin deepened to a golden mahogany hue. The Prince followed the glow to Plinus' face and was astounded when his eyes began to radiate with a golden light. Regealth released his grip on the cuff and stepped away.

Plinus stood still for a moment, then slowly touched his chest and face with his hands as if relishing the feel of himself again. He beamed at Regealth, the smile changing his features dramatically. Jael had only regarded him as a meek and humble servant, but now he saw who Plinus really was.

"You are fortunate I have forgiven you for that delicious sleeping draught you sent me. Ruby Metheglin? You spared no expense!"

"I had to be sure you'd drink it," the little priest murmured. His face darkened, and he frowned. "You know I had no choice, don't you?"

Regealth patted Pinus on the arm. "I do, I do." He turned to Jael, his eyes narrowing with concern. "Where is Amarynn now?"

Jael set the bowl down and ran a hand through his hair. "I don't know. After what just happened, I have no idea what's been done to her or where she is."

191

"What they've done to her? Tell me — what do you mean?" Regealth joined Jael by the hearth, firelight accentuating the lines of worry that creased his brow.

"They took her high on the mountain, on a ledge. Gave her all her weapons, then they forced her to try to fight one of those atranoch, the biggest."

"Try?" Regealth questioned.

"The beast refused to attack. I think we encountered that same atranoch in the forest on our way here, and the same thing happened. Afterward, she said she thought it was a Traveler."

Plinus stepped forward. "Venalise has been trying to summon Travelers like your Amarynn, but she has only succeeded in calling beasts, and most recently, the atranoch."

"That means she was right," Jael murmured to himself. He looked to Plinus. "Why would Venalise want them to fight each other?"

Regealth turned and eased himself back into the chair. Plinus stepped forward.

"Venalise wants to understand Amarynn. She is trying to learn from her. She thinks she can tease out the nuance of the magic that brought her and the other humans across."

Regealth tilted his head and studied Jael where he stood, leaning one shoulder against the hearthstones. He spoke softly. "A bond has begun to form, am I correct?"

Jael exhaled. There was no doubting that. He reflected on the emotions he felt whenever Amarynn had been threatened or injured, and it became even more evident.

Regealth continued. "I sensed you two were drawing together. Like blood and water, your bond is strengthening. It would have happened eventually, but the unfortunate circumstances in which it is manifesting have come at a most dangerous time."

Jael pushed off from the hearth and began to pace. Regealth followed his agitated stride.

"Jael, you need to get us out of this place quickly."

Jael threw his arms up in frustration. "I can't leave! Plinus must take you. I have to get Amarynn, as well as the stone." He stopped in front of Regealth's chair. "I will not leave her here with Lors and Venalise. She won't be 'studied,' she'll be tortured!"

Regealth dropped his eyes and picked at his robes. He breathed deeply, then looked up at Jael. "My boy, that is precisely why you must leave this place as quickly as possible. They cannot have both of you."

"What do you mean both of us?" Jael narrowed his eyes.

"You are tied to her, boy, in ways you don't even know. But if you come with me now, we can take one piece of the puzzle away from Venalise. One she doesn't even know she has."

Jael shook his head. "No. I'm not abandoning her."

"Lord Jael, if I may?" Plinus stepped forward. "Your Traveler is immortal. Venalise cannot kill her. Better that she has her than you. You can die, or had you forgotten?" The priest's tone was hushed but firm.

Jael knelt by the hearth and stared into the fire, counting his breaths and forming his strategy. Regealth needed to get away from Athtull Keep. He was out of the dungeon already; therefore, he was halfway to his freedom. Plinus was with them now, but his absence would be noticed quickly. While Lors and Venalise were distracted by the events on the mountain ledge, he must take advantage of the diversion.

As much as he hated to, he would have to be the one to get Regealth out. Once the mage was safely away, he could come back for Amarynn.

Jael stood. He held out his hand and pulled the old man to his feet.

"We don't have time to discuss this. I'm getting you out right now." Jael turned to Plinus. "You have keys, I presume?"

The priest nodded and pulled a ring from one of his deep pockets. "The large one opens almost any lock."

Jael released Regealth and grasped Plinus' hand as he took the keys. "I knew I could trust you. We will get you out, too. I swear it."

"I have survived many years here with only limited access to my magic. I can survive a while longer." He raised his arm, brandishing

193

the now-defunct iron cuff. "Especially now that Venalise can no longer harness my talents."

Jael paused at this, but Plinus waved him off. "Another story I will tell when we are away from Athtull." The priest pressed a small, folded paper into Jael's hand. "Directions to get you to the bailey yard. Now go before any of us are discovered." He turned and opened the chamber door for them.

Jael exited his chambers, Regealth following just behind. He unfolded the paper, and together they wound through a maze of back hallways and hidden stairwells. When they reached the bailey, just inside the outer gates, Jael motioned for Regealth to wait inside the doorway, concealed in shadows. He strode across the yard toward the corner tower be believed to be where Amarynn had entered the Keep. The door was ajar. Just when he stepped into the opening, a soldier carrying a bundle of arrows burst through, colliding with Jael. Jael tensed and turned his face away as quickly as he could. The soldier cursed under his breath and barreled on, paying no attention to who he had run into.

Jael made a quick pass inside and checked behind the stores of weaponry and dry goods to ensure there were no more surprises, then peered outside to signal Regealth to join him. He stepped back into to tower to wait. Minutes later, shouts went up from the tower, but Regealth had not yet made it inside.

The door to the tower opened, filling the small room with the cacophony from the yard. Jael rushed to crouch behind several large grain bags just as two guards rushed through the opening. They each grabbed double armloads of arrows and returned outside, leaving the door wide open.

He had almost given up on Regealth when the old mage finally slipped inside and carefully closed the door behind him. He was out of breath but not as frail as a man his age might be given the circumstances. His powers were clearly strengthening.

Jael rose from his hiding spot. "What's going on out there?" he whispered.

"It seems they've spotted riders approaching the Keep."

Jael lost no time questioning him. Instead, as directed by Plinus, he felt along the wall until he found a knothole in the heavy wooden wall that concealed the latch to the hidden door. He leaned in with his shoulder and motioned for Regealth to come closer.

"Now, when we step out of here, you must stay against the wall," he commanded. "I'll tell you when to move, but when I do," he lowered his voice, "you move as if shadow demons are behind you."

Regealth, warned by his serious tone, nodded. But then something seemed to catch his eye, and he pushed past the Prince, scurrying to a pile of broken longbows. Jael spun around. "What are you doing?" he hissed.

"Ah-ha!"

Regealth grinned as he pulled back the burlap covering from something laying among the broken pieces. "I knew I saw something!"

"Frost," Jael breathed as Regealth pulled the broadsword from the pile. Jael reached for the sword, Amarynn's blade gleaming even in the dim light of the storage room. He recalled her standing to face the atranoch, fearlessly leading him through the cave, standing proudly in defiance of his father before she was sent to the dungeon.

His resolve swelled. He would not leave her here. He wrapped his hand around the ornate grip and slid the sword through his belt. Frost, the ice-forged blade of the first Traveler, Essik, belonged in her hands. As the heavy blade settled on his hip, he vowed to return for her.

CHAPTER 26

She was shivering.

Flashes of memory screamed through her mind.

Fragmented, piercing pricks of light exploded behind her closed eyes while icy, shrieking pain blasted through every nerve.

She was back in the summoning chamber in Calliway. Crackling sounds assaulted her ears while the tang of iron and sulfur soured her nose and mouth, making her gag. Rivulets of cold water ran down her face, and she tasted blood on her tongue.

She was shivering, naked on the stone floor. A wave of energy pulsed through her, and she sucked in a breath as if it were her first taste of oxygen. Her eyes snapped open and immediately locked onto another pair — these one's stormy grey — wide with wonder and fear.

The eyes changed. Their color lightened to a startling silver, upturned at the corners, ripe with sympathy and curiosity.

Amarynn began to breathe again.

In and out, in and out.

Little breaths.

Sip at the air. You are fine.

The silver eyes blinked, and so did Amarynn. Her breaths were coming hard and fast, but they began to ease as she let the memory slide away.

She was not in Calliway. This was not her crossing.

197

She was lying on the floor of a chamber she had only seen once, and the girl kneeling beside her… she did not know.

Amarynn sensed movement from behind. The girl looked up, then scrambled to her feet, stepping back. She heard a huff and snort as a bear cub clumsily scuttled out of her way. Amarynn placed her palms on the floor and pushed herself up, bringing her knees beneath her. The weight of the iron shackles around her wrists pulled, but still, she sat straight, carefully testing the chains that hung from them. They were anchored on either side of her to the floor of an enormous chamber carved into the stone.

There was just enough slack to allow her to rise to her knees, but no more.

"I took the liberty of having you brought to my aethertorium." A voice, velvety and sickly-sweet, slithered into her ears from behind her.

Venalise took slow steps around Amarynn until she was standing in front of her, just a few paces away. She beckoned to the child.

"Sia, darling, come here."

The child stepped to Venalise's side, but not before scooping up the mewling bear cub. Sia was a tiny slip of a thing with dark curly hair that framed her broad, angular face. There was a sorrowful depth to her silver-colored eyes, but there was also a spark there. Amarynn could see she was hiding a kind of deep, quiet strength, one that she, herself, was familiar with.

Venalise continued, "I will be honest with you, Amarynn. I intend to learn how you were summoned. You will tell me, or I will dig through your mind until I find what I am looking for."

Amarynn said nothing. She leveled her stare at Venalise, and her lip curled into a snarl.

Venalise raised her eyebrows in amused surprise.

"So much anger! Was the memory I just uncovered that uncomfortable?" She glided forward, then kneeled in front of Amarynn.

She leaned forward, close enough for Amarynn to smell her lilac perfume, and whispered, "I haven't even begun."

Amarynn drew herself erect in front of Venalise, her hands clenched, chin held high in defiance.

"This will be difficult for you... to give me what I seek." Venalise arranged her face into a pout, feigning sympathy.

Amarynn met Venalise's gaze with a glare. She channeled all her rage, all her pain into her words. "Listen carefully." Amarynn's voice was ice. "This is the last time you will *ever* hear my voice. I will not tell you anything."

She strained against the chains and made herself as tall as she could. She continued to stare Venalise down, refusing to blink.

"No matter what you do, I will not cry out. I will give you nothing. Whatever you want, you will have to take it," Amarynn sneered, "if you can find it."

Venalise chuckled to herself and stood.

"As I said, I haven't even begun. We shall see just how strong you are."

Dusting her skirts dismissively, she turned and took Sia by the hand, and the two disappeared through the arched entrance to the adjoining chamber.

Once they were out of sight, Amarynn sagged back to rest on her heels. Her heart was beating wildly, and she breathed heavily.

I haven't even begun.

She would never admit how much Venalise's words terrified her. For as long as she could remember, she had wanted a release from her immortality – either through death or a return to wherever she had come from. But if Venalise could draw out a twenty-year-old memory so quickly, so vividly, what if she could tap into her past memories?

It was one thing to know she had lived another life, but not knowing anything about it allowed that past to be kept at a distance. There were no names or faces she could miss, and Goddess-forbid, she had loved someone. But if she still possessed memories of her old life and Venalise could find them, Amarynn was confident it would destroy her.

She would rather stand against an entire army alone than face an eternity of remembering what had been taken from her. Things had changed, however. Jael had planted a seed of doubt about her quest for finality.

In the past days, traveling with the King's son had become some sort of subtle balm for her soul, despite her attempt to deny it. He sparked an allegiance she had never felt in her twenty years as a King's bonded Legion Traveler. Lasten did not inspire a primal urge to protect as his son did, which made no sense; all Travelers were bound.

Jael was somewhere in this place — no doubt plotting a rescue — and probably developing a plan that would do nothing but get him caught. She knew he would try to get Regealth out of the Keep, but now she also knew he would do something stupid and return for her. She couldn't let that happen; she must do whatever she could to prevent him from returning, from risking his life for hers, again.

Regealth had spoken of the young girl, Sia. Maybe she would help her.

It might be enough if she could convince her to deliver a message to Jael.

As far as she knew, the Gate Stone was still hidden, but as long as there were no water or sky wielders to focus their power through it, they were safe. The stone could be recovered another time.

But Amarynn sensed something in Sia. Regealth said she was powerful — untapped but powerful. She could not allow Venalise to keep the girl, not if the witch was trying to call human Travelers. If Venalise possessed Amarynn's knowledge and the Gate Stone, Sia could be the last link in the chain. The reality settled in. If Jael was coming back for her, he had to get Sia out — not her.

Amarynn slid her legs around to sit cross-legged and give her knees a rest. This chamber was cold and damp — the opposite of the dungeon cells. The chains attached to her wrists were just long enough for her to rest her arms on her knees. She stretched her neck forward and back, trying to loosen her muscles so they didn't cramp.

As she rocked her head from side to side, she thought of Sia. It seemed that the girl was not entirely in league with Venalise. She had a hesitancy about her that gave it away. Amarynn had no doubt now that Jael needed to focus his attention on the girl. Now, she just needed a way to let him know.

Venalise leaned over and rested her knuckles on the table. Sia sat across from her continuing to toy with the crystals and other paraphernalia in front of her, absently shooing Thera away as she nipped and tugged at her sleeve. Sia knew the mage wanted to know what other magic she possessed, but she still did not trust this woman and did not want her to know that she felt energy everywhere. Sia didn't know what that meant. She wished she could talk with Regealth and continue her lessons with him.

"Let's you and I go for a walk," Venalise said, standing and extending her hand. "I want to show you something." Sia reached for Thera, who tried to scramble off the bench, and tucked her under her arm before taking Venalise's outstretched hand. As they exited the alcove and made for the chamber door, the mage paid no attention to the warrior chained in the middle of the room.

As they left the workroom alcove, Sia glanced across the chamber at Amarynn. The little girl fixed her eyes on the warrior. Sia remembered Regealth speaking of her on the ship, of how she was not only immortal but a very special immortal. She wasn't as big as she thought she'd be. She just looked like a very strong woman, though her heavy chains hinted she was much more dangerous. Venalise tugged on Sia's hand, and she stumbled a bit, trying to catch up. The two stepped through the double doors and into the depths of the Keep.

Together, they left the chamber and climbed the stairs that never seemed to end. The bailey yard was close, but Venalise turned the other way, and they wound around a long hallway until it opened into a glass-windowed atrium.

Sunlight filtered through the panes. Plants hung from the rafters and sat along the windowsills, their multicolored blooms dripping from green stems and fronds. The room smelled of earth and dampness.

Sia had never seen anything like it. Most of her life had been spent on the ship or her family's farm in the scrubby foothills. Venalise released her hand and signaled that she was free to explore. She took a few tentative steps into the room, feeling the life and the water droplets that hung in the air. Inhaling deeply through her nose, she started to reach out with her magic but stopped.

She didn't want Venalise to see everything she was working so hard to hide. Instead, she knelt in front of an ornate stone basin that overflowed with vibrant blue and yellow flowers. Multicolored birds chattered as they flew in and out of two large fruit trees.

Shouting from a remote part of the glass room broke the quiet reverie. "Lise!"

King Lors and two of his guards burst through the greenery, knocking over several ornate pots and urns. Sia flinched but stayed down, making herself as small as possible. She was startled and frightened, just like she had been on the ship when Venalise discovered her looking for the Gate. She felt light-headed and gripped the stone basin to steady herself. The cold began creeping in from all sides.

"Lors!" Venalise whirled around to face him. "What is it?"

"He's gone!"

The King's eyes were wide with a crazed fury. He paced in circles around Venalise, unable to contain his anger. "They are both gone!"

"Who?" she probed, trying to calm him.

"Jael and the old man," Lors spat.

Venalise raised her eyebrows in surprise. "Did you think the son of King Lasten would just sit here and wait this out? Knowing his father was most likely on his way?" Venalise laughed.

Lors spun and gripped Venalise's shoulders, roughly pulling her to him.

"Did you know they would escape?" he whispered, his voice ragged.

"Did you not?"

She put her hands on his chest and shoved him back. She studied the King for a moment, then snickered. "I didn't need the old man, Lors," she said.

He looked at her, clearly confused.

"I only needed the stone." She touched the amulet around her neck, "…And the Traveler."

She turned and sauntered over to where Sia cowered.

"The only way to get Amarynn to come here was to use Regealth as the bait. He would never have cooperated," she said, her back turned away from Lors.

Venalise looked down at Sia. She was still crouched, looking up at Venalise with wide, frightened eyes. Tiny water droplets dripped from her hair into a growing puddle at her feet, and all around, blossoms and leaves turned their faces toward her.

Venalise smiled wickedly and turned back to Lors. She gestured to Sia. "And now that I've confirmed this little one is a source of water magic, I have everything I need."

CHAPTER 27

All the tower guards were focused on the front wall of the Keep. Angry shouts, raucous taunts, and the clattering of swords and bows filled the evening air. Jael took advantage of the distraction to lead Regealth across the clearing into the trees. Regealth followed, flagging as his breaths came heavy. Jael pushed onward through the undergrowth, pausing periodically to confirm that Regealth was still with him. By the time they came near enough to the road leading away from the Keep, the deep red and orange sky gave way to the black of night. They were a reasonable distance from the Keep now, and Jael's confidence in their escape strengthened.

Passing through a small clearing, he happened to look down just as he stepped into the pale moonlight. His sharp intake of breath caught Regealth's attention.

"What is it, boy?" he asked breathlessly, coming from behind.

Jael leaned down and retrieved a long auburn braid. He held it in his hand, his thumb gently running along the coarse strands. Just like her, he mused — strong, woven together with complication, skill, and beauty. Without thinking, he held it up to his nose and breathed in, remembering her scent from when he held her back, not far from where he stood now.

"She will survive this, you know."

Regealth put one hand on Jael's shoulder. The Prince nodded and tucked her braid into his belt.

"The immortal have a tolerance for pain that is different from you and me," he continued.

Jael turned to Regealth.

"Pain is still pain, and she's had enough, don't you think?" His voice was strained.

"We'll do no one any good talking about it, now, will we?" Regealth said dismissively, patting his shoulder and walking to the edge of the clearing. Jael scowled as he followed, stepping to the lead to hold back a thick bundle of branches so the old mage could pass. Just as Regealth ducked through, Jael heard the faint jingling of bridles and stirrups on the road the two were following.

"Wait—" He put his hand out.

The noises were getting closer.

Jael pushed ahead of the mage again. "Wait here," he whispered.

He carefully picked his way as close to the road as possible without being seen. Half a dozen horses were stopped along the roadside. All but two of their riders were mounted, and only one of them wore livery. Jael's heartbeat quickened when the man turned in his direction, revealing a blue tunic emblazoned with the bear and thunderbolt of Karth.

"We'll have to work on your scouting skills, My Lord," a familiar voice whispered.

Startled, Jael turned to find Bent with a sly grin on his face.

They clasped hands, and then Bent beckoned for Jael to follow.

"Wait," Jael said. "I need to fetch Regealth."

"Nioll's already got him," Bent replied. "Where's Rynn?" he whispered.

The look on Jael's face was all the answer Bent needed.

"Ah, lass," he muttered under his breath. He turned and led the Prince back through the thicket away from the road.

Jael nodded, and they made their way over a rocky hill to their camp. They had chosen to keep their campsite simple — no tents or fires. Jael counted at least four dozen troops, including several Travelers. Their spartan setup was proof they did not intend to stay in the Darklands long.

He walked past a few men removing saddles and stowing gear for the night. They were busy but quiet and purposeful in their movements.

"Good to see you alive, My Lord."

Ehrinell, the only other female Traveler in the Legion, flashed him a warm smile and casual salute as she bent down to open her bedroll. She was the opposite of Amarynn in nearly every possible way, except for her skill. The two were closely matched, with Amarynn her superior only by a margin. However, where Amarynn was brute force and strength with a blade, Ehrinell was stealthy and cunning in the shadows.

Jael returned her greeting with a grim nod and moved to the group's center. Regealth was sitting on a tree stump, and Nioll kneeled in front of him, unwrapping the mages' ankles and feet from their filthy bindings. Regealth tried to shoo him away, but his efforts were futile.

"I am fine, I tell you! Just get me some water, and I can heal myself!"

Nioll continued his ministrations and looked up at the mage, grinning. "Oh, I'm sure you can, magician. But if you'd ever suffered from the trench foot, you'd know to get these disgustin' cloths off yer' feet as fast as you can, magic or no!" He continued unwrapping and peeling away the layers.

Regealth scoffed.

"Oi! Lad!" Nioll called to one of the Legion men nearby. "Fetch me a water skin."

Bent joined them just as Nioll was finished with Regealth's feet. He shifted his position to allow Bent space to kneel beside him. The young soldier trotted up and handed Nioll a skin heavy with water. Before turning away, he produced a wineskin and handed it to Jael with a nod. He took it gratefully and sat down next to Regealth, taking several deep, long swallows.

"Nice outfit, m'Lord." Nioll motioned to the Darklands sigil on Jael's chest.

Jael glanced down and winced. He had forgotten he still wore Lors' colors. He sighed and lowered his face into his hands, chasing his thoughts for a moment. He raised his head, a questioning look on his face. "If you both are here, what was all the commotion at the Keep about?"

"We sent a couple of Travelers ahead to toy with them." Nioll grinned mischievously. "You know, get them fussin' and hollerin'."

"I suppose my father knows what's happened?" Jael asked, not looking at anyone in particular. He took another pull on the wineskin.

"Aye, and he was not pleased," Bent answered.

"Oh, I imagine not," Jael mumbled to himself.

While Regealth sipped his water, Bent told the group how he and Nioll decided to go back to Karth and return with reinforcements. "I decided going back for help was better than returning to tell your father you'd gone off and gotten yourself killed," he added. Bent stood and put a hand on Jael's shoulder. "Now, tell us how they captured her so we can figure a way to get her back."

Jael drew in a breath and told them everything he knew: how she had slipped inside the Keep dressed as one of the guards. He told them of his attempt to coerce Lors into giving up what he had stolen. Then he told them how Lors put a dagger into Amarynn's chest. After a long pause, he confessed to the killing of his men; recalling that moment nearly broke him.

"What about the child?" Regealth asked, putting one hand on Jael's arm. Just as he had when Jael was a boy, he sent a gentle stream of magic, a cool caress of lapping water, to help calm him.

"Child?" Jael asked.

"Venalise has a little girl with her... a tiny thing. Her name is Sia," he explained.

Jael recalled the ride into the hills when Amarynn faced the atranoch on the ledge. A child was riding with Venalise. He remembered her smiling at him.

"Yes, there was a child. She was with the mage," he answered. "I didn't see her but one time, though."

"Well," Regealth cleared his throat, "we must see how we are going to retrieve her." He sat up and straightened his robes.

"After Rynn faced that beast, I don't know where they took her," Jael said. "Either one of them."

Regealth took a moment to respond.

"I'm not talking about Rynn, boy. I'm talking about the child." Regealth's mouth was set in a determined line. "Amarynn can handle herself, but that child is extremely rare and powerful. We must not allow Venalise to hold her."

Bent, who had remained quiet throughout the discussion, now spoke. "Aye, Rynn can handle herself in any fight you throw at her, but against magic?" He looked back and forth between Jael and Regealth. "Are you suggestin' we leave her?"

"Absolutely not!" Jael immediately cut in.

Regealth was silent.

Jael turned to stare at Regealth. He could hardly believe what the mage seemed to be suggesting. The thought of abandoning Amarynn was beyond his capacity to comprehend. Nothing could convince him to turn his back on her, not after what he'd witnessed.

Finally, Regealth spoke. "Gentlemen, I'd like a moment with his Highness."

Nioll stood, then he and Bent stepped away and headed to join a group of Legion men settling in for the night. Regealth followed them with his eyes, then turned his gaze to Jael. The Prince was stonefaced, jaw clenched, and his expression hinted at a dangerous edge.

"Jael, there is more than one reason I cannot allow you to go back inside that Keep. A reason you do not know and were not supposed to know for many, many years. But I am afraid if I don't explain this to you now, you will go and do something even more foolish than you already have." Regealth gestured to the Darklands colors Jael wore.

"You feel connected to her, don't you? But it's strange, isn't it?" he whispered, leaning in close to him. The grime of the days held captive in the dungeon filled the wrinkles around his eyes, his lips still peeling from his former dehydration. "You haven't been around her long enough to feel responsible for her the way you do. Yet, you do." Regealth sat back and looked him up and down. "Now, why is that do you think?"

Jael had no answer for him; the old man spoke the truth. He had never felt so connected, so drawn to anyone as he did to her in his twenty-five years. The two of them had never socialized back in Calliway, save a few interactions related to the Legion. He could not remember when they said more than a handful of words to one another until he visited her in the dungeons just a few days ago.

"Jael, do you know how I summon the Travelers?"

"You use magic and channel it through the Gate Stone," Jael replied.

"Yes, that is part of it, but I do not do it alone. " Your father plays a part," he said, "almost every time."

"I know that." Jael nodded, then shook his head impatiently. "What are you saying? How does that have anything to do with me?"

"My boy," Regealth laid a withered hand on Jael's knee. "Your family has magic running through it as old as these mountains. Your father was just more ambitious than his father and his father before him. He was not the original source in his generation, you know."

"I know this as well. Magic is passed through blood, and families can only hold one living source at a time. My father's sister, Dyaneth, wasn't just a source; she was a mage — a powerful sky mage — that helped you create the Gate. She took the power when my grandfather died."

"Yes, you are correct. But when *she* died—"

"I've heard this story." Jael leaned forward and rested his elbows on his knees. "Dyaneth had no children, so my father inherited whatever magic she still possessed after creating the Gate Stone with you." Jael shook his head and lifted his hands. "What are you trying to tell me?"

Regealth's gaze lingered for a moment on the Prince. "Dyaneth was an anomaly. Her power manifested well before your grandfather's death. And she was not just any sky mage. She was the most powerful wielder of sky magic in many, many lifetimes. Old blood coursed through her, and her powers were boundless. When she and I created the stone, she did not infuse all her power into the Gate. If she had, it most likely would have killed me."

"Then my father is a potent source, as I have suspected, given that you can summon Travelers now without Dyaneth."

"I do need a strong source, and yes, your father is exactly that. However, I do not think you understand the magnitude of the power your aunt possessed. If all her power had transferred to Lasten alone, it would have killed him."

"So where did the excess magic go? You? The Gate"

Regealth grasped the Prince's arm.

"Jael, what were the circumstances surrounding your birth? Do you recall?"

"I know there was a terrible storm. Mother always told me it was a Vhaleesian omen that predicted the birth of a great warrior." Jael chuckled. "I always thought she made that up just to bolster my ego."

"Perhaps so, but what else happened that night?"

"Wasn't that the night you created the Gate?"

"It was."

"Then that means it was the night Dyaneth died." Suspicion crept across Jael's face.

"Yes, do you see now?"

"That means..." Jael stopped.

"Yes," the mage whispered. "You possess ancient, deep magic, boy. You will wield as Dyaneth did."

"But I—" Jael suddenly rose to his feet. He looked down at Regealth, the mage's words not quite registering. His mind was whirling with memories of his childhood, trying to find any indication that Regealth spoke the truth.

"You've had— I put a dampening spell on you when you were very young. Ever since—"

"Ever since Amarynn was summoned," Jael breathed out, almost to himself, his eyes wide. That day when he was five years old flashed in his mind. He had gone with Regealth to his aethertorium, where the Gate Stone was kept. Now, it made sense why he had felt what she felt — the cold and the fear.

"You two are connected, my boy." Regealth stood. "They already have the most powerful Traveler Karth has ever known and the Gate Stone, but if Venalise has you both, she will have more power than Karth will ever have in its possession again — the same source used to summon her. A source who can also wield. They will have themselves the first and only mage King."

Jael felt like he had been punched in the gut. If Regealth weren't holding on to him, he might have gone to his knees. Everything he had just been told made his entire life a half-truth. All he could think to do was look at his open hands.

Did he possess magic? That was only supposed to happen at his father's death. And what did Regealth mean, mage King? He slowly turned his hands over, clenching his fists. He needed to sort out his emotions and make sense of what he was told before he could even look Regealth in the eye.

"Does my father know?" he whispered, not looking up.

"No one, not even your father," Regealth said. "Though I think he suspects. Your mother, too. She is very wise."

Jael finally leveled his eyes at Regealth. "Take it off."

Regealth looked confused.

"Remove the dampening spell."

"No, Jael. I cannot. Your father—"

Jael was standing now, towering over Regealth. "Take. It. Off."

Jael's words were quiet but brimming with rage. Regealth stared at the Prince for several seconds, eyes narrowed at Jael's sudden command. Around them, the noises of the forest quieted. Even the men hushed themselves amidst the tension that radiated between the mage and the Prince.

Realization crept across Regealth's face. "This is about Amarynn, isn't it?" He leaned closer so only Jael could hear. "You are untrained. You wouldn't know how to use your power, and there is no time to teach you anything that might be useful."

In an instant, Jael's dagger was drawn, pointed at Regealth's heart. His voice was still low but startlingly vicious. "I will choose for you, Regealth. I am the Crown Prince of Karth. I am to be the first mage King.... you said so yourself."

He was confident he had the mage's full attention. Amarynn would not be left behind. Power or not, Jael was going back for her.

Sheathing his dagger, he said, "As your Ruler, I command you to remove the dampening spell. *Now*."

CHAPTER 28

"Well, I hope you are rested, Traveler."

Venalise glided into the stone chamber, Sia following discreetly behind her. Thera snuffled and lumbered behind Sia, distracting herself with dust motes in the air. The girl kept her eyes fixed on the floor this time. Amarynn feared she had been frightened into subservience, which did not bode well for her.

The Traveler was still sitting cross-legged on the floor, her head still and erect. Her forearms rested on her knees, chains stretching from iron rings on the floor to the shackles on her wrists. Venalise stopped directly in front of her, but Amarynn kept her gaze focused on the space between them.

"Oh, I remember," the mage said, irritation lacing her tone. "We aren't on speaking terms."

She stepped away for a moment and returned with a low stool. She sat, taking an inordinate amount of time to arrange her skirts around her. Glancing back up at Amarynn, she said, "No matter, I'm not looking for conversation. I'm looking for information."

Amarynn dropped her eyes to the floor, concentrating on the patterns in the stone. She drew in a slow breath and steeled herself for whatever might come. The last time Venalise was in her head, the witch had taken her back into her earliest memories of Regealth's aethertorium, a memory chosen by Venalise. But she had been unconscious when Venalise wormed her way into that memory — Amarynn was conscious now and did not know what to expect.

At first, you'll only hear my voice.

Amarynn's eyes snapped up on instinct, and she cursed herself for it. She didn't want the mage to see her affected in any way. Venalise wore a smug little smile on her lips, and Amarynn would have given anything for a blade in her hand at that moment.

While I am in my element, I can do many, many things. Water mages may be able to reach out to life-force, but so can I. Earth magic is just as bound to living things as water.

She tried not to show her surprise. Amarynn had learned about the basics of magical power from Regealth; he'd taught her that water magic had a natural connection to all life. He never shared that earth magic did, as well. This meant that Venalise had more in her arsenal than she thought.

You have no idea how powerful I am.

Amarynn stiffened and clenched her jaw, but before she reacted, she tried to clear her mind. She chose one thing to concentrate on: Frost. She recalled every rune inscribed on its blade, the direction the leather-wrapped around the hilt, even the tiny nicks and scratches along its forward edge.

She attempted to lose herself in the feel of its weight in her hand, how the leather warmed in her palm… and how satisfying it would be when she could bury it in Venalise's chest—

Ah, emotions. You hate me, don't you? That's good.

Amarynn hesitated. She wanted her hate to reverberate with the force of a thousand armies, but not if a reaction was what Venalise wanted. She drew herself back and focused on her other blades. Her short sword — standard Legion-issue — and her two daggers — were acquired when she won a bet against Ehrinell almost fifteen years ago, when she was the least angry when she had found some joy in belonging somewhere. The bet was a small thing — an easy way for the only two women Travelers in Karth to bond. She recalled

Ehrinell's grinning face as she shouted at her across the training yard, looking for a fight.

The entire Legion had come out to see them spar. Both were still new, Ehrinell barely a year and a half into her service. She was a cocky thing, all blonde curls and always smiling. She always fought above her abilities, but perhaps that was smart. How else could she learn quickly and climb the ranks?

Amarynn had won the fight, leaving Ehrinell bruised and bloody but still smiling. After that day, the two women held respect for one another, unrivaled in the Legion Traveler ranks.

"Why can't we remember anything from where we came from?" Ehrinell had asked Amarynn one evening after a long day of training.

Amarynn shrugged. She was afraid to even try to remember where she came from. Travelers didn't know their pasts; many didn't even know there were pasts to remember. She often wondered why they weren't given some sort of story to placate their curiosity. They were clean slates, so why not make their histories for them?

"I was cold; I remember that," the golden-haired Traveler said.

"I was, as well," Amarynn replied.

"And it hurt so much, like ice and fire all at the same time," she continued. Amarynn just nodded.

"The King was there, waiting for me. He was so angry at Regealth," Ehrinell continued. "I know he was not expecting me to be a woman." She flashed that smile of hers and chuckled.

"No, he wasn't." The firelight danced along the rim of her metal tankard, and Amarynn watched the light moving across the surface of her ale.

Ehrinell picked up one of her throwing knives and used it to pick at her nails. "Was he angry when you crossed, too?"

"The King wasn't there when I crossed." Amarynn gave her an odd look.

Everyone knew that Amarynn's crossing was the only one the King had not personally witnessed. That was just one of the distinctions that

217

set her apart, made her feel unwanted. She was only just beginning to realize who might have been there with her.

"Who was it, then?" Ehrinell leaned in. Funny, she didn't smell of sweat and dirt from the practice yard. She smelled good — clean, with the faint scent of lilacs.

"Why would you ask that, Ehrinell?" An icy edge tightened Amarynn's voice.

"Who was there when you crossed?" Ehrinell was getting insistent, almost pushy.

The room began to close in.

"*Who?*" Ehrinell's voice was changing.

Amarynn's eyes opened. She could not remember closing them. Venalise sat in front of her, one eyebrow arched. It had taken only one stray thought for Venalise to find a way into her mind. The Traveler refocused her efforts to clear her head, concerned at how deceptively easy it seemed for the mage to simply wander in and out of her memories.

She chose something instinctive and straightforward to focus on: Legion broadsword guard positions.

Shoulder guard, straightforward oncoming attack.

She visualized the position and felt her muscles extending and contracting at the thought. She breathed in.

Heavens guard, attack from above.

She imagined Frost's weight in her hands and felt the pull from its reach. Like in the dungeons in Calliway, she put herself through the motions in her head to keep from focusing on her surroundings.

Body guard, close-range fight.

She visualized pulling her sword close, so close she could see herself in her blade. A defensive move in a close-quarters situation. She could have used this in the dungeons if she held her sword then.

Demons guard—

"Close range from below." The voice was achingly familiar. Its warmth surged into comfort that spread through her body, around her heart.

Jael.

"I watched you when you worked on your drills."

The scene in front of her shifted. She was no longer in the mage's stone chamber; she was in the practice yard. She saw the Prince standing in the shadows of the castle wall. He could only have been six or seven years old. He shielded his eyes against the sun to see her, his blond hair ruffling in the breeze.

"I know why you left." His voice drifted past her ear, sending a shiver down her back. She wanted to hear that voice again, next to her.

In his early teens, he sat at a long table strewn with books and parchment. Regealth and one of the many palace tutors hovered over him while he strained his neck forward to watch her and two other Travelers walk past the doorway to the library.

"I remember your crossing."

He was so close; she could smell the spice and leather of his scent, hear his footsteps, soft on the stones. She yearned for the weight of his hand on her arm in the forest again.

"You are my Kingdom's greatest warrior. And I know that you feel alone. I remember."

She wanted to protest, but then he was behind her, his voice at her ear. At her back, his body pressed forward, and she couldn't help but lean into him.

"You are a legend, yes, but no one wins unless you tell me who was with you in that chamber.

"Was it me?" he whispered. He wrapped one arm around her waist; she could feel his breath, warm on her neck. She felt the eagerness in his embrace as he tried to pull her close.

"No," she breathed. "That didn't happen, you slippery bitch."

Amarynn snarled as she opened her eyes. Venalise's smile stretched across her traitorous face.

"Oh, have I struck a nerve, Traveler?"

The stool tipped back as she stood. Venalise came as close to Amarynn as she dared, given the rage radiating from Amarynn's eyes and her clenched and quivering fists. Kneeling to eye level, Venalise gave a light laugh.

"I think I might know who was with you in that chamber." She stood. "Yes, I am fairly certain that handsome young Prince was there." She turned and started to walk around her.

Just as Venalise disappeared from her periphery, movements in the shadows drew her eyes toward the far wall. Sia was there, clutching her bear cub. The conflict was etched across her face as she hugged the bear tighter. Her eyes darted from Amarynn to Venalise.

"For such a fierce warrior, you are far too easy to read," she said over her shoulder. "But I was looking through the information you remember — things you know. I wonder how difficult it will be to open the door into what you don't."

Despite her efforts to appear unaffected, Amarynn's head dropped. Her tormentor's footsteps were behind her. She flinched as she felt the mage's cold hand clamp onto her shoulder, then blinding pain roared as a dagger was thrust into her lower back, its end protruding from her left side. Sia leaped to her feet while the bear cub clutched to her chest, wriggled, and growled.

She sucked in her breath as the weapon was pulled out, refusing to reveal her pain; hot blood began to pour down her clothing, spilling onto the stone beneath her.

"Before we begin looking through your pretty little head for those secrets, I think we should weaken your resolve just a bit."

The dagger clattered to the floor just beyond Amarynn's reach. Venalise sauntered back around in front of Amarynn, a feigned apologetic expression on her face. She knelt in front of her again.

"Tch, tch," she clucked as she shook her head. "This doesn't have to be so difficult, you know." Venalise rose again, straightened her skirts, and held her hand in Sia's direction. "Come, child."

Sia hesitantly stepped forward, then hurried to her side, casting quick, uncomfortable glances at Amarynn's sagging form. The little cub had gone still, its head buried in the crook of the child's arm. Together, they walked across the stone chamber toward the door. Amarynn's breaths slowed, and her vision blurred, but she could still see Venalise and the child's silhouettes in the chamber doorway. Venalise paused and turned.

"Take your time, Traveler. We'll be back after you've had a chance to die."

CHAPTER 29

 It will take some time, Prince," Regealth muttered.

"I need to prepare."

Jael stood in front of the mage, unmoving.

"It's not as if I can just wave my hands and make it disappear," Regealth snapped. "Magic as complicated as the spell you've carried within you for nearly twenty years doesn't just fall away like an old cloak." The old mage stood up and picked his way toward the woods.

"Where are you going?" Jael started to follow, but the Regealth stopped and turned, raising his hand to stay him.

"I will do this alone, boy." He noted the look of skepticism on Jael's face. "Leave me to my work."

Jael stood and watched, listless, as the mage turned back to the forest and pushed his way into the trees. He could do nothing but wait, and the longer he did nothing, the greater his anxiety became.

"I couldn't help but hear," a lilting voice said from behind.

Jael turned. Ehrinell was there, hands on her hips. She was joined by two other Travelers, dressed and ready for battle.

"My Lord," she took a step forward, "we are loyal to the Legion. Others might turn the other way, but we will not stand by and leave our sister in the hands of that kind of evil."

One of the men, Finn, stepped closer and nodded his agreement. Jael looked the three of them over, and he couldn't help but think of Aeric and Barrim. His stomach sickened with the pain of their sacrifice. He was almost ashamed, even as his heart swelled with pride. Amarynn was convinced there was no love for her among the Travelers. And yet, here stood three, ready to go into the Keep and do whatever it took to bring her out. He cleared his throat.

"I would ask if you were prepared to commit treason, acting against orders, but—"

"We would be following you, m'Lord. And last I checked, it's not treasonous to follow your Crown Prince." A roguish glint danced in her eyes.

Jael smiled. For the first time in days, he began to feel a little more like himself. He gestured for the three to follow him. They found Bent talking with several Legion men.

"Bent," Jael began, "I need you to send a man up the side of the mountain after Amarynn's horse and a couple of Karthians we stumbled upon." Bent didn't question the Prince. He simply turned and called for one of the men.

"This is Benji," he introduced the soldier to Jael, who clasped his shoulder in greeting.

"I need you to retrieve two horses and the two people tending them. They are up there," Jael gestured to the side of the mountain at their backs and proceeded to tell the young soldier where he would find them. When he was confident the lad knew where to go, Jael reached into his belt and pulled out Amarynn's braid. He pressed it into the soldier's hand, saying, "Let the big gelding have a sniff of this, and he'll follow you anywhere."

The young soldier grinned and nodded as he stuffed Amarynn's braid in his pocket and snatched up a pack. He was off and into the trees in minutes.

Ehrinell snickered behind the Prince.

"We ought to just send that damn horse in after her instead of going ourselves. Goddess help anyone who gets in Dax's way!"

"You are going after Amarynn?" Bent's eyebrows were raised. "I thought we agreed to get the youngster back first."

Jael sighed. He had hoped to slip away without having to have this conversation. He took Bent by the elbow and guided him a few steps away from the others.

"Yes. We are going back for Rynn — and the girl, if we can find her." Jael ran his hands through his hair and looked around the campsite. "You all should keep here, to the trees. You'll know if we've been successful," he added.

"Ah, My Lord, I'm not so sure this is the best idea." Bent pinched the bridge of his nose with his thumb and finger. "Surely, Lors would be on you in a bleeding minute if you walk back in there. You should stay back and let the Travelers go in your stead."

Jael knew the older man held his best interests at heart, but of all people, he had expected the Blademaster to understand.

"Bent, if you witnessed the things I have, if you saw what Lors did to her, you'd want to castrate the bastard yourself. I cannot just sit out here and wait like pampered royalty for the Travelers to fetch her. I won't!"

Jael sucked in a breath to stem the flow of his anger.

Nioll, who had been watching their conversation from afar, trotted over.

"Oh, I've seen that look before, My Lord," he said, shaking his head. "You're about to march yourself back into that Keep for the Traveler, aren't you?" Nioll grinned. "Well, as much as I love a good, cold night on the forest floor, I think I'd rather go kick me some Darkland arse if it's all the same to you." He jerked his head in the direction of Ehrinell and the other two Travelers. "Besides, you need another mere mortal to bleed with you—those bastards forget to guard your back when they canna' be killed!"

Jael returned his friend's smile. Bent sighed, the worry lines on his brow deepening, and he lifted his hands in defeat. "You have a point," he conceded. "Grab your sword."

225

The room was freezing. Amarynn shivered, trying to brush away the icy air wrapped around her body with her hands, but she couldn't. There was a burst of heat, only for a moment, then nothing, leaving her even colder. She gulped in breath after breath, hungry for air.

A loud clatter resonated in the dark chamber, and she opened her eyes. There, across from her, was a boy. His storm-grey eyes were wide, but not only from fear. He wore a look of shock as if he had just witnessed the impossible.

An arm's length above him, suspended in a cloud of mist, spun a blue crystal. It called to her, its blue-green facets refracting tiny pinpoints of light, casting thousands of shimmering fractals on the walls in its slow rotation. She wanted to hold it, disappear inside it, become lost in it instead of being in this cold, dark place.

Go to the crystal, Amarynn. It's safer there. Better.

She kept her gaze fixed on the beauty of the blue-faceted stone. As it spun, she felt warmer, lighter. She was so cold — and now she felt better. Her body relaxed as she focused on the light. Brilliant colors burst from its facets, and she became lost in their splendor. The chill dissipated, fluttering away from her.

Yes.

A new kind of light surrounded the glittering stone. A corona of blue-green incandescence coalesced and expanded, at first just near the crystal. But then, tendrils of foamy light reached toward her, blocking the boy and the room from her sight.

She was so warm.

But now the light shone too bright — it hurt. She threw up one arm to shield her eyes as its core pulsed into view. The spinning, reverberating mass of molten light glowed more brightly with every turn. She felt her heart flutter, then slow; her movements began to feel forced, like she was treading water. A high-pitched ringing started as a whisper, then crescendoed until she thought her eardrums would burst.

226

She cupped her hands over her ears, squeezing her eyes shut and pulling herself into a ball. The sound, the light — it was too much. She could feel the pulsating light on her skin, the ringing sound making the hairs on her arms stand on end. Then, the air was sucked from her lungs. She convulsed, arching her back nearly to the breaking point.

And then there was nothing.

She was nothing.

There was nowhere.

The blackness that wasn't entirely black enveloped her, and she retreated into herself, into the silence.

"I can rid you of that."

The voice surrounded her, gently pulsing into existence, then sharpened with a surety that startled her into an unfamiliar scene. An old man, vaguely familiar, stood in front of her. She was on the street surrounded by soaring stone and glass towers. There were no people, just the old man and her.

He tapped her chest just above her heart. "I can rid you of that," he repeated, smiling. Amarynn felt the warm sun on her face filtering through her eyelashes, making it difficult to see. The old man peered at her expectantly. He placed the palm of his hand on her forehead. A stranger reached for her, yet she didn't flinch. "And that." He offered a kindly smile.

It seemed as if he had been expecting her. He smiled so warmly, like an old friend. He said nothing but simply looked at her and studied her for a moment. Then he took her hand, patting it lightly.

"Will you come?" he beckoned. She made no protest, following him like an obedient child. The world gently sloughed off her, blowing away and leaving her empty.

Then, images flashed through her mind.

People, names, emotions, loss.

She was caught up in a wave of light and felt a spreading warmth — then, without warning, the cold returned.

Her body was wracked with convulsions, and when they subsided, she found herself once again shivering on a cold and wet stone floor.

Amarynn gasped for air.

The pain was too much this time, even for her. She had sworn she'd make no sound, she'd not cry out, but as memories came flooding back, faces and places, memories of who she had been, her heart broke into a thousand pieces.

A high, keening sound broke the silence, and she realized it was coming from her own throat.

So much to have lost.

She broke, again and again, sobs overtaking her like so many demons tearing her apart from the inside.

She wept until she couldn't breathe.

She wept until her body refused to move.

She lay face down, shackles on her wrists, her cheek pressed into the cold stone. She was done. Eternity could have her.

"You know, I almost feel sorry for you."

Amarynn's eyes slowly opened. Just in front of her, Venalise's skirts brushed the stone. She could see where the fabric wicked the moisture from the floor.

"Almost," she said sweetly.

Amarynn turned her head away, pressing her forehead to the ground. She gathered herself and called on her aching muscles to draw her knees beneath her. The effort was tortuous, but her rage-fueled her. Venalise's footsteps tapped lightly as she walked a slow circle around the Traveler's hunched form.

The footsteps continued. Once her knees were beneath her, Amarynn placed her palms flat on the stone. She pushed against the floor and pulled the tension tighter and tighter in her belly.

"Sia?" Venalise was just about to step in front of her now, her tone imperious. But the mage was careless in her overconfidence; she had stepped far too close.

Amarynn's legs shot out in less than a second, striking Venalise near her knees. The mage fell forward, the sudden and unexpected attack preventing her from stopping her fall. A loud crack resonated in the chamber as her head struck the floor. She lay there, motionless.

"Sia." Amarynn's voice was a hoarse croak.

Amarynn scanned the edges of the shadows for Sia. She saw nothing. Then, the child appeared. Amarynn pulled her legs back beneath her as Sia rushed forward. She stopped just out of the Traveler's reach, pausing just long enough for Amarynn to notice.

"I won't hurt you," Amarynn whispered. Then it started again, the images of people and things she remembered. She squeezed her eyes shut as if that could block them out. Silent sobs threatened to erupt, and she shook from the strain. She opened her eyes and looked at the little girl pleadingly. She wanted to tell her to run, but she couldn't form the words. Sia stepped closer. She set her cub down and knelt in front of Amarynn, careful not to touch the fallen woman's unmoving body.

Amarynn couldn't control her trembling muscles, but she tried to speak anyway.

"Y-you have t-to leave." Her teeth rattled against one another, and the lack of control frustrated her. She nodded towards Venalise. "While you c-can."

"I'm sorry she hurt you." Sia looked over her shoulder at Venalise. "She's not all bad," she whispered, almost to herself. She reached out and placed her hands on either side of Amarynn's head.

A strange numbness poured over Amarynn, like water running over her skin. A cooling sense of nothingness fluttered through her mind and her heart. She blinked and looked at the tiny little girl who stood in front of her, silvery eyes wide open, unaware of the magnitude of what she had just done. It became clear why Regealth was so adamant about getting Sia away from Venalise and Athtull Keep.

A nudge at Amarynn's knee drew her attention, and she watched the bear cub butt its head against her leg. It was a stone bear, if memory served her correctly. She let her hand drop to touch its grey-white fur, and it nipped at her fingers. This must have been how Venalise had convinced the child she was looking after her best interests. Amarynn ground her teeth and clenched her jaw, sucking in a breath to steady herself. "Sia, she is bad. She is the very meaning of bad, Sia. You must go and find Regealth and get away from here."

Before Sia could respond, a sudden stirring from Venalise sent her scurrying back into the shadows, the bear cub lumbering after her. The mage pushed herself up to a sitting position and then scrambled back on her hands out of Amarynn's reach.

The rage on her face was unmistakable.

"You," she spat. "You will pay for that." She stood, unsteady. Casting her wild eyes around the chamber, she spied the dagger she had used to stab the warrior in the back. She staggered over to retrieve it.

Venalise returned to face Amarynn, the dagger in her hands. She held it out, laying the blade across both of her upturned palms. She closed her eyes as she mumbled. The mumbling grew into chanting, then shouting, in a language Amarynn did not recognize. She had transformed from calm and emotionless to maniacal, with her disheveled hair and the spreading bruise on her temple. The shouting became a shriek, then slowly, the dagger floated from her palms and began to spin. It whirled away from Venalise and spun in an arc toward where Amarynn was still chained, disappearing over her shoulder. A razor-sharp pain sliced through her as the dagger drew its sharp tip across her upper back. Amarynn hissed in pain.

A satisfied smile bloomed on Venalise's face.

"You will stay here as long as I wish, Traveler. But don't worry, you'll have your dagger to keep you company," she sneered. Amarynn jerked against her restraints as the searing agony of healing snaked across her skin. "I have spelled it, so it will never stop its assault on you. Healing hurts almost as much as the injury, doesn't it?"

She laughed as the dagger struck again, marking a thin red trail along Amarynn's arm. "Farewell, Amarynn," Venalise drawled. "I'd say 'till next time,' but I just don't know if I'll ever return. Enjoy eternity."

Venalise whirled around and snatched Sia up by the wrist. They reached the doorway, and before Venalise could reach for an ornate brass lantern that hung by the door, she stopped to steady herself. She lifted her free hand to the side of her head for a moment, and she snatched the lantern. They both disappeared into the Keep without looking back, leaving Amarynn with the bewitched dagger, chained to the floor in painful darkness.

CHAPTER 30

"Rest here. Breathe slowly, normally."

Regealth motioned for Jael to sit on one of the many fallen trees scattered on the forest floor. Jael dropped to his knees instead.

The old mage placed both of his hands on Jael's head. They trembled slightly, though he hoped the Prince did not notice. He was tired. The drain of the past week and then the sudden rush of power this evening was almost too much for his aging body to bear.

Jael and his band of warriors were making final preparations to leave for the Keep when Regealth returned from the forest. The Prince might have already left if it hadn't been for Bent's quiet counsel. The older man could sense the urgency in his every move.

Regealth began the quiet litany of chants and phrases needed to channel the power he was drawing. He felt the magic coalesce, reaching down his arms like tendrils of living things seeking the light.

The magic lines tightened and escaped through his fingers, weaving a fine net around Jael's head. The net grew, and Regealth gave a gentle push to widen its circumference. Slowly, it cascaded around the Prince from the mage's hand down to the ground.

Regealth adjusted his stance. There would be backlash when the 20-year-old dampening spell was drawn away from Jael. The mage needed to absorb the shock and the residual magic when it did. He only hoped he was still strong enough — the spell he cast now might make room for the surplus of power.

He checked his casting one last time, then uttered the words that would release Jael's power.

Jael heard the words Regealth spoke over him, feeling the mage's presence like a pillar of familiarity. The tone of his voice, the fragile whisper-like sound, had been a part of his life for as long as he could remember. This voice was almost as comforting as his own mother's.

A sudden kernel of white-hot energy flickered in his chest, then faded. For a moment, he thought that might be all there was, and he couldn't help but feel disappointment. But then, another spark formed in his mind, and this time the energy was more robust, brighter.

The power in his chest returned, only now it felt like more of a surge than a spark. It grew, stretching itself into every part of his body. His tissues sang with the energy; his very bones felt like they glowed. The magic sought out his body in a primal way — he needed it, and he could feel his body drink it up with a desperation he didn't know it possessed.

Regealth took a step back, and Jael knew that all of the magic he felt reverberating through his body was wholly his own. When he finally opened his eyes, he saw the old mage standing back with Ehrinell and Bent.

The Prince had been transformed. When Jael lifted his eyes to the group, they shone with a wildness they had never seen in him. The King's son was now complete.

Jael stood but took his time doing so as if he was new to his body. The forest was still. After several long minutes, Ehrinell approached, stepping forward to stand in front of the Prince. She dropped her head and began to lower herself to one knee, but the Prince stopped her before she was able, clasping her arm in the Legion manner.

"Tonight, we are equal," he said softly. "You were the first to offer your blade to help me, and for that, I will forever be in your debt."

She said nothing and moved to stand at his side. The two other Travelers, Finn and Stavin, joined her.

"You've magic, eh? Looks like I'm at a disadvantage now," Nioll grumbled. He extended his hand to Jael, "But I'll still have your back, even if you won't need it from the likes of a plain human anymore."

"I'll always need someone like you standing beside me, friend," Jael grasped his arm and pulled him into a quick embrace.

Bent looked over the group sternly. "Well, now that's over with, why don't we see about getting this underway. I, for one, am ready to get what we came for and get out of these Goddess-damned mountains."

Jael bobbed his head in agreement and turned to address his newly assembled team. "I know how to get in. Once we are inside, I'm going after Lors first."

"Doesn't it make more sense to just get Amarynn and be gone as quickly as possible?" Ehrinell asked.

Jael's mouth was set in a grim line. "Yes, it does, but I don't know where they've taken her. Lors will know where she is. Besides, there is a debt to be paid by him, and I will see it collected."

Ehrinell raised her eyebrows in surprise at Jael's tone. "As you wish, My Lord."

"I only ask one thing. When we find him, he's mine."

All four nodded, then began their short trek through the forest. In less than an hour, they arrived at a vantage point that overlooked the tower which contained the secret door. Ban and Ahai were high in the sky, the former cradled in the crescent horns of its larger counterpart. The blue glow of Ban mingled with Ahai's pale yellow to cast an eerie green glow. Their combined light was waning, making it difficult to see the shadowed surface in which the door was concealed.

Before they left camp, Bent sent word to the handful of men and Travelers tasked to agitate the Keep's contingency of Darkland soldiers. While those on the tower wall were focused on the front of the Keep, they left the sides unguarded.

Jael cocked his head and heard the calls and taunts from the other Travelers as they harassed and occupied the Keep's guard. He looked back to the others and grinned. "Time to go."

They moved with stealthy precision and were in the side door in seconds. Once inside the tower storeroom, though, they needed a plan to gain entry to the Keep. Even with Travelers at the entrance to Athtull, there was a measure of uncertainty about the state of the bailey yard. They wouldn't know what to expect until they were inside the bailey walls.

"Stavin and I can create more chaos," Finn offered. "We can hold our own against more than what's out there, even on a slow day."

"You'll need me with you, most likely," Ehrinell added, looking to Nioll and Jael. "If you want to find Amarynn without drawing too much attention, I have the skills to do it."

She was right. She was a trained assassin in the Legion, proficient in situations where brute force and full Legion assaults were counterproductive.

Jael gave a quick nod of agreement.

"Stavin and Finn, you head out and do what you do. Once you've seen that we are in the Keep. You can duck out."

"We may stick around," Stavin joked, his low voice rumbling, "if we are having fun." He flashed a rare smile. Finn chuckled and punched him in the arm.

"Let's go, you lout," he said, reaching out to gently pat where he struck. The two smiled mischievously at one another and stood. They drew their swords and were out the door, from where sounds of shouts and metal clashing quickly followed.

Jael arched an eyebrow questioningly at Ehrinell.

"Those two are inseparable. It is what it is," she said. Nioll and Jael took positions by the door, waiting for her signal. She focused her attention on Jael.

236

"You lead once we are out there. I don't want to waste any focus looking for some damn door. I'll be right behind you. If anyone tries to engage, you let me step in," she directed.

"Aye," Nioll interjected. "She steps in, and you fall back. I'll be behind you. Wouldn't want to give any Darklands bastards access to that pretty face of yours."

"Yes, but to be clear, I want Lors. Without a doubt, I want him to know that I was the one to end him." Jael's voice was low but intense.

Ehrinell held up her hand. "We go," she said, "now."

She grunted as she threw the door open, and they ran out into the chaos. Most soldiers were still up on the ramparts, but many of those still in the bailey yard was preparing weapons for an assault. At least, they had been until Finn and Stavin arrived. The two Travelers were engaged with several men, their blades whirling, several Darklands men already on the ground behind them.

"Go!"

Ehrinell gave Jael a push, and he ran toward the entrance to the Keep. They might as well have been invisible. Not a single soldier stopped them as they charged across the yard and into the door.

Once safely within, the outside din lessened. Without hesitation, Jael ran for a flight of stairs and bounded up, with Nioll and Ehrinell close behind him. He wasted no time, running straight for the throne room. He knew Lors would be there with his precious maps and plans.

He skidded to a halt just before the open double doors and ducked inside, striding confidently into the chamber.

Lors stood at the far end of his long table. The Darklands King looked up as Jael appeared.

The Prince approached him, chest heaving from the run up the stairs but savoring the look of surprise on Lors' face. He adjusted the grip on his sword and stepped forward. Lors, acknowledging the danger, reached for his sword, which lay on the table among the maps.

"Where is she?" Jael's voice was quiet.

The room was almost silent. In the distance, sounds of soldiers in the bailey yard and the fall of footsteps in quick succession wafted in and out of earshot. Lors, sword in hand, leaned casually against the table's edge and cocked his head to the side, "Who?"

Jael was stoic. He refused to play Lors' game.

The King's eyes glinted with amusement. He cleared his throat. "Am I to assume this is a rescue?" He pushed off the table and took a step forward. "Did daddy finally arrive?" Lors flashed a knowing smile. "I bet he was pleased with your handiwork."

"Where." Jael took a step forward. "Is." And another, his voice stronger. "She!" He was shouting now.

Lors threw his head back and laughed.

"Oh! This is *rich*," he exclaimed. He strode to the center of the room casually. "You approached me," he pointed back toward the throne, "in this very room. You demanded I return your precious stone and warrior to no avail, and now you return and make more demands?" His expression darkened. "You'll have to kill me."

Jael lowered his chin, never breaking eye contact with the King. He could feel the unbridled magic in his blood thrum in response to his rage. It wanted release.

"Done," he whispered, then charged.

Lors had no chance. Jael was on him in seconds. The King brought his sword up to block Jael's attack, but the Prince effortlessly knocked it out of his grip. Jael felt the power in his body infusing the sword. He brought it around to strike Lors on his unprotected side in one fluid motion. The blade bit through the leathers and found his ribs. Jael could feel the metal scrape bone as Lors fell back onto the stone floor.

The King staggered and reached for the dagger at his belt, but Jael swung his sword, magical energy arcing behind his swing. The dagger clattered to the floor.

Lors cried out, one hand pressed to his side to quell the blood seeping through his tunic. He scrabbled backward toward the dais as Jael came for him, unrelenting. Lors pulled himself up the steps, and in an instant, Jael was there. He stood over the King, breathing hard, his sword pointed directly at the fallen King's chest. He paused. Lors lifted his chin in defiance, but his bravado was erased as he winced in pain, grasping at his side.

Jael dropped his sword as he knelt over Lors, one knee on the trembling King's chest. He pulled his dagger from his belt and held it to the hollow at his throat.

Lors stared at him, suddenly perceiving the magic in Jael's eyes, pulsing and twisting. His panic was unmistakable in his widened gaze. His breath caught, and he whimpered. "Please."

Jael's eyes narrowed. His mouth turned up in a snarl. "Where is she?" Jael's voice was ice.

"Lise!" Lors cried out, his breathing quickening as he tried to push backward and wriggle away. Jael stopped him, slammed his left hand down on Lors' shoulder, and pinned him in place.

"Your mage isn't here to protect you, m'Lord," Ehrinell taunted from the doorway just as Jael leaned in close enough to see the stubble on Lors' quivering chin.

"Since you refuse to answer my question, I have another." The dagger drew a drop of blood as Jael pressed harder on Lors' throat. "Do *you* even have a heart?" Jael whispered, tightening his grip on the hilt of his weapon.

The Prince's eyes glittered as he drove the dagger into Lors' chest, just below his throat. Jael's magic surged as metal bit into flesh, raging through his limbs, threatening to burst. Ice-blue energy skated across his hands and traveled down the dagger's hilt into Lors' body. The magic disappeared into the wound, and Lors convulsed, his mouth contorting into a silent scream. Jael's eyes lingered on the King as the magic dissipated. He stood, retrieving his dagger and wiping it on his breeches as he watched the King's blood pour onto the floor. Lors lay there, writhing and drowning in his own blood, the panicked look on his face mirroring Amarynn's when she endured the very same.

"Before you die, know this." The Prince leaned over and retrieved his sword, sheathing it. He drew himself up. "I, Jael, First Son of King Lasten and sole heir to the throne of the Kingdom of Karth, hereby claim the Darklands. Your throne is forfeit, and you are deposed."

Without another glance in Lors' direction, Jael tossed the dagger to the side, then turned and walked out of the room.

Jael did not stop in front of Ehrinell and Nioll. He did not need to. He was going to find Amarynn, and he would bring her home.

CHAPTER 31

Ehrinell caught up to Jael at the bottom of a double flight of stairs. They were deep within the mountain, past the dungeons. The screams and cries of the caged atranoch broke the hot and heavy silence.

"My Lord, do you know where you are going?" she asked quietly, fully aware of his agitated state.

He said nothing.

She laid her hand on his arm. "Maybe you should take a moment. Let me do what I do best."

He studied her in the dim light of the passageway. Her face was fine-boned; she looked more like a lady of the court than a highly-skilled assassin. However, the glint in her eyes revealed her warrior's edge.

"But—" Jael began.

Ehrinell gripped his shirt and pushed him back against the wall. "Do you want to find her? Or do you want to run around this Keep, playing hide and seek?" Her challenge struck a nerve.

"You're right," he conceded. "We'll wait here."

"If I haven't returned in five minutes, go on without me."

She faded into the shadows before Jael could reply. Nioll leaned back against the stone wall and sighed heavily.

Jael did the same, pressing his head against the wall and closing his eyes. All he could envision was Lors, his dagger in the King's throat,

241

shock frozen on his face. It was not a comfortable thing, taking a life. But the bastard deserved it, Jael told himself. He deserved to know the horror he had put Amarynn through, and Jael was more than happy to deliver the lesson.

Then the image changed to Amarynn's hazel eyes widening when Lors' blade struck her in the same place. Jael could not escape reliving the helplessness he had felt at that moment. A knot of dread formed in his belly. A sensation, like a gentle tug, overtook him. He pushed off the wall and stepped toward a darkened passageway to his right. The pulling relented. He replayed the memory, stepping back toward the wall, and the sensation returned.

You two are connected, my boy.

Regealth's words resonated as Jael stepped to the left, towards a staircase that led downward into shadow. The pull strengthened, almost to the point of being painful.

"Unbelievable," he breathed. He took a step back, and it lessened.

Nioll reached out a hand to stop him as he paced forward again, a quizzical look on his features.

"What is it?"

Jael looked through Nioll, a fire in his eyes that hadn't been there when they entered the Keep. "Wait for Ehrinell here. When she returns, I want you both to leave the Keep. Find Bent and help him."

"Leave? My Lord—"

"Just do as I ask, Nioll."

Jael was running down the darkened passageway before Nioll could say another word.

Pain, relentless, coursed through Amarynn's body. The dagger was locked in a slow dance around her, darting in and out as it sliced perfect, painful marks she could not dodge. First, there was the cut that burned a fine line through her flesh. Then, the bite and sting as magic pulled muscle and skin back together. It happened over and over again; Amarynn had lost track of time.

When Venalise left her in the darkness, she tried to listen for the blade. Immortal or not, she did not seek out pain. Immortality offered no guard against suffering — only against ending it.

She tried to dodge the blade, but the dark made that nearly impossible, and the chains on her wrists chafed and pinched and only allowed her to move so far in any given direction. The worst of all was when it found her face. That had only happened twice, but she jumped in surprise as it found her lip, making the cut that much deeper and more painful to heal.

Amarynn dropped her head as she focused, chin to her chest, and sat back on her heels. If she found a way to sever her hand, to get free of the chains, it wouldn't be restored by the same magic that healed her other wounds. Limbless Travelers weren't unheard of but being unable to wield her weapons would be torment. Immortality was hard enough to bear when she had something to offer. An eternity of uselessness was unthinkable. There were no weapons near her, save the dagger, anyway.

The dagger struck again, this time across the back of her neck. She hissed and arched forward. Her head swam.

The room turned bright. Someone was shaking her with heavy, rough hands. They shoved her shoulders back, and she stumbled.

"Lazy bitch! What do you do all day!"

The low, raspy voice made her stomach clench. The sun was setting — purple and orange streaks appearing across the early evening sky. A loud crash made her turn while her heartbeat hammered in her chest. An older man was in front of her, reaching for her, and when she escaped his grasp, he swung. She tried to dodge his blow, and it caught her just behind the ear instead of on her cheek where he'd intended.

A child was crying. He was screaming from somewhere she couldn't see.

Where was he? Oh, God!

Amarynn cried out, and the memory diffused into mist.

Her heartbeat was erratic, like the flight of the dagger. She still heard cries, but this time they were that of the atranoch, not of a child. Their screams and cries had been building since Venalise left her here. Maybe they cared, she thought to herself. She laughed at her absurdity. The dagger struck again, but this time she didn't flinch. She began to welcome the agony, to enjoy it.

She was slipping into the battle rage that would render her numb — impervious to the pain — and she embraced it. The darkness closed in again, and this time, she dove willingly into it.

The pull became overpowering.

Descending the staircase, Jael turned off several times down various passageways but felt his insides contort until he could barely breathe. As he changed direction and returned to the stairs, the feeling would subside. It became clear that his magic was guiding him somewhere. He could only hope that it would lead him to Amarynn and that alone kept him moving forward. She was somewhere deep within the mountain, and he put his trust in the magic to find her.

The stairwell ended at the very bottom of the keep. Here, the air was thick and heavy, and the short corridor, lined with sputtering sconces and the occasional tattered tapestry, ended with a single door. Now, the magic was all but singing in his blood. The hairs on the back of his neck stood straight up. The magic was responding to her. It had been all along, but now that she was near, there was no mistaking it — she must be close.

He reached the door and pulled on the heavy iron handle. The room was pitch black, so he snatched a lantern from the wall. His body was vibrating with a resonance that could only mean one thing.

He had found her.

There was a groan from the heavy wooden door, then light — a lantern shining from the doorway — and it moved closer. The lantern's glow barely reached the center of the vast cavern where she was bound, casting an otherworldly illumination on Amarynn's form. Rivulets of sweat and blood mingled with the damp chill of the chamber, dripping from her body to the stone floor. Sagging against the chains, she was immersed within herself; her concentration focused on listening for the blade's next approach. Her sides heaved as she fought her battle with the dagger, and in her rage, she found a discipline that pulled the world away, allowing her to focus on survival without distraction.

The light finally reached her face, and she squinted towards it, its radiance too much for her eyes after being in total darkness for what felt like days. The figure holding the lantern was only a dark shadow, but as her eyes adjusted, she saw him. Jael was striding into that dark, cold chamber with the force of a thousand armies. His eyes shone with an icy glow— he had no fear.

Amarynn shook her head as she let her battle rage fall away. She was finished, and Lors had won. The King had the mage, the stone, and the child, and now there would be no stopping him. Amarynn grunted between clenched teeth, "No, Jael! Go!"

The Prince knelt just outside the etched stone circle where Amarynn knelt, chained to the floor. Blood trickled from her skin and mixed with the cold water that dripped from above. He set the lantern down.

"Go," she whispered, pleading. "She's gone with the child. Find them and leave me." She was shivering, the cold, healing magic of her immortality unrelenting as the spelled dagger spun and twirled around her, nearly missing Jael's face in its merciless path. Without Regealth, Amarynn knew there was nothing he could do. Venalise's magic was simply too powerful.

Jael's eyes left Amarynn's only for a moment. He looked down at his hands as he lifted them, moving in slow motion. He looked back to her and pushed his palms forward toward the spinning fury of the spelled dagger. It widened its orbit around Amarynn's shoulders, moving toward Jael. She strained against her chains, trying to block its path, but it tumbled just out of reach. As it arced closer to him, she pleaded, "You can't stop it! Leave me! Go!"

Jael stood still, arms held out in front of him, eyes closed, the muscles in his jaw working as he inhaled and drew himself up. Something was changing — Amarynn could feel it in the charged air around them. Just as the dagger whirled into his outstretched hand, there was a hiss; the knife vibrated as if it struck stone. Amarynn's eyes widened as the air around her rippled and her mouth and nose filled with a metallic tang. Confusion flooded her mind as the realization hit her full force. Jael, untried on the battlefield and untested in the world, was wielding magic the likes of which she had never seen. It was impossible, yet he was doing it right in front of her.

What he had said that night in the stables flashed through her mind. *I remember your crossing.* Pieces slammed together. Everyone knew Regealth never brought the Travelers across on his own, so why had she been fooling herself all these years? He always used the King as an anchor to draw out the magic of the Gate — common knowledge. But the little boy — the stormy eyes that had been there the moment she opened her own. Everything slipped into place and became clear. He had used Jael when he brought her to their world.

The dagger, its spell broken, clattered to the ground. Amarynn slumped forward against the chains, her breath coming in great heaves. Jael dropped to his knees in front of her and gripped her shoulders. Their foreheads pressed together.

His hands moved to her face.

"I would never leave you," he whispered.

Amarynn was trembling as she looked up and saw the storm-grey, the intensity, the new blue lines of electricity that now danced in his eyes. Never in her wildest dreams would someone care enough to risk everything to save her. Even Bent would know better. He would have left her if it meant getting Regealth safely away.

246

Jael's thumbs brushed her cheeks, wiping away the blood and water. Her chest rose and fell rapidly while the Prince searched her face, his eyes full of concern. She did her best to hide her pain. She was Amarynn, the Immortal, but there was too much hurt to hide now that Venalise had opened the floodgates of her mind. But now, even as she was chained to the floor, she knew she was willing to risk everything, even her eternity, for him.

"Leave me. Find Sia and the Gate." Her stomach turned at the weakness of her voice.

"You saved me in the forest. Now it's my turn." He reached down to her wrists and placed his hands on the thick metal bands. Amarynn felt another surge in the air around her as the shackles fell away. She fell forward into him, released from the tension of the chains.

Jael's arms wrapped around her, supporting her. It was over — she was free. Amarynn pulled back and looked into his eyes. All her fear and every ounce of her pain tumbled through her. Her heart shattered open, and she leaned into him, her lips seeking his. Jael's hand curled around her head, pulling her to him as they found one another, his energy consuming her, completing her.

An undeniable need overtook her. She could taste her tears and blood on his lips, but it didn't matter now. Nothing mattered now except that she was free and Jael was here. He pulled away to look at her and smooth her hair away from her face, tucking the short strands behind her ear. The atranoch screamed in the distance.

"We don't have much time." He stood and reached to pull her up. Amarynn stumbled, her legs shaking from their time on the cold, stone floor, but she steadied herself on his arm. Her movements were slow and deliberate, shock replacing the adrenaline trickling away. Jael grasped her by the shoulders. "We have to run."

Jael's request did not register.

Jael gripped one of her hands and pulled her toward the doorway. Amarynn's whole body screamed in agony, but she pushed on, gaining strength from his warm grip. They raced up the staircase, but once

247

they arrived at the top, instead of turning toward the broad hallway leading to the outside, they immediately changed direction when they heard shouts and footsteps running toward them.

They turned to the left and sprinted into one of the dark corridors near the bottom. Soldiers passed by their hiding place rather than returning to the stairs. The pair kept to the shadowy passageway. With every step, Amarynn felt the wounds from the spinning dagger closing and her physical strength returning, but the thoughts and memories that had flooded her brain under Venalise's hand threatened to drop her in her tracks. She heard strange whispers and saw faces in the shadows that weren't there. Occasionally, she glanced behind them, a new paranoia pervading her thoughts. Jael held her hand tightly, her arm tucked under his own. They took one last turn before exiting the narrow side passage and entering a wide corridor, where they heard, again, the atranoch wailing in the distance. Jael stopped for a moment, unsure which direction to go, but Amarynn pulled on his hand in the opposite direction of the beasts' cries.

"We're getting out of here, now."

CHAPTER 32

Jael could feel the pull of Amarynn's hand wane the farther they ran. She was struggling, though she wouldn't admit it. When he spied a dark alcove, he ducked into it, pulling her to him.

"Will you be all right?" he whispered into her hair.

She breathed in and out, then pushed away from him.

Jael looked down and grimaced when he noticed her entire left side was covered in dried blood. He reached out, but she caught his hand before he could touch her.

"I'm fine," she said sharply but regretted her tone, noticing the hurt in his eyes. "Venalise had to weaken me, to get into my head," she added in a gentler tone. "She used my dagger to bleed me out."

Jael studied her in the dimly flickering light of the torches. Even immortality required rest and sustenance, neither of which she'd had. Her face was gaunt under the streaks of blood and dirt, and dark circles had formed beneath her eyes. Her skin was dull, and her lips cracked and bruised.

She had been the model of strength and bravery when they'd entered the Keep, but she seemed much different now. Her wild look of dread and desperation had unnerved him when he found her in the chamber.

Sudden footsteps from around the corner made both of them jump.

Jael instinctively reached for Amarynn to pull her back toward him, and, surprisingly, she complied. He positioned himself in front of her and turned his back to the corridor, pressing them both as far into the shadows as he could. His magic hummed in response to the danger. Moments later, three Darklands soldiers ran past the alcove.

"Move," she growled, working her hands up between them. She grunted and tried to push him away, her breaths coming faster, sounding almost panicked.

"Easy," Jael whispered, his lips near her ear. "I've got you."

Even as he said the words, they seemed out of place. She was one of the most feared warriors their world had ever known, but at this moment, she appeared as fragile as a child.

"I know." She stilled and exhaled. "I know."

Amarynn looked up at Jael, and he grasped the back of her head, pressing his forehead to hers. "You are safe now."

He leaned down and let his lips briefly brush her forehead. "I don't know what she did to you, but know this," he locked eyes with her, "there is no one — no magic, no beast, no mage in this world who will hurt you again." He pulled his other long dagger from its scabbard and pressed it into her hand. "Right now, though, I need the fiercest Traveler in the Legion. I need you, Amarynn."

She lowered her chin to look at her hand, wrapped around the blade's grip. Amarynn lifted her head again, with a tiny spark of fire flickering in her hazel eyes. It wasn't much, but he saw a hint of her old self. She nodded.

"Now, let's get out of here, shall we?"

Sia tried to keep up with Venalise, but her tiny legs were no match for the mage's long stride, and the bear cub was wiggling in her other arm. She struggled to keep from dropping Thera at such a hurried pace. They wound through the Keep, following passageways she was unfamiliar with — dank, narrow, and unused for some time. At last, they climbed the staircase to the throne room. That much, she could tell.

Panting as she climbed, she couldn't help but think about Amarynn. They had left her chained to the floor in that chamber. No matter what Venalise said, it didn't feel right to leave her like that in the dark. She'd tried to help her, but she didn't know what to do except help make Amarynn forget. She wasn't sure she even knew what she was doing but reaching for the warrior's head had been an impulse, and she let her instincts guide her through the rest, imagining cool water and quiet peace. Sia didn't even know who Amarynn was. She knew that Regealth had talked about her on the ship, and he seemed to care for her very much.

They rounded the last corner, and Sia saw the doors to the throne room looming ahead. Soldiers were running in all directions while a handful of men stood around the entry. When they saw Venalise, they stiffened and parted for her to pass. But Sia saw the dais steps before Venalise; her breath caught in her throat. The King lay sprawled out on the dais steps at the foot of the throne, surrounded by a pool of blood. A tug on her hand broke her shock, and Venalise pulled her through the throng of soldiers.

Venalise was unaffected by the sight. She let go of Sia's hand and delicately picked her way around the gruesome scene, lifting her skirts to avoid the blood. Sia clutched Thera and lowered her eyes, burying her face in the cub's soft fur. Venalise leaned down to tug the silver circlet from Lors' waxen brow. She paused as she clutched the crown and looked up at Sia, peering at her through Thera's fur, her brows furrowed.

"Honestly, this saves me the trouble," she said, straightening. Stepping carefully back around to the floor, she added, "I assume this is the work of Jael, who is most likely looking for the Traveler as we speak."

Tucking the circlet into a pouch tied to her belt, she knelt in front of Sia. "My dear," she said, "we are leaving this place. If the Prince finds Amarynn and we are still here, I fear what they might do to you." She frowned.

Sia lifted her head, eyes widened. "Me?"

"Oh yes, my love. The Prince told me he thinks you are very, very dangerous."

Venalise stood and straightened her skirts. "And I am sure the Traveler would cut out my heart, given a chance," she muttered.

"But Regealth told me Amarynn is good. She's special," Sia said, confused.

"Well, she's good to him, my love," Venalise purred. "And after spending time with us, I'm sure she's none too pleased. Especially if the Prince has had a chance to whisper in her ear."

Sia tried to imagine why the Prince might think she was dangerous. Venalise, she could understand, but Sia hadn't done anything to make him think she was terrible. He had seemed so kind when she smiled at him on the hill. It didn't make any sense.

"Where are we going?" Sia asked, her voice sounding small.

"I know a place where no one will find us, not until we want them to." Venalise smiled down at the child. She held out her hand. Sia looked up at the mage, then took it, following her as they exited the room, leaving the King's body behind.

Corridor after corridor took Jael and Amarynn through parts of the Keep they hadn't known existed. In their frantic search for an exit, they had pushed themselves further into the mountain and closer to the atranoch, despite their efforts to find an exit. Each room they found was smaller than the last, and an oppressive feeling of being buried alive began to snake its way into Amarynn's thoughts.

Where are you going?

She caught her breath and reached out to the wall to steady herself. "Did you hear that?" she breathed.

Ahead, one pathetic torch sputtered, and she flinched when an angry face formed within the flickering light. It scowled furiously at her, then melted back into the flames. Amarynn shook her head forcefully to keep her mind focused on the present — she needed to rid herself of these unwelcome, intrusive thoughts.

Her heart raced, and sudden pain shot up her spine. The hallway in front of her vanished, and she was in a room built from wood and stone. The sound of footsteps forced her into the corner, and she made herself as small as possible. They were getting closer. She could taste the bile in her mouth. She had vomited so many times from the pain that nothing was left in her stomach.

"Useless bitch."

Her hands trembled over her eyes.

"Amarynn!"

Her eyes shot open wide at the sound of her name. *Her name* was not the name she had heard in her head.

Jael knelt in front of her.

"What is it? What frightened you?"

Disoriented, she cast about and realized they were still in the dim corridor; only she was curled into a ball against the darkened floor.

Jael took her hands in his and squeezed. "We have to keep moving."

She couldn't speak, her mind still wracked with fear. *But fear of what?*

She nodded absently at Jael as he pulled her up to her feet. They heard more cries from the atranoch ahead but had no choice but to move in their direction. The light brightened as they neared the passageway's end. Jael cautiously peered past the end of the hallway, then beckoned for Amarynn to follow.

They stepped out into a chamber, an intersection of several corridors. Amarynn saw etchings on the floor like the lines in Venalise's aethertorium and sucked in a breath, sidestepping the center. "We need to get out of here."

Jael followed her eyes to the floor. "These look like—"

"Yes, I know." Amarynn's mouth was set in a firm line. Her next sharp intake of breath alerted Jael to danger. He glanced across the chamber and recognized the two silhouettes rushing out from one of the passageways. Venalise bolted from the shadows, followed by Sia, who awkwardly scrambled to keep up while clutching Thera to her chest. They stopped when they saw the Traveler and the Prince already in the chamber. Venalise grabbed Sia's hand.

Amarynn broke the silence. "Sia!" The warrior stepped toward the little girl and held out her hand.

"Rynn! What are you doing?" Jael hissed.

She turned back to Jael. "Regealth wants the girl!"

Amarynn took another step toward the center of the room while Sia swung her head to look at Venalise, then back to Amarynn. The little animal she held began to mewl and wriggle in the child's arms as she stood frozen, clutching the mage's hand. She put one hesitant foot in front of the other, but Venalise squeezed her hand, pulling her gaze back.

"My dear girl, go if you want." Her smile dripped with sweetness as she dropped the little girl's hand. Then she changed her expression to appear regretful. "But I won't be here to help you if you regret your choice."

"Let her go, witch," Amarynn hissed.

"She's free to go, Traveler." Venalise's eyes glittered with malevolence.

Sia took another step.

"We need to leave, Rynn." Jael's voice was low, but the urgency unmistakable.

Amarynn stepped into the circle of the room, her hand still outstretched. Sia looked back at Venalise.

"Well?" Venalise looked down at Sia and arched her eyebrow.

Jael moved to Amarynn's side. "Come or not, Sia, but we are leaving." His voice was clipped, agitated. Amarynn could feel prickles of energy radiating from him.

When she did not move, Venalise laughed. "That's what I thought."

Venalise stepped forward and gripped Sia by the elbow, dragging her into one of the many passageways. She pushed her ahead, then let go of her arm and turned back toward Jael and Amarynn, almost as if they were an afterthought. Then, raising both of her hands, she began to murmur.

Directly above their heads, the stone began to quiver and shake. Amarynn looked up as gravel and pieces of rock began to fall.

The room reverberated with the cracking and groaning of stone. All around them, fissures appeared, and large cracks began to form across the chamber walls. A massive ceiling piece shuddered and shifted, causing the floor to heave. Amarynn instinctively dropped to a crouch just as part of the stone overhead gave way.

Jael was on top of her just as her knees touched the floor. The magic inside him surged, and he threw his hands out. Bolts of blue and white energy radiated from him, shattering rock into dust, but the most significant pieces had yet to fall. Another loud crack followed, and two enormous slabs shifted and dropped, halting unexpectedly when they started to drop to the floor below. Just before Amarynn was entirely covered by Jael, she raised her head to look through the dust across the chamber.

Sia had fallen to her knees, the strange little bear cub scrambling to get back to her. Her hands were planted firmly on the chamber floor, and her body shook from strain. Eyes closed, she panted heavily. Amarynn could only assume she was drawing magic from the stone beneath her feet. In the pouch around Venalise's neck, the Gate Stone pulsed and began to glow. A loud snap made Amarynn duck her head back to the floor, abandoning her observation.

Amarynn and Jael braced for the crash of the slabs, the floor quaking as massive pieces of stone made impact. Jael held his breath, waiting for the crushing blow, but it never came. Amarynn strained to lift her head from beneath Jael's defensive position when the room quieted.

Jael sat up, pulling Amarynn with him. Together they looked at the space where they had been crouching. Only one torch remained lit, allowing them to see the floor in a perfect circle around them. Little bits of dust and gravel gave evidence of the massive rockfall.

"How?" Jael breathed. "I didn't do this," he added.

"Sia," Amarynn said quietly. "I saw her just as the rocks fell."

The rest of the chamber was filled with pieces of stone. Boulders, slabs, and rock blocked the passageways, including where Sia and Venalise disappeared. The only opening still exposed was the one directly behind them.

"They're gone," Amarynn whispered.

Together they stood, carefully climbing over the debris to their only way out. Amarynn leaned back against the wall to catch her breath when they cleared past the rubble. "She has Sia and the Gate, Jael," she said, running a hand through her hair.

"I know, but we can't do anything about it while we're trapped here," he said, peering down the dark corridor. "Where does this lead?" Jael asked.

Amarynn shook her head, but a sudden shriek reverberated down the passageway and echoed through the remaining space around them. She readjusted her grip on the dagger still clutched in her left hand.

"The atranoch. This must lead to their holding pens." She held up the dagger. "I'm going to need a bigger blade."

CHAPTER 33

The atranochs' cries and calls echoed down the corridor, frenzied in response to the chaos that had erupted throughout the mountain keep.

Amarynn gripped Jael's sword with both hands. His offer to trade weapons strengthened her resolve. Somehow, the comforting weight of the blade helped her keep her focus on the present and ignore the voices tumbling around in her head.

The passageway was narrow, and the rockfall caused by Venalise had triggered more minor tremors all over the mountain, leaving patch after patch of rubble to navigate. As they neared the end of the corridor, an eerie orange and red glow bathed the passage walls in an otherworldly light. A pungent animal odor hung in the air, heavy and thick. Amarynn and Jael slowed their approach, cautiously peering into the enormous cavern that housed the atranoch.

There was no way to estimate the number of creatures in the aerie. If they hadn't been in a race to escape the mountain, the sight of so many winged beasts would have given her pause. High in the mountain, a few crevices let in filtered sunlight, watery and dim. Smaller beasts, no bigger than mountain cats, fluttered at the top of the cavern while the larger atranoch clung to the many rock outcroppings lining the vast walls of the enclosure.

Amarynn's skin hummed with relentless electric ripples as every head in the aerie turned in her direction. Jael, watching his feet as he stumbled after Amarynn through the rubble, nearly pitched past her before her arm shot out to stop him.

"Don't move."

Jael lifted his head. "Goddess," he murmured, stepping back with one foot.

She scanned the area. The exit was a large, barred opening to the far-right side, but they would have to cross the open enclosure to reach it. With all eyes fixed on her, there was no possibility of stealth. Amarynn rubbed the back of her neck to try and relieve the uncomfortable sensation of electricity that continuously crawled up and down her spine.

Two atranoch near the passageway exit shifted and lumbered in Amarynn's direction. They were well-muscled. Their charcoal and green scales rippled with iridescence. The pair huffed in and out loudly as they adjusted the wings folded tightly against their backs. Nostrils flared as they scented her, and their irises' crystalline orange and blue whirled. The vertical slits of their pupils narrowed. Amarynn held her breath, unsure of what she was waiting for.

One of the smaller atranoch flying in the center of the cavern bellowed a call, taking Amarynn by surprise. Then the floor shook as a tremor rolled through the mountain.

She turned slowly to face Jael.

"Do you trust me?"

"What are you going to do?"

Amarynn looked out at the enclosure and then to Jael. "Two times now, I have encountered these beasts, and not once have they threatened me," she said quietly. "Not once."

Another tremor shook the chamber. She reached for Jael's hand. "We are going to walk out of here. I don't believe they will attack. I think they are just as confused and afraid as when I crossed, and they know I am one of them."

"Are they—"

"Yes," she nodded. "I am certain that they are Travelers, too."

She squared her shoulders, then stepped out of the shadows, pulling Jael with her. She clutched his hand and pulled him close. "Stay as close to me as you can. I know they won't hurt me, but I don't know about you."

They steadily walked across the cavern, passing the smaller atranoch, who did nothing more than watch with curiosity.

Halfway to their destination, a low rumbling rolled from deep in the mountain. Several of the creatures flapped their wings in agitation and lumbered toward the barred exit. The rumbling continued, growing in intensity.

A sharp crack sounded, and a large piece of the rock wall detached, crashing down to the cavern floor. One of the small animals panicked and barreled forward, crashing into Jael and Amarynn, sending them both flying. Amarynn was thrown backward into the cavern, but Jael landed only feet from the bars.

They were separated, and a group of agitated atranoch whipped their heads around to eye the Prince, who lay alone on the ground.

"Jael!" Amarynn cried. "Run!"

She watched him scramble to his feet and sprint towards the metal gate. Fortunately, the iron bars were wide enough apart for him to squeeze through. She breathed a sigh of relief and stood, ready to join him.

The distant rumbling from the mountain grew closer. More tremors rolled across the cavern floor, testing Amarynn's balance. A stalactite crashed down just to her right, and she stumbled. Another rock fell, landing a glancing blow on her left shoulder. The atranoch in the air were converging, pressing towards the exit. Her heart skipped a beat.

Her vision faded at the edges, images forcing their way into her line of sight. She dropped to one knee, slamming her hands to the ground to try and stop the oncoming memory. Paralyzing cold shot out from her chest and claimed her body.

"Look at me when I'm talking to you, whore! I told you to have this place clean by the time I returned! What is this?"

A clay cup hit her in the temple and shattered into pieces.

"And this?" Another hit her in the arm.

She clutched the boy to her chest and dropped to the floor. She lay on her side, dropping her chin over his head, and pulled her knees up to protect him. He was crying. So was she.

"Give me the boy and clean this shite up! "

She didn't move. She couldn't. She didn't dare even to breathe.

She just wanted to make it stop. She'd do anything to make it stop. Stop!

"Amarynn!"

Jael. She could hear his voice. He was frantic.

"Amarynn! Get up!"

The light wavered through the sheen of tears that filled her eyes. She was on the ground, breathing hard. Blinking away the tears, she could see more rocks falling, but none were near her. She pushed her confusion aside and slid one arm out to raise herself to a sitting position.

Her hand connected with something hard. A rock, she thought at first, but as she tried to push it away, the palm of her hand felt the smooth, curved stone attached to something big. She lifted her head and saw her hand was resting on the onyx-scaled foot of the largest atranoch in the cavern.

More rocks were falling, some striking the atranoch's back and wings. It flinched but refused to move, and Amarynn didn't understand. She was trapped. She ducked, waiting to feel its teeth.

A deafening crash sounded as a large slab detached and fell, hitting the atranoch in the shoulder just above its wing. The massive animal went down on one knee, twisting slightly to avoid crushing her. The beast wasn't moving in to attack her. It stood over her, protecting her from the falling debris. The atranoch ducked its head, allowing one of its massive eyes to find her. It swung his head toward the iron gate, then looked back at her.

It was telling her to run.

She looked for Jael. He clutched the bars, and she could see he was on the verge of running back in for her. She shook her head and pointed to the large metal latch.

"Open the gate, Jael!" she cried.

The Prince didn't hesitate. While he worked the latch, Amarynn launched herself from the safety of the beast and sprinted, dodging the scaled bodies that were crowding the exit.

Just as she was about to clear the opening, one of the giant beasts pushed ahead of the others. Amarynn pumped her legs harder and then dropped, sliding the last few feet underneath the atranoch's belly. She came to rest at the bars just as the latch mechanism sprung. The gate groaned and began to swing open as she rolled out of the way and pressed herself to the side of the mountain.

Great, scaled bodies poured from the cavern, launching themselves into the rose and indigo dawn sky. Amarynn looked to the entrance just as the last atranoch emerged — the one that had saved her. She couldn't tell before, but now she realized that it was the same creature she'd encountered on the ledge when they were expected to fight, the one she'd met in the forest.

The atranoch swung its head to look at her, and then it bellowed a call to the others as it heaved itself off the cliff, spreading its massive wings. It gained enough altitude to catch up to its kin in two great beats.

Amarynn and Jael watched as the weyr of atranoch beat their wings, pushing themselves higher and higher. The biggest one glided to the front then banked, the others following, as they sailed past the closest peaks of the Dark Mountains and into the endless sky above the Stone Reaches.

CHAPTER 34

The steady patter of rain woke Amarynn from an uncomfortable sleep. She pulled the blanket up over her head and tried to bury herself deeper into the pillows.

A thunderclap startled her, and she sat up. She ran a hand through her stiff hair and swung her legs off the side of the bed. The room was dark, and the warm glow from the hearth cast lazy shadows on the walls.

They had returned to Calliway that evening, and she had been surprised when Jael insisted that she stay in the castle. The trip back from the Dark Mountains was excruciatingly slow and painful for her. Her body had been pushed to its breaking point at the hands of Lors and Venalise. After the massive rush of adrenaline she had experienced during their escape began to dissipate, it was nearly impossible for her to ride back to Karth. She insisted on trying, in any case. Regealth placed a potent sleeping spell on her just so Jael could get her off Dax's back. She fought him the whole way down.

A flash of lightning lit up the room, then the slow roll of distant thunder shook the glass in the windowpanes. Amarynn stood and walked to the hearth. Her legs were still unsteady, and she sank into one of the oversized, overstuffed chairs. She pulled an embroidered throw off the arm of the chair and tucked it around her.

Staring into the fire, she plucked absently at her shirt — Jael's shirt — the scent of him lingering on the fabric. He had carried her to the room where he and Ehrinell stripped her of her torn and bloodied clothes. Jael had pulled his shirt off and offered it to her until more suitable clothing could be arranged. She had been too exhausted to object.

Over the three days it took them to travel back to Karth, her body tried its best to repair itself. She was in constant pain from the immortal magic that coursed through her; with it came flashes of memories she didn't understand. Memories filled with fear and pain made up the majority, but a few didn't hurt. She was relieved when Regealth visited her as she tried to sleep a few hours ago. He used his magic to quell the strange new noise clattering around her head.

Right now, her mind was quiet. The healing pain in her body had subsided, and though she was reluctant to give in to the safety and peace of her room, her body demanded it. Her eyelids were heavy when she sunk back into the cushions and pulled the soft blanket up over her shoulders. The sound of rain soothed her, and the distant rumbles of thunder ushered her into a deep and dreamless sleep.

"You're not so scary now, are ye?"

A lilting, melodic voice woke Amarynn. She was still in the big chair, her legs thrown over one arm. She opened her eyes to find a plump, matronly woman standing beside her, her hands on her hips.

"Wh— who—" Amarynn tried to find her words.

"Audra, Lady."

Amarynn pushed herself up in the chair. "Do not call me *lady*," she growled.

The woman narrowed her eyes and crossed her arms in front of her. The two appraised one another for a moment. Finally, the older woman sighed and touched her hand to her chest. "I'm Audra, and I am here to look after ye and see you rest and heal up nicely! We'll start with a bath," she said. "Can't have ye dirtying up any more sheets and blankets, can we?" She wrinkled her nose.

Amarynn spied a small table by the chair, a tray of fresh pastries piled high. She looked at her hands. Dirt and blood were caked under her fingernails, and she could feel the taut, dried blood on her skin under the shirt. She didn't even bother to touch her hair. She could smell it.

Amarynn nodded in wordless agreement and stood to follow. Together, they went into another small room that adjoined her sleeping chamber, where a steaming bath was waiting. She was scrubbed and fed an hour later with a new pair of pants and a fresh linen shirt. She stood in front of the floor-to-ceiling mirror and looked herself over.

Her rough-shorn hair fell below her chin in dark auburn waves. She was thinner than she'd been in years, and her face was haggard. But there was a color in her cheeks that felt new. She was still weak, but for once, she didn't feel unsettled.

A soft click caught her attention, and she turned just in time to see Jael slide through the door. He pushed it closed and turned toward Amarynn.

"You look better," he smiled.

She looked down at herself and shrugged. "Well, I certainly smell better."

Jael crossed the room in two strides and swept her up in his arms, burying his face in her hair. He breathed deeply and then pulled back to look at her. "Oh, I don't know," he grinned, "lavender is nice, but I prefer the smell of dungeon rot and atranoch piss on a girl."

Amarynn pushed away from him and playfully punched him in the arm. She sat down in the overstuffed chair and leaned over to the small table to grab a pastry. Jael sat across from her and leaned forward, his elbows on his knees.

"Did you sleep well?" he asked, a hint of worry in his eyes.

"I did," she answered, nodding.

"Any more of those ..." he trailed off.

"Memories?" she said quickly. "No."

She popped the pastry in her mouth and dusted her hands on her pants. Restless and uncomfortable with the conversation, she stood and wandered to the window.

"Jael," she started, not looking at him but staring down at the practice yard where the recruits were training. "Why am I here? I should be in the Legion quarters. Why, the food, the servant, and the clothes, all this?"

She turned back to Jael, and he stood to face her.

"There's so much to tell you." He gestured for her to come back and sit. She sighed and returned to the chair, crossing her legs underneath each other. Jael sat back on the edge of the chair opposite her.

"You know Regealth used his magic to help you while we traveled back." He looked up at her with sympathetic eyes. She inclined her head.

"Do you remember anything after we got out of the Keep and found Bent?" he asked her.

She remembered some, but she had pushed those memories as far away as possible. The climb down from the Keep was challenging, especially after their narrow escape from the atranoch enclosure. She was plagued with flashback after flashback the entire descent through the forest, slamming into her with such intensity and frequency that she couldn't tell what was real. Jael did his best to reassure her, to soothe her, but she was confused and humiliated. First, to have been reduced to a whimpering mess by Venalise and now finding herself incapacitated from pain and exhaustion; these were not feelings she was accustomed to. She resisted his efforts until she could hardly stand. Jael all but dragged her the last mile before they found a Legion scout.

"Did the whole mountain come down?" she whispered.

"Nearly," he said, raising his eyebrows. "We think Venalise caused it so she could get away with the girl."

The mountain had been massive, with chambers and tunnels connecting to the adjoining Keep. To bring it down would have been an undertaking worthy of legends. Venalise was powerful, but Amarynn hadn't realized the full extent of her power.

"I know what you're thinking," he added, "and we think Sia and the Gate magic must have helped her. And that," Jael stood, "is why we will find them."

"Who is 'we'?" Amarynn asked cautiously.

Jael shook his head, "That hasn't been decided yet."

"And your father?" Amarynn arched one eyebrow. "You haven't said one word about him."

He rubbed his face with his hands.

"My father is furious with me for helping you escape and taking on Regealth's rescue without telling him." Jael moved away, restless. He leaned against the edge of the fireplace. "But I think the fact that I handled Lors' assassination myself impressed him enough that he's holding back a little."

Amarynn's heartbeat quickened, and she was on her feet instantly.

"Lors' assassination?"

Jael's expression was nothing short of dangerous. "He paid for what he did to you. I made sure of it."

Amarynn had never seen that sort of fierceness in Jael. He was the diplomat, the negotiator, and the kind-hearted Prince who spoke kindly to Morning Hill's innkeeper. But the new ruthlessness in his eyes resembled his father, and it worried her.

"What is to become of me?"

"My father has conceded that because you were willing to sacrifice yourself for Karth and me, he is willing to extend a pardon to you. But you cannot return to Legion service." Jael arranged his expression to one of regret.

"What?" Amarynn snarled. "I was willing to sacrifice everything, but that's not good enough for him?" She stepped forward toward Jael.

"You are to remain here, in the castle—"

"A prisoner?" she hissed.

"With me." His smile was both beautiful and infuriating at the same time. He reached out and pulled her to him. "You are to be my personal guard, my protector," he whispered, just near her ear. "Because I cannot be apart from you, Amarynn."

He pulled back, his eyes locking with hers. He touched the fine line of the tattoo under her eye and traced it down to her jaw with his thumb. He rested his hand on her cheek and brought the other behind her head to tangle in her hair.

He leaned down and let his lips gently touch hers. She reluctantly pulled away from him and stepped away.

"No."

The hurt in his eyes was unavoidable. "Amarynn," he stepped toward her.

"No, stop," she said, choking on her own words. "I can't..." She crossed her arms and looked away.

The confusion on his face gave way to anger. "What do you mean?"

Amarynn closed her eyes, choosing her words carefully. "This bond you feel. It's not love. We are magically bound — that much I learned from what Venalise did to me."

"Bound or not, that doesn't change my heart."

"Yes, it does," she whispered. For the first time in her Karthian life, she felt wanted and cared for. She was truly seen. But Jael's affections were veiled in a shroud of magic that kept him from understanding the truth. "You are the Crown Prince of Karth, and just like all the other Travelers are bound to your father, I am bound to you. You are going to rule this Kingdom one day. I'm a fighter, yours to command, and I'm immortal. Don't mistake my loyalty for more than it is."

Jael threw his arms up in frustration. Then he placed his hands on his hips and began to pace in front of the window. "So, you are immortal. Now we know that I am a mage of some significance. With enough time and Regealth's help, you will see our bond is more than the kind my father shares with the other Travelers!"

"But what if it isn't?" Her voice was barely a whisper.

His back was to her, but he spun around at her words. "Amarynn," he growled, "I would move a thousand mountains for you. I swear I will find a way."

She leaned back. Magic roiled in his grey eyes like tiny lightning bolts writhing and twisting across a stormy sky. He was beautiful, but he was reckless — he had tasted the power hiding within. She hated to deny what she felt, what he wanted, but she needed to help him see reason. Something inside her had awakened, and she could not deny that she wanted to be as close to him as she could, but she knew better. Now that Venalise had gotten inside her head and released dark demons of her own, there was no guarantee that together they would be anything other than destructive.

"Jael, we need some time to regroup. You are a mage! *A mage!* And I have things of my own to sort out. We should give ourselves time to adjust to this new reality. I *will* be your guard, and I will protect you. That will never change."

Her heart was breaking with every word she spoke. Yet another hope dashed by her cursed immortality. She almost wished Venalise had broken her beyond repair to spare her this moment. "Go on and be the Prince. Go learn how to rule this Kingdom to become a better King than your father. I'll be right beside you."

Jael stared at Amarynn for a long while. He cleared his throat and reached out to touch her face.

"Rest," he said. "You take all the time you need." He walked to the door and opened it. He turned back to her. "There will never be anyone for me but you. I will show you how this can work. You'll see."

CHAPTER 35

"Lady Amarynn?"

Amarynn glared at the young servant boy. She was cleaning up after several early hours in the practice yard, and she was tired, hungry, and in no mood to be called "Lady."

The boy waited, not sure what to do. Three other boys stood behind them — all carrying wooden boxes of different sizes.

"Are these for me?" she asked him impatiently.

"Ye-yes..." he stammered.

"Well, don't just stand there!"

She stepped back and opened the door. The boys rushed in and set the boxes on the table near the hearth, then quickly left, eyes averted. As the last one exited, he handed her a note.

Amarynn walked to the table and eyed the boxes. There were four of them — ornate, with beautiful silver latches. She opened the largest one and stared.

Nestled on a bed of burgundy velvet was a short sword. While her fingers trailed along the blade, admiring its beauty, she lifted the letter.

I'm sorry your weapons were lost when the mountain fell.
I hope these will be acceptable replacements. -J

Amarynn set the letter down, a smile tugging at the corners of her lips. She opened the others. Two long, slender boxes each held daggers,

271

and the larger square box contained three simple but deadly throwing knives. They were beautiful and well-made. But one was missing.

"I couldn't find a big enough box for this beast."

Amarynn turned at the sound of Jael's voice. He was standing in the open doorway, holding her broadsword.

"Frost!" she exclaimed. Jael came toward her and placed it reverently in her hands. She looked at him questioningly. "How did you get this? I left it in the tower room."

"Regealth found it, actually," he said. "When I was smuggling him out of the keep."

She looked up at him, her eyes shining brighter than ever.

"I can't have a weaponless personal guard, can I?"

"I also lost my sword belt and scabbards," she murmured.

"Go see the swordsmith," he said. "They've already got all of them started, but they needed your measurements." He held up his hands. "My estimations weren't good enough for Selwyn."

She turned back to Jael. "Thank you."

He smiled and winked, and she cursed herself for almost getting sucked into his charm. She took a purposeful step back and turned to the blades as a plausible distraction.

Jael followed her, and she felt him move closer. He leaned in and placed a small kiss at her temple, his hand on the small of her back.

"Go get your sword belt, Lady Protector," he whispered.

She whirled around, giving him a half-serious glare, and he laughed, stepping back.

"A group of Vhaleesian dignitaries are arriving this afternoon, and we are all required to attend their welcome. It will be your debut as my guard." He turned and walked to the door. Before he closed it behind him, he grinned and added, "And wear something pretty, my Lady!"

He laughed and slammed the door shut as a throwing knife landed on the door frame, just where his head had been.

Amarynn wandered through the hallways, stopping in the kitchens to grab a piece of bread and crumbly cheese on her way to the swordsmith. The whole palace buzzed with excitement and activity. She overheard some of the kitchen staff chattering about who might be arriving.

"I heard it was the Queen's sister," Magga, the head cook, said to one of the kitchen girls. "Maybe she'll bring that handsome son of hers!"

The girl giggled as she picked up a tray.

"Maybe the Prince will finally get a match," she said. "He's so handsome! I can't believe he's not married yet! The Queen must be beside herself!"

Amarynn bristled at the girl's comment. She shoved past her and out the door into the stable yard, her talk about Jael striking a nerve. She smirked. If she only knew Jael's future was already decided by him, the King and Queen's wishes be damned.

As she stopped and leaned back on the fence, their last, brief kiss replayed in mind. The way he held her, the conviction in his voice and his eyes. His attention was almost enough to make her believe he would find a way to make things work for them. For the first time in the twenty years of her life in this world, she couldn't deny that she felt a glimmer of hope for her future whenever Jael was with her. She felt like there *was* a future.

Maybe Jael was right — perhaps they could be something more. She snorted to herself. She could just imagine the court's reaction to their Queen lopping off someone's leg on the battlefield.

If Jael was a mage and the future King of Karth, she could try to believe there might be the possibility. It wasn't completely implausible. Queen Feramin's mother had been a Vhaleesian warrior, so there was a precedent — and after everything she'd been through, didn't she owe it to herself to try? But with so much uncertainty on the horizon, with the Gate Stone and Sia still unaccounted for, Amarynn doubted there would even be time to think about matters of the heart.

She pushed off the fence and crossed the yard, stopping by Dax's stall on her way through to the smithy. He was lazily chewing on a mouthful of oats when she ducked into his stall.

"Forget the Prince. You are the truly handsome one, aren't you?" she scratched beneath his long forelock. "Maybe I should marry you, hmm?"

The war horse blew out and shook his head. Amarynn laughed, "No?"

She patted his neck and held out a handful of sugar lumps she had stolen from the kitchen. His soft nose tickled her hand as he took them from her. Amarynn leaned on him for a moment, savoring the comforting smell of her horse and the fresh hay. She ran her hands over his shoulder, feeling his strong muscles while he craned his neck around to nuzzle her pockets, looking for more sugar.

"Stop it, you child!" she laughed, pushing him away. "I'll be back later, and we'll go for a run, yes?" She gave him one last pat on his neck and then left the stables to collect her belt and scabbards.

The swordsmith's shop was dark, illuminated only by a tiny window and the fiery glow of the forge. Two men stood around the anvil in deep discussion. The smith's back was to Amarynn, but the other man looked up at her as she walked through the door.

He was dark: dark hair, dark clothes, and he looked familiar. She couldn't place him at first, but then she realized who he was. Aron, the brooding Traveler who came with Bent for her in the Northern Reaches.

"Amarynn," he said.

"Aron," she inclined her head in greeting.

"I hear you're to head up Lord Jael's personal guard." He was standing in front of her now. She had not realized how tall he was. "Good luck with *that*." He chuckled under his breath before turning and walking out of the shop.

She watched him leave. As he stepped out the door, he hesitated for just a moment. Amarynn waited for him to turn, but he continued, disappearing into the busy throng of people. Her eyes lingered on the empty doorway, but then she turned and waved at the smith, who offered his hand in greeting.

"Amarynn," he smiled. He reached across his worktable and retrieved the most beautiful belt she had ever seen. The work was simple but elegant in its design.

"The Prince said to spare no expense but that it shouldn't look delicate," he said.

Amarynn chuckled as he handed her the belt. She started to buckle it around her waist but stopped. "Didn't you need to take measurements?"

"No, Lady," the smith said. "My father made your first belt, and I crafted your new blades myself. He kept records of everything he made, so it should fit you like your last one."

She thanked him and buckled the belt first, then the thigh scabbard. They were exquisite. The smith disappeared for a moment, then returned with one more item.

"For Frost," he said, handing her a cross-body strap with a beautifully tooled leather scabbard down the back. "My father made that broadsword, too. One of the best he ever forged, may the Goddess hold him close."

"Thank you, Master—" Amarynn looked at him questioningly.

"Selwyn, my Lady."

She clasped his hand. "Thank you, Master Selwyn. I'm sure the Goddess has him closer than most, as talented as he was." She took Frost's scabbard and returned to her rooms in the palace as quickly as she could. She was eager to feel the weight of her weapons again.

But when she arrived at her room, the door was ajar, and Audra was there, laying out clothing on the bed.

"Oh! La—" she stopped, then puckered her mouth, grimacing. "Amarynn, I mean. Hurry now!" She ushered Amarynn into the room. "We need to dress you, and quickly! The entourage from Vhaleese has arrived, and King Lasten will be receiving them shortly!"

A new pair of black leather breeches and an embroidered linen blouse were laid out next to a fine-fitted jacket and boots. The

275

ensemble was a bit much for her tastes, but she was relieved to see it wasn't a dress.

Audra insisted she bathe; then, her handmaid attempted to make sense of her hair after she dressed.

"It's so short!" she cried in frustration. "What am I supposed to do with this?" She finally settled on two close braids on either side of her head, pulled behind her ears. She wrapped the ends in burgundy and dark blue leather to honor Karth's colors.

"It's fine, Audra," Amarynn consoled. She slid her new blades into their scabbards. When she was ready, she went to her door and paused, unsure where to go.

"It is customary for a monarch's guard to escort them from their private chambers." Jael was striding down the hall, a smile on his face.

"It is also customary for the monarch's guard to know where the monarch's private chambers are located," Amarynn retorted.

Jael laughed, "Fair enough!"

He was beside her, one hand touching the braids in her hair. The formal jacket he wore made his shoulders seem wider. He was washed and shaved, the scent of spice stronger than usual. He leaned in, placing his lips at her temple, and this time, she didn't pull away but accepted the kiss. She stepped back, arching her eyebrow at the jewel-encrusted sword belted at his waist.

"Strictly ceremonial," he explained. "Not to be used for fear of losing a sapphire." He gestured to the hallway. "Shall we?"

"Should I walk in front of you or behind you?" Amarynn asked.

He thought for a moment, then shrugged. "You know, I have no idea!"

"I'll stay just behind you," Amarynn said. "But we'd better hurry, or Audra will drag us both by our ears." She grinned, and they started down the corridor.

They stopped at the doors to the throne room and realized they were the last to arrive. King Lasten and Queen Feramin were already seated. A gaggle of royal relatives milled about, and Regealth sat in a chair near the dais, two apprentices standing just behind him.

Jael turned to Amarynn and whispered, "Follow me. When I go to stand by my father, wait till he acknowledges you. Then you will take your place by Regealth." He gave her a quick wink.

Amarynn pulled on the bottom of her jacket to straighten it, then placed her left hand on the sword at her belt. Jael squared his shoulders and walked forward to the dais. He stopped, gave his father a short bow, then bounded up the two short steps to give his mother a quick kiss on the cheek before moving to stand behind the King.

Amarynn stood motionless in front of King Lasten. He sent her to the dungeons the last time they faced one another. She looked uneasily towards Queen Feramin, who held her gaze for a moment, then lifted her chin as if to lend Amarynn courage. She was a strong and beautiful woman in the way that only warriors could be. Amarynn, bolstered by the Queen, looked back to the King.

He eyed her warily as if he was questioning his decision to offer her pardon. Finally, he spoke.

"Amarynn of the Legion of Karth, we hear you have been quite busy," he began. She kept her chin up and her face stoic. "For escaping my dungeon, we should have your head, though I hear you were given some unprecedented assistance." He cast a sidelong glance at Jael, who tried to hide his amusement.

"For taking it upon yourself to try and infiltrate the Darklands Keep and rescue our most precious mage, you may keep your head. And for seeing to it that our only son and the Crown Prince of Karth made it out of Athtull Keep alive; we acknowledge your loyalty."

The King dismissed her with a wave. With an indiscernible sigh of relief, she took her place beside Regealth.

All eyes now turned to the double doors, where a group of Vhaleesians gathered. A man and woman stepped forward first. They were tall, like the Queen, and both wore the long, dark hair typical to the Vhaleesian people.

Behind them was a young woman. Her willowy form was taut with lean muscle, and her light-colored hair was done up in hundreds of tiny braids, all gathered at the nape of her neck in a knot. She wore an ornately-decorated longbow slung across her shoulders like the forest hunters of Vhaleese.

King Lasten and Queen Feramin stood as they approached.

"Welcome, Lord Haryk and Lady Nephinae," the King said.

Queen Feramin stepped down to embrace the Lady Nephinae.

"We hope you traveled well, cousin," she said warmly.

The Queen and Lady Nephinae stepped back as Lord Haryk beckoned for the young lady behind them to approach. He took her hand and escorted her to the steps of the dais.

"May I present my daughter, Caeda."

Amarynn studied Lord Haryk's face. He appeared to be bursting with pride as King Lasten gestured for Jael to join him at his side. His daughter seemed entirely disinterested.

Something was wrong. Amarynn tensed, and her hand went to her sword.

As Jael stepped forward, the King reached for Caeda's hand.

"My son, may I present Caeda, your newly betrothed and the future Queen of Karth!"

The wind was howling through the mountain pass when a pack of riders reached its narrow passage. The small group did not stop; instead, they pushed on until the trail leveled off on a flat glacial plain of blinding snow and ice.

Seated atop the lead mount, the mage Venalise scanned the horizon.

"Mistress," a small voice called from a bundle of blankets in front of her. "I-I'm so cold!"

"Hush, child," she chided the bundle in her lap. "We'll be by the fire come nightfall."

A small face peeked out from the blankets. "Couldn't I just make a fire right here?"

Venalise pulled her cloak tighter around her shoulders and stared down at the girl. "Sia, dear, you'd burn yourself out fighting the wind up here." Venalise looked up at the grey, sunless sky, then back at the girl. She raised her eyes to scan ahead toward a low rise in the distance.

"Settle in, child. We are in the Suhonne lands now. In a few hours, we will reach their stronghold. In the meantime, I'd say you could try to warm yourself by calling your fire, but we both remember what happened last time."

Sia frowned. She was learning to call her magic but being able to differentiate between the elements was still proving problematic. The last time she tried to call her fire, she gave three of their men frostbite. Venalise was only helpful with the earth energy of stone and metal, making the child's instruction all the more difficult.

A piercing scream echoed off the mountains, and she shielded her eyes against the light that reflected off the snow-covered rocks. Atranoch glided high above them, banking and circling in and out of the lesser peaks. The creatures had been following them at a distance ever since she and her entourage left the ruin of Athtull Keep. Venalise narrowed her eyes for better focus, noticing that the big one, their leader, was still absent from the weyr.

Her eyes left the sky to survey the snowy plain ahead. Any minute, she expected to see riders appear. In fact, she was counting on it. The Suhonne was one of the seven houses of the Stone Reaches, and as the southernmost, the proud horsemen patrolled and protected the mountain border. The House of Suhonne had singlehandedly kept each of the seven great families secret from the rest of the world for hundreds of years.

Sia groaned and pushed herself as low as she could in the saddle. Thera squirmed beneath the blankets until Sia allowed her to poke her head out through the top. Venalise shook her head and urged her horse forward, signaling the others to follow. Together, the small band stepped out onto the snowy expanse and continued their journey north.

A few hours later, just as the horses began to slow, a smudge appeared in dusk's orange and red glow. The smudge grew larger until Venalise could make out a contingency of Suhonne riders, approximately fifteen in number, approaching from the north. Within twenty minutes, the two bands of riders met.

The leader of the Suhonne walked her horse forward after the others stopped some distance from Venalise and her men. She was small in the saddle, but her stature commanded attention and respect. She eyed Venalise for a long time before speaking.

"You are not from the Below," she said in the Eorath dialect.

"No," Venalise said, lifting her chin. "I am of Stone."

The woman raised her eyebrows at Venalise's use of the common tongue of the Stone Reaches.

"House?" the horsewoman asked, still skeptical.

"Korr," Venalise said, her tone curt and commanding.

The leader scoffed, unbelieving.

"You wear too many blankets to be Korr," she huffed, still speaking Eorath.

"I have been Below for a long, long time."

"Tell me your name, would-be Korr," the leader squinted in the dusk.

"Tell me yours," Venalise countered, lifting her chin imperiously.

"I am T'Suhonne Sashtra, second to T'Suhonne Vash. I lead this patrol."

Venalise dropped the blankets from her shoulders and sat tall in her saddle. She eyed the woman named Sashtra, then scanned the faces of the others behind her.

"I am T'Korr Vena," she said in Ceadari, the high tongue of the Stone Reaches, her voice strong and clear. She waited a moment to allow her name to register. "I have returned from many years in the Below. I bring important news for my mother, Empress, T'Korr Uhll."

One by one, the horsemen bowed their heads and pressed their fists to their foreheads. Finally, the patrol leader did as well.

Venalise smiled to herself. The wind whipped her cloak, flecks of ice collecting like a crown on her hair.

After all these years, she was going home.

ACKNOWLEDGMENTS

I'm not going to lie. Writing the acknowledgments is the hardest part of completing a novel, especially one that has taken nearly a decade to complete. Who will I forget, hmm? I'm sure there are people I'm missing! I'm a nervous wreck trying to acknowledge everyone who played a part in creating this book. I'm going to start with myself. The entire idea of Amarynn began as a mental image of a woman in a forest, out of time, out of place, and needing to find the strength to find her way. So many different circumstances in my life led to her creation that it is difficult to pinpoint what truly brought her story to life.

Now, I must thank my parents for fostering my creativity and telling me I could do anything I put my mind to. More importantly, I am grateful that they made me *believe* I could. That gift has paid dividends in more ways than just completing The Gate. They taught me that my imagination was boundless and not to be afraid of climbing out of the box and going my own way. "Thank you" doesn't quite do it. And to my brother Steve, thank you for the encouragement and your belief in me.

Of course, I could have never completed this book without the support and patience of my husband and children. No one rolls their eyes when I ask, "Can I just read this one thing to you?" even after hearing the same scene fourteen times; it is a testimony to their love. My husband, who savored every word (and made me re-read everything at least three times), was an endless supply of ideas and different perspectives. His willingness to listen again and again meant the world, and I'm devastated he will never see the story that lives and breathes because of him. My daughter, the writer, who fought tooth and nail to keep scenes I threatened to cut and who helped me maintain sensitivity as an author. Her investment and encouragement are priceless. My youngest son, a worldbuilding and magic system-creating genius, kept me on my toes and pushed me to deepen the scope and depth of Karth and everything magical within the world of The Gate. And my oldest son, who refused to read it "until it was finished." Suck it up, buttercup – you've got a book to read, now! And Dax, you are immortalized now. May your snaggle tooth and protective streak never die.

I couldn't have gone through the painstaking process of editing and repeatedly revising if it weren't for my friends. Gayle, your support means so much. You kicked my butt whenever I doubted myself. Jen, I'm glad I have you as a draft reader. For a math teacher, you sure can write! Elaine and Tara, thank you for listening to me drone on and on about this publishing thing. Writing is not a sport, but it *is* an endurance activity! Ella, one day we're going to write that novella with Erisi and Amarynn doing what they do best! The San Antonio Writer's Roundtable peeps — you saw it first. You tore it to shreds and helped me build it back up. And Irene, thank you for dragging me along to that writing conference at UIW. Hearing an agent speak about opening lines changed the entire trajectory of The Gate for the better.

Way back when, in middle and high school, my English teacher told me, "You are a writer." Those words replay in my head every time I think I can't do it. Thank you, Leila Meacham. As a teacher myself, I am acutely aware of teachers' impact on their students, and my experience as your student is no exception. You lit the fire in me to write, and I will be forever grateful.

This brings me to the strangest thank you I have. Thank you to my 7th-period Pre-AP science class at Jackson Middle School (2018-2019). Ben, Audrey, Devora, Dean, Xan, and all the other beautiful souls that dared me to finish and asked me every day, "What's your word count now?" Keep an eye out, Schonbergers! You're in this story and the books that follow, just like I promised. And to my Fredericksburg Creative Writers and Digital Publishers — you kept me going through the pandemic and all the fallout that ensued.

Thank you to Max for the #PitMad like and for requesting to read the first draft of The Gate. Thank you for seeing its potential. Because of your endeavor, I now have the good fortune of being in an actual literary girl gang. LOI Ladies... LaNae, if you hadn't been brave and struck out on this publishing adventure, The Gate would still be sitting on my laptop — untouched and unrefined. Thank you for pushing me to make it better and including me in your band of crazy ladies! Karen, thank you for all the questions I never thought to ask and for reminding me that the world will always need more bears. And finally, Kaleigh. You are a visionary artist who captured Amarynn and her story so well. You blow me away with every video and image you create. Lights Out Ink, thank you for giving The Gate, and the books that follow, a home.

And to you, the reader, thank you for taking a chance on Amarynn's story. I hope you lose yourself in her world as I have. Maybe we'll bump into each other while we're there!

ABOUT THE AUTHOR

BRANDI SCHONBERG has always written stories, but this is the first one she has completed. The Gate is her debut novel and the first title in The Immortal Coil Saga. She teaches science and creative writing in Fredericksburg, Texas, with her children and far too many animals than anyone should be allowed to keep.

She can be found at:

https://www.BSchonbergAuthor.com

FB: BSchonbergAuth
T: @BSchonbergAuth
IG: @BSchonbergAuth